Until the Clock Strikes Midnight

ALSO BY ALECHIA DOW

Just a Pinch of Magic

Until the Clock Strikes Midnight

Alechia Dow

FEIWEL AND FRIENDS
NEW YORK

QUICK NOTE ABOUT CONTENT WARNINGS:

While this story stands as a cozy, romantic fantasy, it's important to note that within these pages, there is an exploration of the nature of life, loss, and love. It contains a character with bipolar disorder, and all this might entail for those living with this disease as I do: intrusive, negative spirals of thought, difficult emotions, oscillating moods, and brief self-harm and passive suicidality. There are mentions of off-page parental abandonment and death, loss, grief, and one very small, reproachable comment of fatphobia on page 167. While I do my best to handle these topics with nuance and compassion as they are all within my lived experience, please take care of yourself while reading.

A Feiwel and Friends Book
An imprint of Macmillan Publishing Group, LLC
120 Broadway, New York, NY 10271 • fiercereads.com

EU representative: Macmillan Publishers Ireland Ltd, 1st Floor, The Liffey Trust Centre, 117–126 Sheriff Street Upper, Dublin 1, D01 YC43

Our books may be purchased in bulk for specialty retail/wholesale, literacy, corporate/premium, educational, and subscription box use. Please contact MacmillanSpecialMarkets@macmillan.com.

Library of Congress Control Number: 2025015208

First edition, 2026
Book design by Meg Sayre
Feiwel and Friends logo designed by Filomena Tuosto
Printed in the United States of America

ISBN 978-1-250-37577-3
10 9 8 7 6 5 4 3 2 1

TO ANYONE WHO HAS EVER BEEN TOLD TO

SHINE A LITTLE LESS BRIGHT,

LAUGH A LITTLE LESS LOUD,

BE A LITTLE LESS BOLD . . .

AND SAID NAH.

THIS ONE'S FOR US.

CHAPTER ONE

Darling

It's not a celebration if there isn't a cake. That's just a fact. No cake equals no joy, and no joy equals *Why are we even doing this?*

My stomach rumbles and I shift in my seat, glancing to the back, where empty tables stand against the bare wall. Not only is there no cake, there's no platter of cookies either. Not a chocolate chip in sight. Not even a whiff of something delicious nearby.

Yes, I know that celestials appreciate solemnity, but this? This is dull.

I lean toward the girl next to me, my voice a whisper. "Do we think there'll at least be snacks later? I'm starv—"

The Guardian, maybe a few years older than me with light brown skin and straight black hair, rolls her eyes and turns away sharply. Such a cheery bunch. I settle back into my seat and look around at all the blandness. I understand that for a lot of students at the Mortal Outcome Academy this is just a formality, but shouldn't it be more vibrant than this? They could have at least sprinkled confetti or have a banner that reads YOU DID IT! This *is* graduation day, after all . . .

The beginning of disappointment swirls in the pit of my stomach. This is supposed to be one of the biggest days of my eternal life and look at it. The auditorium is tan, as are the seats. The stage. The carpet. And everyone's dressed without an ounce of imagination. Only their golden halos stand out, polished and gleaming above perfectly coiffed hair of every color.

At the podium, Head Guardian Honour prattles on about duty and morality. About how we are the first generation of Guardians to embrace change and diversity. About how a new era has dawned. About how we should be proud of ourselves as we begin the next step of our journeys. There's not a smile to be found anywhere in the place. Only complete reverence.

We're all meant to represent our titles and status as the very best Happily Ever After has to offer by looking and acting alike for the sake of consistency.

It's just . . . conformity's not really my thing, and I've never been particularly good at it. Sure, I got the memo to wear something formal, but no one said which shade or that I couldn't embellish. With some quick wand flicks, I'd made a well-tailored white, frothy mini-gown tapered at the waist with a pearly sash. I'd shimmied into my lucky rainbow-striped leggings and brilliant purple ankle boots. My voluminous cloud of curls spills from the highest, fluffiest bun imaginable, and my lips are glossed bubbly pink. If no one else will, *I'll* bring the party to the party.

My outer appearance must always reflect my inner reality . . . or at least the reality I want to feel. No one looks too hard at what's behind the smile when you cloak yourself in colors.

I would have never fit in anyway; I'm a halo-less head taller than most of my classmates, my hair kinkier, I have wings tucked into my back, and my general vibe is more spirited. I'm what celestials often call *loud*, *ridiculous*, *a character* (which I think is supposed to be an insult?), and *too much*.

Do I care? No.

Well . . . not *right now*. I'd prepared for this moment, and I won't let anything ruin it, especially not my illness, which wants nothing more than for me to collapse into a blubbering mess of anxiety and/or rage.

Nope. This is my day. Honour's correct: A new era has dawned, and I'm at the forefront of it.

"For several reasons, this is a momentous occasion. Not only will you receive your provisional licenses . . ." Honour pauses, building suspense. "You will be the first to hear an incredible announcement that could change the very future of our leadership."

I sit up taller—the mentorship. What I've worked for since I arrived. My plans are ambitious, yet attainable—*if* I stay on course and don't let any dark clouds hide my sunshine.

As if Honour is listening to my thoughts, her steely blue-eyed gaze meets mine. She shakes her head. Blond flyaways wave briefly in a nonexistent wind before falling back into place. Her alabaster skin glistens in the spotlight, making her look every bit a stereotypical Guardian. *Oh sprinkles*, is she listening to my thoughts right now?!

"For the first time in three generations, the Mortal Outcome Council has decided to grant a privilege to the pupil who has achieved the highest cumulative score ever received from this institution. Someone who is . . . oddly unique . . ." She nods at me for show. My classmates turn my way, their mouths dropping open. Though I can't hear thoughts or sense emotions like they can, I know they're making judgmental comments in their minds to giggle about later.

Let them. I'm above such impertinence, for I am a gracious paragon of magnanimity.

While most twist back in their seats, one person's glower lingers across the rows. Virtue's lips pinch together as if she's holding in a string of curses. I resist the urge to smirk, preferring to take the high road by clutching a hand to my chest in faux surprise. I cannot believe I ever kissed those lips. I cannot believe those lips ever unpinched long enough for me to kiss them.

"When the Mortal Outcome Council allowed the first fairy in centuries to enter our academy on the Guardian side, it was met with bafflement. Fairies are known for their opinionated stances regarding not only morality, but the role of eternals in helping mortals choose their destiny. When she decided to join us, we never expected her to be determined, impactful, or different than what we'd learned."

Guardians bob their heads. It *is* true that the only time most fairies want to deal with mortals is when we prank them for a bit of entertainment. We are, what some have called, a very "unserious" species. We're also not very helpful. If you asked fairies about their personal moral philosophy, it would be: "Destiny is what you make it," followed by: "A little chaos keeps things interesting." However, fairies and celestials do agree that choices can make a life better or worse. Which is why I'm sitting here. I want to help mortals make good choices.

"Still," Honour continues, "she has redefined how we interact with mortals. She has her own style and a success rate we are keen to see replicated in the realms. It is for that reason the Mortal Outcome Council has decided to offer Darling—" She stops suddenly to clear her throat.

I know it's because of my full name. They did give me the option of using only my first name. I declined.

They'll just have to deal. I may sit with the Guardians but I'll always be a fairy. My lack of halo proves that. As do the wings magically tucked into my back, only hinting at their presence by a light purple outline wrapping around my shoulders.

"Darling Sparkleton," she says with more authority, "the chance to obtain the Mortal Outcome Council's coveted mentorship if she succeeds with her first independent case. Darling, will you please rise and join me on stage?"

There's a collective gasp as if it was offensive that she said my name or that I am now one step closer to the Mortal Outcome Council. There's never been an instance when a chosen mentee doesn't ultimately take a seat on the council. From there, I'd have a real, meaningful—and powerful—voice. With it, I'm going to challenge our perceptions of Happily Ever After. My name's going to be added to *The Book of Compassion and Care*, which sits in the center of the Mortal Outcome Council chambers, where the most powerful group of five celestials convenes to decide the fates of mortals. And I will sit there among them. As an equal.

No one will doubt I belong ever again. As the first fairy in history to have this position, I will not only rework the system to be more inclusive, I'll lead generations in my style.

I bounce up on my feet and plaster the biggest smile on my face. *Your outer reality reflects your inner reality. Keep your cool.*

After pocketing my glitter wand—all fairies have one; they're impossible to break and you can change their appearance anytime you like—I try to squeeze down the row. Angry faces greet me as my ample body bumps into their limbs.

"Sorry," I mutter. Their mouths curl into snarls, jealousy spiraling around the room. Their negativity seeps into my body, causing a sudden burst of nerves that shakes my legs, and I nearly trip over someone's oversized foot. *Deep breaths. None of that.* I catch myself and don't bother apologizing again. They don't care and neither should I.

Once I've made it into the aisle, I release the stomach I'd been unsuccessfully sucking in. Head forward, smile radiant. I sashay up to the stage. Avoiding the glares is easy when you've been doing it for years. It's even easier because most of them—besides Virtue—never liked me to begin with. Never thought I was worth their breath or energy.

My family and friends back in Whimsia feel the same. They don't talk to me anymore either. They cannot believe I'd degrade myself by working with celestials or mortals when there's no imperative for fairies to get involved in matters beyond our realm.

Whimsia has everything you could ever want; why leave home?

Celestials are so dogmatic.

Unoriginal.

They get to live forever, and they want to work with mortals?

Which is when I reminded them that celestials need mortals to thrive. While Whimsia has magic at its core, making every fairy eternal and powerful, the fate of celestials is bound to the fate of mortals. Their magic comes from life energy, the light and the dark between the stars. We had a whole class about it. Admittedly, I wasn't paying too much attention about the specifics, what with Virtue sitting next to me being all cute.

Anyway, it makes sense that they work to create stability and predictability. And why the Mortal Outcome Council tasks celestials who become Guardians with helping mortals find their Happily Ever Afters, and the celestials who become Misfortunes with helping mortals make the difficult decisions that'll lead them away from unpredictable Unhappily Ever Afters.

It's my task to show MOC leadership that fairies can *and will* make the mortal realms better too. One good decision, one swish of a wand, and one heartfelt, caring discussion at a time.

That thought adds a little more pep to my step as I walk toward Honour. She's smiling down at me. We both know she's secretly boiling. If she had her way, I'd be back home no longer burdening celestials with my presence.

With one purple boot after the other up the stairs, I reach for the golden coin from Honour's outstretched hand. Today, all of us will be given our coins granting entry to every realm. This coin will be with me until I no longer wish to keep it, even if I fail this one assignment.

And finally, it's mine after years of giving my energy to

outperform everyone else and their biases. I had to work twice as hard for half as much, and I still came out on top.

Honour pulls back and leans into me for a hug. "You're going to fail." Her tone is sharp and would have pierced me like a knife if I hadn't worked so hard to maintain this carefree disposition. "You'll realize you don't belong here and go back to your little village—what's it called, Curious Canal?" The snark in her voice is breathtaking for someone perceived to be righteous.

I let out a laugh and squeeze her a little tighter, the steel walls I've built around myself holding firm. If I let every slight affect me, I wouldn't have been able to accomplish everything I have, and will.

"Paradise Pines. But don't worry, I'll do this better than any celestial ever could." There's a smile in my whispered words as I take the coin from her hand.

"Funny you should say that." Honour sneers.

The coin firmly in my grasp, I step up to the podium. "It is such an . . . honor," I say with a wink at Honour, "to receive my provisional license and take on my first client. To have this opportunity and chance at the Mortal Outcome Council mentorship is a dream come true. I can't wait to get started. I can't wait to usher in this new era . . ."

There's a moment where I wonder: Should I do it? Should I be bold, even if it means they'll hate me more? But boldness is my brand, and who would I be if I didn't stay true to my ambitions?

"It's a privilege to help mortals," I continue. "Not just those deemed worthy by leadership—*all* seeking help and kindness and Happily Ever Afters!"

No one claps, but their silence is an afterthought as the coin heats my palm and I glance down. A name, location, and date are etched into the metal. My first solo assignment. Lucy Addlesberg. The Kingdom of Lumina. Seven Midnights.

Get ready, Lucy. I'm going to change both our lives.

CHAPTER TWO

Calamity

Mortals love making bad decisions. That's a fact.

I try not to grimace as I bend down to whisper into Phred's ear. "All in."

A sigh escapes between his teeth as he considers his choices, and *I* consider him.

Phrederick Shadowlock is not my client—I haven't gotten my first solo client yet—he's merely a diversion at this point. Not too unlike the cards on the misshapen wooden table in front of us.

"Come on," I goad. "You'll win."

Phred shakes his red-haired head. Some part of him knows that if he loses, he'll lose more than the silver in his pocket. And yet, he can't stop himself either.

Because mortals are inherently, inexplicably disposed to act against their own self-interests. Which makes my job as a Misfortune at times comical, at other times predictable, and at all times necessary.

Far more necessary than our celestial counterparts, Guardians.

While Misfortunes nudge mortals into making bad decisions for the greater good, Guardians nudge mortals into making good decisions for their personal good. The only overlap is the subjective term *good*.

Good to Guardians means working with Happily Ever Afters to make them *even* happier using daylight magic, thus their golden halos. Good to Misfortunes means working with Unhappily Ever Afters to become Ordinary Ever Afters, using night magic, thus our shadowed eyes. For some inexplicable reason, Guardians fancy themselves imperative to the future of the realms, while Misfortunes often go unappreciated and unseen.

In theory, the goal of *all* celestial work is stability, only it's the Misfortunes who contribute significantly more. We prevent chaos, which is becoming far more difficult as the realms develop and change.

And so here I am in a gambling hall in the nether realm of Barfaris. Gambling on its own is already a bad decision. What would possess a mortal to risk their silver for the slim, almost impossible chance of winning more? Especially in an underworld filled with magical creatures and mayhem. Greed, sure, but also self-sabotage. It's safe to say mortals would be doomed without us.

Particularly Phred, who is currently weighing his odds with a profoundly silly expression on his pale white face. A look he wears often, no doubt, along with the finest silk robes one can buy, that oozes just enough wealth for peasants to be wary of him.

I like Phred. Wait, let me rephrase—I like the idea of ruining Phred's destructive nature. The moment he gets this out of his system, the better his life will be. He'll never find true happiness, but he'll survive.

Currently, he's on the brink of disaster.

When Phred turned sixteen, his father named him his successor on the royal council. He would get invited to the very best parties at the palace, have respect, his choice of suitors, and the finest of food and horses. His father only had one condition: no mistakes. Phred really wanted to meet that demand, truly . . . but it was boring.

Then one night a few weeks ago, he and his noble friends skipped lessons to sneak into a gambling hall. Phred was hooked. It inspired feelings in him he'd never felt before; the risk, the thrill of the unknown, the slumming it with the lower classes—he loved it. He loved it too much. He lost several hundred silver in one very unfortunate hand. Which is why he *had* to keep coming back before his parents found out. If he didn't return it soon, his father would know. His parents would take everything away and name his sister the successor instead. Choosing a daughter over a son would be humiliating, and his sister didn't even like parties! So yes, he had to gamble. It was the only solution, really.

However, the pressure was getting to him, and he'd been making careless mistakes. Last week, he gave his mother's ruby bracelet to his girlfriend, Diane, after she caught him kissing her best friend and servant, Maeri. His mother blamed the family maid for it and arrested her. Phred could've—should've—told her the truth. I mean, what if his mother ran into Diane wearing it? And yeah, he should also feel guilty about the maid, but to him, that's the nature of things.

Then just this morning, he forged his parents' signatures

on his rejected proposal for peasant rehousing outside the city. Several councilors called it uncompassionate and others implied that if he proposed anything similar again, he would not be welcome on the council, regardless of his family. He needed to recoup his losses fast. After that, he'd get his focus back. He'd fix everything. All of this would be forgotten.

Here's the rub: In doing all these things, Phred began walking the path to Unhappily Ever After. If he keeps courting tumult, he could literally and/or metaphorically die. Not just die, he'd continue hurting his family, hurting his friends, and hurting himself.

When I saw him—by accident, I'm technically not supposed to be here, I just don't want to go home—I felt the urgency of his situation. Knew he was on course to be well and truly ruined in a matter of hours. And if there's one thing I love to do, feel compelled to do, it's to stop mortals from completing self-destruction.

Phred's time is running out. He's so reckless—because again, mortals are the worst—that his misfortune was just too difficult to pass by. Now he has me. And, as a bonus, it'll be a nice little boost on my final score. Un-dooming someone my own age from an Unhappily Ever After shows initiative. Determination. Someone worthy of more than just a provisional license.

I had to latch onto Phred. Mortals only see me when I want to be seen—which is never. He can hear me though. Well, he can hear my words in his own voice in his own head.

I add a little more edge. "Come on. If you win, you can replace all the silver before your parents see . . ." His brows pinch together. Ugh, I'm going to have to lay this on thick, aren't I? "You could also buy Diane that necklace she admired in the jeweler's window. She may even grant you a kiss. A betrothal between your families would be most advantageous."

Phred frowns. Okay, Diane doesn't inspire him. Hmm. "What about Maeri?" At this, Phred's eyes brighten. Snippets of fantasies flood his mind, and I sift through them, picking one that'll drive my next words home. The words leave my lips lazily, adding a bit of sleaze Phred seems to appreciate. "You could buy her a trinket and she would be very grateful. You could have a routine dalliance with her. Diane would never know."

A candle flickers to life in Phred's mind. Yes, I've got him now. Decision made. He pushes more silver into the pile on the table. The dealer shakes his head while the other players perk up. They're thinking this kid is either a genius or dense. And I'm thinking this is just what he needs.

They flip their cards. Phred wins with a trio of griffins. Good. Now he's feeling confident. As painful as these next steps will be, they'll be the most helpful too.

"All you can do is win," I say with a trickle of arrogance. "Another hand." I needn't try so hard. Phred is already caught hook, line, and sinker. Still, it never hurts to give voice to their desires. Keep them on track.

Phred wins another round because I make it so. With a snap of my fingers, I can switch the players' hands, mix up the cards lying face down. Just a little bit of parlor magic; Misfortunes don't normally need to use much.

Smoke circles the ceiling while Phred gambles. I wander

around looking at cards, listening to conversations. The candles flicker and drinks splash over heavy mugs as a minotaur waitress stomps through, wiping down grimy tables. We're in a hidden club beyond the palace walls. I'd been walking in the village using an old coin I stole from my father's wallet, when I followed my instincts here. I love the nether realms. They're alive and rife with chaos that I desperately want to fix. With more time, I could turn this place around one client at a time. Watch it transform from an Unhappily Ever After to an Ordinary Ever After.

Phred sits up. He recouped his losses. He could quit now. Walk away. Everything would be as right as rain.

"Another hand?" the dealer asks, lifting an eyebrow.

Phred smiles.

The round begins and he has good cards, ones I didn't have to arrange. There's a zeal in his movements. In his gaze. He's not thinking about his parents or Diane or even Maeri. He's thinking he's about to change his life. Maybe he wouldn't take the council spot. Maybe he would open his own exclusive tavern frequented by the royals and nobility—the only people he deems worthy of joy. The pile of silver is high. It would be enough, and he wouldn't even have to finish school or learn the politics of creatures he believes are beneath him.

"It's all going to be yours," I murmur.

Phred tries to keep his hands steady as he pushes the last of his winnings in. Oh, this is it. This is his chance at something better than what his parents could give him. After this win, he'll be swimming in pretty girls and riches. At least that's what he thinks.

Cards flip. Phred's winning. About to have a four of a kind. He's nearly there, and for a moment, I wonder if I should restrain myself. The card—a black serpent—is on the table. I could let Phred have his dreams come true for a moment. This would be giving him exactly what he wants.

But then . . . he doesn't deserve that. No mortal does. If I gave him everything he wanted with this one hand, he would never learn to be less self-centered. He's seventeen and already a cheater. A bully. Spoiled rotten and yet always wants more. Privileged and wealthy, but never donates to anyone asking for help. He abhors peasants and any unbeautiful creature that crosses his path. If he gets everything he wants, would he turn his life around? No. He will never be satisfied with what he has. He'll die at an early age creating more Unhappily Ever Afters for those unlucky enough to encounter him. He will create chaos.

Phred doesn't deserve to get what he wants. He deserves to get what he needs.

I tap my finger against the card, changing it from the serpent into a sphinx.

When it's revealed and another player wins, Phred deflates. All his silver is gone.

His thoughts are loud. *My parents will know. They'll take the carriage. Take my council spot. Disgrace me. I'll have nothing. Be nothing.* What he says aloud though is, "*Fuck.*"

After excusing himself from the table, leaving all the chips behind, Phred hobbles outside. The moon is high and somewhere in the distance, wolves howl.

Phred is feeling low. He's thinking about how unfair it all

is, how this cannot be happening to him, how he's the victim, really, when I tap his shoulder. He's no longer on the path to Unhappily Ever After.

Phred will take this disappointment and the punishment coming his way. He will cry. He will languish in his room for a while. And then he will learn to work. Appreciate less. He will find new, attainable, predictable dreams to chase.

He will have a perfect Ordinary Ever After.

Joy settles in my heart. Power surges in my chest. All in all, this was a good day. A great day, really. I saved this poor soul. He'll never know how close he was to catastrophe. I'm glad I prevented this one.

My work here is done. I grab hold of my coin in one hand, snap my fingers with the other, and dissipate in a cloud of dust. For a brief few seconds, I'm in the space between realms, the Liminal, where it smells foul and looks like dull stars in a sea of nothingness. I've heard it's a reflection of your mood.

When I re-form, I'm back in Malespero. Standing in front of the ash-coated window overlooking The Dark Mile, a moat of used-up coins from former Misfortunes tossed into a river of dirt. It's probably the nicest view any of us have here. It's . . . oddly hopeful.

I stretch out my long limbs, yawning. Realm jumping always makes my body a little tired. After a deep inhale, I glance around at the bareness of my room.

It's impersonal save for a few books borrowed from the Mortal Outcome Council library. There's a stack on statistics, intuitive mind reading, strategizing the future using probability and predictability, and some on understanding the mentality of mortals.

I take a seat on the edge of my bed and look up at the clock, although it serves no purpose. Time is irrelevant here. It's always night. Everything's in shades of gray. Even the air whiffs of neutrality.

Malespero shares a border with Avalonia, where the Guardians live. The next closest realm is Whimsia, which is the stuff of nightmares. Pure chaos.

"Home" for my kind is where we Misfortunes live and eat in between hopping to mortal realms. It's a stop-and-go. It holds my clothes, gives me a place to rest my body and magic.

It's also where I submitted unfun assignments until today. I'd skipped graduation in favor of actually helping people. There's no need to congratulate ourselves for ending training. That's precious time lost, better used to keep mortals safe.

While illegal to use my father's coin, no one can fault me for being diligent. And it's not like I could run away with it. I still have to come back here every day to my father's house to recharge. Although I would never call it home or him my family. The concepts of home and family don't exist. Not for me. Not with *him*.

I chug the glass of stale water that's beside my bed and fall back against the headboard. My eyes briefly close and I picture another place. Imagine myself in the center of a bustling village as mortals meander around me and droplets of cold rain patter my cheeks. What would it be like to physically exist there? To be seen there? To *feel* there?

Sudden laughter bubbles in my throat. What would I do if I was surrounded by all that life and color? The thought runs circles in my mind. Who would I be if I wasn't working? I'd be restless. The mortal realms may have food and color and smells and sights, yet they are cruel without guidance. It's becoming the nature of mortality. They *want* to suffer. And I won't let them.

There's a sudden knock on my door and I startle from my little escapist daydream. I peek again at the clock on the wall, which swings around concentrically, never stopping to rest. Still, even I know that it's not the right time for a visitor. I should be asleep.

With a deep breath, I cross over the room. I steady my breathing. There's only one person it could be. The only person who, unfortunately, matters in my life.

I twist the door open and Blight rushes in, knocking the knob out of my hand. The wood crashes against the stone wall. A yelp leaves my lips before words join it. "About the coin, I only went to Barfaris and I—"

Blight only shakes his bald head. "Not now, child. I don't care about your little exploits." What he doesn't say, and I know with all my being, is that he doesn't care about me at all. He glances around the room, happy with the lack of personality within it, and then slides another gold coin from his pocket. "We've a deadline."

My brows thread together as I take Blight in. He's a short, dark brown man with an impeccable black suit that only high leadership could wear. I look nothing like my father, which is just as well since I'm not allowed to call him that outside the house. The lack of resemblance helps him keep his distance from his unwanted nuisance of a son when it suits him.

I glance down at the coin and then back to him. It could be a test. He loves testing me and watching me fail. "The academy didn't mind that I skipped today?"

"I told them you were preoccupied." Blight tuts, thrusting the coin into my palm. "This coin comes with your provisional license, but also orders from leadership. They were impressed with your work in whatever nether realm you unlawfully visited. Really impressed. You tied for first place at the academy, near-perfect score. You've now qualified for a chance at the mentorship."

"*The* mentorship?" Despite this possibly being a farce, excitement flips in my gut. This is what I've been wanting since before I could walk. Back then, I wanted to be like Blight. Prove to him that I was worthy of being called his son. Now, if I got this mentorship, it would be the official start of a great career. This is huge. I could travel the realms at will, whenever I wanted, using my magic without recharging. I'd have access to everything. I'd have freedom from Malespero. I'd make decisions. I could create lasting, impactful change throughout all the realms. We could decrease Unhappily Ever Afters to a record low, perhaps even eradicate them completely—

"Settle down, it's a test," he says gruffly, and my excitement shrivels. "Pass and you'll get the mentorship seat on the council. Fail, and you'll be stuck here longer than either of us would like, continuing to assist me until you get your full licensure." Blight holds my gaze, though he's a good foot shorter than me.

"This could be a case that'd give Misfortunes the last spot on the Mortal Outcome Council. We could have the majority for once."

I chuckle mirthlessly, my stomach upset at the thought of failing and continuing to live here with—and worse, assist—a father who hates me and a nonexistent mother who made sure he would. "No pressure."

"I'll tell you this, given our . . . connection. You are a strong Misfortune. You've helped twenty-two mortals cement their OEAs within the same time it takes anyone else to cross seven. And that was just within a school setting." He steps closer to me; his polished gray shoes sink into my dingy white carpet. There's almost pride in his voice. Almost. "This won't be straightforward. Your client will be at a pivotal juncture. You'll only have seven midnights to turn it around. And you'll have to use more magic than you're used to, and far more charm."

"I'm not too worried about charming a mortal, Blight." It's not like the mortal will see me. But . . . I scrub a hand over my lips at his words. There's a reason they're picking me. The destiny must be difficult to strategize. A challenge. If anyone could do it, it's me. I'm great at finding the right angle, the bad decisions that'll lead to a decent life. If I didn't, I wouldn't be nearly as confident. And Blight wouldn't be here telling me that I'm in consideration for the mentorship.

"It's not only a mortal you'll be charming." He cocks an eyebrow as the coin begins to heat in the palm of my hand. "And you'll be in the magicless realm of Lumina. You know how those are—they can be a bedrock of Unhappily Ever

Afters, including a few rare and extremely dangerous Miserably Ever Afters."

I glance down as a name etches into the metal. Before I can read it, Blight coughs, drawing my attention away from my new client.

"Don't mess this up for us, Calamity. With hesitation, I believe in you." He plops his hand down on my shoulder. "I know you can bring us this win and land the mentorship seat on the Mortal Outcome Council. Though the Guardians may be celestials"—he takes a deep breath as if he's on a pulpit commanding his troops—"it's time for us to have a voice in esteemed leadership. It would propel our family into the spotlight, bring respect to our names. Respect our family lost when your mother left for the mortal realms, embraced chaos, and . . ." He doesn't finish that thought. "Do you understand? Do you know what's required?"

"I do," I answer quickly. It's easier for him to believe I'd do this for him and our "family" since I've pushed myself my entire childhood for both. Only I know I'm doing this for me. For mortals. For celestials everywhere. If he's happy in the process, that's even better for me to step out of his shadow and away from him forever. "I've no doubt in my abilities."

"Good." Blight smiles, and it might be the first time I've ever seen him do that. It's not bright or even joyful; if anything, it's a taunt. "Use that arrogance. You'll need it."

CHAPTER THREE

The Mortal Outcome Council's library is vast. The kind of vast that makes it impossible to tell where it begins or ends or how many rooms there are. Even as the sole occupant living in the dormitory above it for the past few years since I wasn't welcome home, I still haven't figured this place out. I did, however, find the most isolated—and *cozy*—study room for my research. Well, as cozy as one can get here.

This one has a standard wooden desk and a hard chair that bites into the backs of my knees and is enclosed by bookcases containing all the books useful to my needs. One of those bookcases pushes open to bring me back to the main floor.

I drum my fingers against the table, staring down at the paperwork Honour handed me.

It would seem there are quite a few stipulations about securing the mentorship—at least that's what I assume are in the thirty-three pages of contractual Celestialese. While I know Celestian and common tongue, this is almost an entirely different language. The dictionary isn't too useful either; every time I define one word, it gets used a different way in the next sentence.

I asked Honour to translate it. She laughed and said, "*Good luck.*"

Magic's no use either; I can't just make myself smarter or fluent in another language.

Ultimately, I sign it without knowing what it says and hope for the best. The paperwork disappears the moment the ink dries, and now I'm shifting my focus to what actually matters.

Lucy Addlesberg and Lumina.

This assignment will require a lot of plotting. Which really means being careful how I use my magic or else I'll fail. And that means adhering to several, frankly ridiculous, rules.

1. Celestials forbid using magic for bad intentions—fairies would say/do whatever feels best, there's no such thing as bad anyway. You can see why this rule will be hard to follow. What if, for instance, I trip a villainous jerk into a pile of manure because it would make my client laugh? Apparently, that's not a good intention?
2. Guardians believe magic can only be cast for making dreams come true, securing a Happily Ever After. For improvements. Now, the idea of "improvements" is vague, which is where the only-good-intentions bit comes in. I could magick water if my client was feeling parched, make her dress extra sparkly if she so desired. But again, if I trip a villainous jerk into a pile of manure because it would "improve" my client's mood and maybe even spread fertilizer onto

a much-needed garden? That's still a bad intention. So annoying.

3. Then I have the single most important fairy rule: Any physical, life-altering improvements I've made for a client must be completed by a True Love's Kiss or the solidification of their Happily Ever After. If neither occur within the specified time, well . . . any magic I've used is undone by that final midnight. Meaning I can't leave Lumina until Lucy Addlesberg secures her fate or else all my efforts will shrivel up like a pumpkin enchanted into a coach.

In conclusion, I'm using fairy magic in a celestial assignment. What feels natural to me might offend the uptight Guardians, who will be only too happy to flunk me.

For my own sake, I should take the advice Virtue gave me once when I was struggling to assimilate, not that it necessarily helped: *Limit your magic*. But applying it here means I could be less likely to break rules, right?

Ugh, I loathe rules. And worse, I loathe researching.

I take a quick bite of my honey biscuit, chewing thoughtfully. Once the delicious flavor washes over my tongue, I slip a triangular white pill from my pocket and swallow it with some tea. Strictly speaking, drinks and food are verboten in the library, but there's no one here to snitch. It's blissfully quiet, a calm paradise compared to where I'm going.

Lumina is an unusual realm. I've always loved magicless kingdoms—they're the stuff my favorite stories are made of. Helping down-on-their-luck protagonists see an entirely different world where dreams can and do come true through changing their perspective and a swish of a wand—that's a blast. Unfortunately, they are very conservative at times. The kind of place where teenagers marry in arranged matches between families because the average life expectancy is short, and they almost never break out in song like in magical kingdoms. It's disappointing—I'd love to be in a place where the villagers randomly perform spontaneous-yet-coordinated dance numbers.

Anyway, the most important quirk: The Kingdom of Lumina is unlucky. You could almost think it's cursed. According to this history book, most inhabitants experience Unhappily Ever Afters. Everything in their realm is set up and structured to make people fail. To cause people to make poor decisions. The climate is rainy—this would be good for growing crops, only theirs stopped growing years ago. Now it's just dark and grim without purpose. The economy is bad, the gap between the rich and poor is bigger than anywhere else. Misery runs rampant there. Everything I read implies it's going to be gloomy for me in Lumina.

I slam the book shut. That's enough reading. The only way to understand this realm is to see it with my own eyes. So I clutch the coin, let its magic swirl around me . . . and then *poof*! I disappear into the Liminal, my body and mind separate into glitter and sparkles, flying down a long tube of stars and wonder.

The air smells like warm chocolate cookies, although I've heard it's different for everyone else.

All too fast, I reappear on the cusp of Lumina in the magical well that sits on the edge of the Liminal. I breathe in and out, letting my heart and lungs settle, letting my legs steady, my eyes focus. With one final long exhale, I push through the magic barrier, climbing up and out into Lumina. Then I grab my wand and tap myself, casting a quick spell to remain unseen. That way I can watch. Observe. Get a feel for the place I hope to change.

What I find is as dour as the book foretold.

Lumina was once picturesque. The sky used to stay blue without a cloud in sight, and beneath it sat a world of brilliance. Now gray, rain-laden clouds hover above patches of dead grass poking through formerly immaculate lawns. Long ago, the streets were lined with beautiful homes of every color, and mortals would smile as they picked up their morning scroll. Now half the houses are either gone or have boarded-up windows.

The mortals still smile, but I sense pain behind it. And the air . . . it used to smell like unending summers of berries and warmth. Joy. Now there are tiny puffs of decay mixed with dirt.

Happiness left Lumina, and with it, hope.

As I walk down the street, gown billowing behind me in the sharp, nippy breeze, I hold my head high. Children playing outside gasp as if they notice me. They call out to their parents that the air feels warmer. The sky brighter. I beam, patting my pocket where my glittery gold wand sits, awaiting further use.

When I pass the signpost with two little arrows pointing in different directions, one to the palace, the other to the village center, I narrowly resist the impulse to restore its shine. The village name, Fulhorn, has been scratched off in places and now reads: FULL O' SHIT. If I weren't here only for Lucy, I would make it my mission to restore this town and have the townspeople change the sign themselves with pride.

However, Lucy is my assignment and I need to be careful. Too much magic too fast will create chaos, and Guardians *loathe* chaos.

Still, I *must* use my magic. It's an extension of who I am. Without it, I lack control. My skin feels irritated, my blood boils. A million thoughts race through my brain, none of them good. I spiral into darkness. Worthlessness. Disappointment. Disenchantment. I want to lay down and never get up again. It's a battle that I'm not confident I can win. Magic makes me feel that at least I can change some things for good. It gives me purpose.

Magic is my armor.

Besides, Lucy's Happily Ever After depends on my magic, and I won't let her down. My success will get that mentorship seat. The Mortal Outcome Council will have no choice but to promote me. I can change the realms. It's important. I cannot and will not fail.

On unshakeable feet and with determination surging in my chest, I tread the dusty road toward the center of the village. The wind yanks at my cheeks as the dirt gives way to cracked cobblestones, and overgrown grass gives way to rows of buildings surrounding a town fountain. No water comes out. I doubt any water has danced from these spouts in a decade.

The shops are just as drab, all shades of warped wood and stone. Rickety titles above each doorway in chipped paint read things like Winifred's Breaderie—I didn't know that was a word—and Shoes by Morris, where all the shoes are either black or dark brown. Ellie's Practical Clothing Outlet is rather busy. There are more than a few strapping lads in the store examining suits. There's a paper store, a candlemaker, a seamstress, a pub. And in the tiny, far corner of the village square, with a metal book dangling from its white stone, is An Enchanted Story. *Lucy.*

I stride past downtrodden people making their way home as the sky darkens in preparation for the rain that'll finally unleash itself on this desolate land. My legs pick up their pace when thick drops drizzle down the windowpanes. I don't enter through the main door but the side one, into a small, near-empty kitchen. It's somewhat neglected. The cabinets are shabby and the floor buckles beneath me.

Not a second after my arrival, I grab a dented mug from the cabinet, tap my sparkly gold wand against the edge, and cast my spell. There's no time to waste.

The air briefly swirls with speckles of glitter. I know, I said I wouldn't use magic superfluously, but hot chocolate is never superfluous. I smile as creamy chocolate fills the mug to the rim. Perfect. Step one is off to a good start.

Though I want to chug it—it's been days since I've had a good hot chocolate, and my nerves could surely use it—I carry it with me to find my new client (!!!), who's somewhere amid the stacks of books.

Through the doorway and into the shop, the atmosphere

changes. One room is dilapidated from underuse, while this one is snug like a home. Shelves line the walls and chest-height cases divide the rectangular room into four. Every available space overflows with books that look loved, polished, with strong spines and embossed lettering. Hints of spices mingle with the scent of opening a brand-new novel the reader is bound to enjoy. Once I glance past the beauty of it, I notice the uneven floor, the old cases, shadowy corners, and the lack of cushioned seating. I can work with this.

The smile continues to linger as I strut over to the romance section, where Lucy Addlesberg lies face down on the wood surrounded by books. She grumbles. *Hmm.* So she's not unwell, perhaps just mortified that a row of dusty books fell on her. It's been a bad day, I gather, and this is the icing on top.

Mmm, icing. I take a sip of the hot chocolate. Yes, that'll help too.

No! Focus, Darling.

Lucy's got long black frizzy braids, dark brown skin, and the most raggedy clothes I've ever seen on a mortal before. An aproned dress torn and patched in places hangs off her frame. There's a hand-written letter crumpled up beside her forlorn form. It interests me, but I can't read it without moving it, and she's not ready to see me yet.

Facts stream into my mind as I meander closer.

Lucy Addlesberg: Seventeen. Smart—she got all the top grades in school before her mother died. She sold their family home, lives in the bookstore, and is unfortunately disconsolate.

She's lonely, worried, and sad. And for some reason, she hasn't made a ton of bad decisions of her own volition . . . so why isn't she already on the path to Happily Ever After? That's odd.

She doesn't notice as I step over her, nor when I twirl my wand once more to create a cushion slightly off the ground. More or less, I want to see her world. See how she lives it. The mess she's in, really. Also, wearing a yellow ballgown strewn with pearls means I can't very well plop onto the floor, but I do want to stay nearby.

Heaps of books envelop us. The titles are in all different sizes and fonts. The vivid illustrations grab my attention. Princesses with long hair tumbling out a window in a tall tower, looking rather glum. Princes in red jackets aiming their bows within wooded paradises. Sleeping teenage maidens awaiting a True Love's Kiss. And on top of each, it says, *Based on the True Fairy Tale*. I squeak. Good golly. While True Love's Kiss *is* true, the other stuff? Yikes.

Fairy tales are just that: stories concocted by fairies in Whimsia and planted in mortal realms for a bit of fun. There's a reason the stories are all dark and twisty and nearly every villain ends up dead or tortured. And, of course, even some of the protagonists aren't spared either. It brings immense pleasure to fairies to not only see our stories entertain mortals, but to watch our tales evolve from a snippet into folklore told to little children so they eat their supper and won't go into the woods alone.

Lucy peeks up with wide eyes. I suspect she heard my reaction and can now smell the chocolate. Magical chocolate is top quality and always seems to cut through a terrible bout of anxiety. It reminds me of home and the advice my mother would give me: If there's a problem you can't yet solve, the first solution is hot chocolate.

I miss her and Paradise Pines. The feeling isn't mutual though.

"Alright, love muffin, it's time to get up," I tell her encouragingly. She'll hear my words in her head and the tone I said it in, but in her own voice. Until I reveal myself to her and we become the very best of friends. Guardians tend not to reveal themselves; fairies do though, and I'm certain the fairy approach is the way to go here. I'm also certain we're going to have a great time together. Starting now. All I have to do is—

"No, stay down there for another moment. Life is hard and you're tired," another person says somewhere behind me. I twist in my seat, my mug nearly falling from my grasp.

I shriek when I see one of *them* standing there. A Misfortune. All in black with sallow gray skin and stringy gray hair that hangs limply by the sides of their face. They meet my gaze. They're tall, leaning against a bookcase as if they've been there the entire time. Wait, how long *have* they been standing there?!

"Begone, devil!" I shout, waving my hands around. "You aren't wanted!"

And then they . . . laugh. The sound is jarring and evil and makes my insides squirm. Why are they here? This is *my* test. Misfortunes only work with those on the path to ruination. That's not Lucy! She's neutral.

"Are you a fairy princess? Where are your wings? I thought fairies had wings." Their voice is deep, strange. Accented, the emphasis on the words different than mine. They cock an eyebrow. "Don't you think that . . . ensemble is a bit much?" They chuckle again.

"Okay, monster." I set my mug down on the floor and jump up, holding my wand out in front of me. "I've had enough of your lip. You aren't supposed to be here."

"Monster? Oh . . ." They seem to understand and tap a finger against their lips. "Sorry about that, I forget to change into my true form whenever I leave Malespero. Let me—" And then they snap their fingers and shift into . . .

Well . . . they shift into . . .

"Oh goodness," I murmur, taking a step back.

They fill in with color—light brown skin, lustrous and messy blondish-brown locks that curl in gentle waves to their ears. They have piercing green eyes and thick, expressive brows. The only attribute marking them as a Misfortune is the inky black sludge that seemingly drips from their eyes and ends just above their sharp cheekbones. Night magic: Misfortunes use the darkness between the realms while Guardians use the light between the realms.

I've been told Misfortunes look quite horrifying, but I find them exceedingly . . . beautiful.

They smile down at me with their beautiful lips. No, not smile. Smirk. Evilly. Like a villain. Because they *are* a villain. They take a step closer. I feel instantly drawn in and hunted. The wand wavers in my grasp.

"Most people don't associate me with goodness as they should, so thank you. The name's Calamity, though my friends call me Calam. I'm he." He winks on that last bit, sliding a few curls behind his ear.

"Misfortunes don't have friends," is literally all I can utter. Misfortunes aren't supposed to be beautiful either, though thankfully my mouth doesn't say that. "And I don't need to know your name. You're leaving. Lucy is *my* client." With the hand not holding my wand, I pluck the gold coin from my pocket and hold it up to his face. "See?"

"Hmm," is all he says, taking a black coin from his own pocket and holding it up to my face. "You did read the contract, didn't you?" Lucy's name is etched into his coin. Meaning she must be his client too. I knew not reading that contract would come back to haunt me.

"Well," I say, adding an air of authority to my tone, "just return to wherever you came from and I'm sure they'll reassign you to someone more worthy of your attention."

"No, thanks. This assignment is important to me."

"It's more important to me and to Lucy." I tap my foot and even I can admit that it's childish. Lucy scuttles away, staring at a book that flipped over seemingly on its own. She's breathing fast and I'm sure she thinks the bookstore is haunted. Oh dear. "She needs help. A guiding hand. Compassion. Not more . . . unfun things. Can't you see that she is not one of yours?"

"Let's get things straight, princess—" He takes a step near me.

I huff. "I'm not a princess."

"Your dress says otherwise." He snorts, standing tall. Not backing down one inch. "We've both been assigned Lucy because she's at a crossroads. This is a test—a game that one of us must win. That's how this works. The winner gets to determine if she has a Happily Ever After or an Ordinary Ever After and receives the mentorship on the Mortal Outcome Council, right?"

I shake my head. "That's not . . . no, you . . . you . . . you—"

"Call me Calam." He has the audacity to look amused. "What's your name?"

My jaw unhinges. Nothing comes out. I'm positively flummoxed.

Then he claps his hands in glee. "No wait, let me guess—it's something like Syrup or Dumpling or Tartlet . . ." He glimpses down at the wand. "What a silly thing."

How dare *he!* I scowl. "My name is Darling, I am she, and I assure you, it's not silly."

I swish it once, scattering magical glitter in the air. It falls on his skin, making it glow—as if he needs anything else to make him prettier. He gags while swatting it away. Lucy squeaks, probably seeing some strange twinkling in front of her eyes. I'm really traumatizing her today, but I'll fix that later. "I'm more powerful than a celestial. So, if you have any good sense, you'll leave before I do something you won't like."

He laughs again. Doubles over, actually, cackling like a wicked witch.

"Stop laughing!"

"*Darling!*" More inky tears stream down his pretty face. "I should have known. It suits you."

I grimace. "Excuse me, *I* am the one being considered for

the mentorship. They wouldn't send two of us. There must be a mistake. Now stop laughing and return to Mals—Malspepi—whatever-its-name-is, or else."

That seems to sober him. He rises to his full height and inches near me. We're so close, I've got no way out. "That doesn't sound very Happily Ever After of you."

Ugh. He has to *go*. "Lucy needs help, not you. Don't you ever lose sleep knowing that you and yours take all the joy out of living? Be bold and do the right thing for once."

"Whether or not you believe it, I'm here to help Lucy too." He stares down at me. Frustration and maybe even a little respect swim in his gaze. "The contract stated rather clearly that there'd be two of us competing. You did sign it, didn't you?"

Honour is the worst. She could've told me.

"Well, then you leave me no choice." I begin swishing my wand, making my good intentions clear in my mind. I'm here to help Lucy, and exposing this monster is the only way I can. This is a bit of tricky magic, causing me to make up a rhyme on the spot. "Make it glitter, make it gleam, take the invisible and make it seen!"

Calam gulps as Lucy's head swivels in his direction, her finger pointing and lips open, a scream ready to erupt.

"You have no idea what you've done, *Darling*." He raises both hands in preparation. The ink dripping from the corners of his eyes shimmer. "I've come here to win."

He snaps his fingers.

CHAPTER FOUR

Calamity

Lucy frantically glances between me and the now-visible fairy before letting out a walloping scream. More books topple out of the rickety case. Everything's so loud, my teeth chatter and my head vibrates.

"You . . . You just appeared!" she hollers, shakily pointing at the two of us. "Like magic!"

I try to scramble away from the sound, but there's nowhere to go in this packed shop. I'm revealed and I don't like it. Misfortunes thrive in shadows and whispers, not when we're seen and judged. To be seen is to be perceived.

I loathe being perceived.

And look, is it my fault? Possibly. I stood there watching the fairy, taking notes when I could've introduced myself better. Should I have used magic to get back at Darling, revealing her like she did to me and making this a thousand times worse? Probably not, but my desire to win that mentorship and save Lucy from a path of chaos is the "right thing" as Darling said. That's what makes me a great Misfortune.

Meanwhile, Darling clutches that wand in her hand as if it's her savior. She's a comically colorful beam of light in this gloomy landscape. Her medium brown skin glimmers against round, rosy cheeks. A messy bun atop her heart-shaped face spills dark brown curls down her neck, skimming her shoulders. She's wearing an enormous yellow monstrosity of a gown, rainbow leggings, and purple boots, and her dark brown eyes are wide. She's a menace. A nuisance. If I want to help Lucy live a life free from unpredictability, leave Malespero behind, freely travel the realms without living in my father's shadow, and change the way the realms operate, I have to outmaneuver this fairy. A plan begins to form. Charm—there was a reason Blight said charm. First, I need to—

"Everything is okay," Darling says in her bubbly voice to Lucy. "Close your eyes, count to ten. The answer will be waiting then."

Lucy promptly stops screaming (thankfully) and begins counting. Damn, the fairy *is* powerful. Guardians don't rhyme or carry wands. And they certainly wouldn't reveal themselves like this.

I'd heard that a fairy had joined the Guardian ranks at the academy, but Misfortunes take separate classes. And even if we were scheduled to, I likely wouldn't have gone, preferring practical over theoretical.

Darling beams at her own handiwork, thinking she finally has the upper hand. Correction, she is an unfortunately *adorable* menace who needs to be cut down to size. I can compete, I just need practice. Like most celestials, I tend to be conservative with my magic. We don't have all that much and worse, this kind of craft is beyond me. It's too powerful. Darling will require me to be clever. Lucky for me, I live for a challenge.

Darling turns my way. "You can go now. She'll come up

with an explanation for why you suddenly appeared—mortals always do that when they see something too weird to be true. Go on. Take the loss, *Calam.*"

I enjoy the way she says my name as if it's a curse. Makes my heart beat a little faster. Like I got under her skin just a bit. Excitement swirls in the pit of my stomach. Oh yes, we are in for a battle.

"Five," Lucy counts softly.

"No way." I shake my head. "You should go."

"Seven."

"Absolutely not." Darling's jaw sets. I find her so . . . obnoxious.

"Nine."

"Well, there's only one way to play this." I double-snap my fingers and plaster a smile on my face. The plan fills in quickly. I know just how I'm going to win: by throwing Darling completely off-center. She's rainbows and laughter and chaos. She'll eschew my natural inclinations for order and control.

"Ten." Lucy opens her eyes.

Some realization dawns on her face as she takes us both in. We resemble mortals now. Me with my princely attire copied from the cover of a book and Darling in a far less poufy gray dress. Save her wand poking out of her pocket, her glittery everything is gone, which, good riddance. It was the best I could do with the time. Darling cringes when she notices and shoots me a glance of absolute loathing—my new favorite. Lucy doesn't notice. Instead, she rubs her head, likely at the bruise from where she was hit by a book.

I was there for that too. Absolutely bad luck.

She takes a few deep breaths. "Wait, I know why you're here . . . You're here to . . . I think I remember. Um . . . Sorry, I'm suddenly . . . quite tired and my brain hurts, and I can't . . ."

"Don't worry," I say, thrusting a hand out to her. She glances down at it as I continue. "We're from a few villages over. We came for the open positions." Yes, keep going . . . "There was a rumor you were hiring, and we would love the opportunity to work here. I'm Calam." I point to myself and then to the confused fairy. "This is . . . well, I call her *Darling*."

"Oh, you're a couple?" Lucy rises to her feet and dusts off carpet lint from her ripped maroon sweater.

Darling gasps. "No, we—"

"More than that," I interject before Darling tries to cut me off again.

Darling sputters. "Wh-what?"

"We've just graduated academy and were desperate to go off into this big world together. Find somewhere new to plant our roots." I share a sly smile with Lucy, who nods as if we're in on a big secret together. "Weren't we?"

In answer, Darling reaches for the now visible hot chocolate on the floor and some sloshes out of the mug before she chugs it down. Clearly, she has a chocolate dependence. Fairies are a bizarre species.

"That's sweet," Lucy says dreamily, perhaps thinking about her own memories or something. Good. I took a wild guess and figured Lucy would love a love story. Meanwhile, Darling is terrified of love, if her reaction to the sleeping beauty memoir is any indication. My ability to act fast on my feet is unparalleled yet again. Adaptable. An asset to the Mortal Outcome Council.

Then Lucy's expression droops, her eyes downcast.

"I'm afraid there isn't enough money in the till for me to hire anyone. You were told a false rumor, Mr. Calam."

"Just Calam," I correct. "We won't need money. Only room and board if possible? We'd love to learn more about Fulhorn and the book business." I sigh with false hope. "I've always wanted to work in a bookshop. They seem full of potential and memories." Lucy truly is a hopeless, sentimental romantic. Sentimentalists make awful decisions. I can work with that. I can use it to get her on track.

"But we understand if this is too much," Darling interrupts, finally catching up. Excellent—this would be no fun if I could keep beating her. "After all, it's clear the store means the world to you, and of course you know nothing about us. We could be perfidious thieves or . . . or . . . drifters with ill intent. And, um, sharing your business with strangers could be daunting."

Lucy throws her head back and chuckles. The sound echoes off dusty tomes and pierces the musty air. She looks free and her age for a moment. "I don't think either of you are perfidious thieves or drifters with ill intent. Not in those clothes, and not if you had any skill at finding silver. My business is by far the least profitable in the village."

"We're just a couple trying to find a new home and community to be a part of," I add, earning a glare from Darling.

Lucy beams again, and I've got her now. Despite my mind being in a jumble from the exposure, I did well. I want to pat myself on the shoulder; the mentorship will be mine. Though I never really had a doubt.

"Still, we don't want to make you uncomfortable with our . . . handholding and, um . . . um," Darling begins, grasping. "Banter?" She winces.

It's difficult not to laugh. Is *that* what she thinks relationships are made of? *Oh, fairies*. Even I, a Misfortune who generally loathes everyone and everything I can't fix, understand mortal relationships and what they entail.

"You wouldn't. It would be nice. And I understand two people trying to strike out on their own. It's like all the best stories." Then Lucy is quiet for a few beats, considering. When she glances up at us, the corner of her lip quirks. "I've an attic that could be used for a bedroom. You would have to share, of course, but I can tell that shouldn't be too hard for you." She winks my way. "And if you're here to work with me to make it better, that would be amazing. I can't pay you or provide you with new clothes or even heat, but I'm sure we can come to some sort of an agreement for food . . ." She trails off, realizing the books are still strewn about the floor. "Oh, I'm sorry you had to see this. I'm usually much tidier."

"We'll clean up," Darling volunteers, touching Lucy's shoulder gently. "Why don't you go make some tea and tend to that bump on your head, and we'll put these back? It's the least we can do since we startled you and gave you such a fright!" She offers a bright smile, which reflects on Lucy's face.

"You did? I can't remember . . ." Lucy taps her temple. "That sounds good. Do you know where everything goes?"

"Definitely," I add with a thick sprinkle of confidence. "Your books are in good hands."

"Thank you. I'll be right back." She drifts off with a slight limp.

When she's finally out of sight, Darling takes the wand from her pocket. She swishes it in the air and the books lift from the ground before sliding back into their right locations.

"There, that's better. Now for this ghastly thing." She touches her wand against her dress, about to cast another spell . . . then she grumbles. "*Sprinkles.*"

I smirk. "Sprinkles?"

We can't undo each other's magic. It's an old rule. One we don't struggle with since we are never assigned the same client . . . normally. Imagine the mayhem of eternals undoing each other's spells, the constant back and forth of intentions. No, Darling is stuck in that dress just like I'm stuck being exposed. Lucy has already spoken to us, seen us. We can't unplant that seed now. Memory magic is difficult, next to impossible.

"It's the right dress," I say with a quirk of my brow. "You look like a young maiden with her possible betrothed."

"This is absurd." Her lips flatten into a thin line. "We're not even—"

"We're in a traditional kingdom, Darling. How else would we insert ourselves into Lucy's life? Why would we both be here at the same time?" I drum my fingers against my thigh.

She grimaces. "You do know this means war, right?"

"What was it you called Lucy . . . *hmm*. My little love muffin." Steam almost whistles out of her ears. "Well, my little love muffin, my heart, my intended, I can't wait to hold hands and banter with you."

"*War*, Calam." Hands on her hips, she juts her chin out. If it weren't for the glittery wand, I might not take her seriously. "You have no idea who you're messing with."

"Oh, *Darling*." I step up to her, my nose nearly touching her own as I sneer. "I think I do. And I think I'm going to win."

"All of this," she counters, shaking her head, "for the mentorship? You would doom poor Lucy to a life without color and joy and happiness? She deserves the best her world can offer." Now there's confusion behind her frustration.

"We agree on that: Lucy does deserve the best her world can offer. Only, you fail to understand the definition of 'best.' Where you see the possibility of a Happily Ever After, I see the possibility of an Unhappily Ever After. Unpredictability. Instability. Tragedy. Imbalance." I lean close to her as Lucy begins walking toward us with two misshapen cups in her hands. Darling inhales sharply, her heart pounding as I nearly brush my lips lightly against her soft, supple cheek. This'll look like a public display of affection, only strengthening our romance to Lucy. She does love a good story. "Happiness is subjective. Survival is a fact."

Her lip wobbles, her gaze meeting mine. "No, that's . . . but, happiness is . . ."

My own heart begins to race. A reaction to being close to someone, no doubt. I swallow, the words almost getting lost in her nearness. My voice comes out huskier than planned. "Happiness has nothing to do with survival. A lesson you'll learn when I win the mentorship."

CHAPTER FIVE

Darling

Air freezes in my chest. There are alarm bells going off in my mind and a spiral that thickens with key words that I told myself I'd never give power to. That I'd never let get to me. My outer reality is reflecting my inner reality, and it's not pretty. I try to steel my face, become impenetrable even as I battle thoughts that want me to bend and break.

Worthless.

Ridiculous.

Useless.

And over and over again, behind all those words, there's a little voice telling me that I've always been wrong. The rainbows I paint on my face and the glitter I dust on my clothes could never cover up the cracks within. Magic cannot fix me. Smiles cannot make a heart happy. Laughter cannot make a mind fun. I'm broken. I don't belong here. Lucy is better off without me. I will never get that mentorship.

No.

I inhale.

No. No. No. It's not about me. None of this. It's about her. It's about making an impact on the mortal realms. Believing I can help anyone get a Happily Ever After.

I exhale.

"No," I say aloud to reaffirm myself. Calam watches me closely, pulling away as Lucy hands us each a cup of tea. If she heard me, it doesn't register as she glances down at the now clean floor.

I try not to grimace as I take the mug and sip the lightly flavored hot water. I need to shake myself from these mind games Calam is playing. He could have totally derailed me.

But I know that there is more at stake than my mental health. Lucy's hopes and dreams depend on me, and I cannot fail her.

Deep breaths in, deep breaths out. I will defeat Calamity the Misfortune. I just need time. And I need to keep up appearances of not backing down, not letting his villainy get me off track.

I am Darling Sparkleton, and I can—I *will* do this.

"No!" I say again with positivity, this time hamming it up for Lucy. "That's such a great idea." I smile. "Calam was just telling me how he would love to help with advertising the store by speaking one-on-one with every single townsperson. It's such a thoughtful offer, and no doubt he will do so well at it." I wink Calam's way and am rewarded with a quick snarl Lucy doesn't catch.

"That would be great." Lucy's face lights up and she slips a frizzy, wayward braid behind her ear. "I've never been able to do that since I have to run the shop." Her voice snags as she glances past the two of us through the storefront's window. I turn slightly to see a thick blond with tan skin flitting by outside as plump raindrops patter down on her. She stops and sees Lucy through the glass. Her mouth quirks up into a friendly smile.

She waves briefly like they may be acquaintances. Lucy does too. It's a weird interaction that makes me utterly curious.

"Who is that?" I ask, pressing closer to Lucy. "A friend?"

Lucy rubs the back of her neck. "She's just . . . she stops in sometimes for a new book."

"Oh?"

Before Lucy can explain—if she was even going to—the door swings open and a little bell jingles above it. The girl's blond waves plaster to her cheeks. Her bottom lip wobbles slightly from the cold. She takes the three of us in while shaking off the rain and unbuttoning her navy cloak. Pools of water form on the warped wood beneath her.

"Sorry," she squeaks. She drops her head, looking down at her muddy boots. "I meant to come earlier but I got held up with my family."

"Hold on." Lucy scampers off to—presumably—get a towel while Calam and I stand there.

"How are you?" I say, tamping down my curiosity. "My name is Darling. I'm—"

The girl's mouth opens and shuts without a sound. Lucy returns, rushing past me and knocking my shoulder.

Lucy's all smiles. "Darling, Calamity, would you mind giving us a minute?"

He and I exchange a glance before we drift back to the kitchen, dismissed. It's just as well; I need a moment to catch up on the day's events and figure out how to win this thing.

Calam huffs, leaning against the shabby counter, where there's a small bowl of oats soaking in water. Everything else is bare space. Nary a crumb nor morsel of other food, plates, or pans. "How do we play this?"

"Beg pardon?" My gaze falls around the room, taking in the rundown cabinets and the lack of a cooling box and stove. What does she eat? *How* does she eat? How is she surviving? While the bookstore is lovely, if this is her home, why is it so inhospitable? And where is her bedroom?

Calamity rolls his eyes and snaps his fingers, though he cringes like it takes a toll on him. I suspect it does. He's a celestial, after all—their magic has limits.

Time seemingly slows. I glance back at Lucy, currently stuck with a rag hovering over a patch of drenched floor, looking up at the mystery girl. Yet the raindrops continue pattering on the roof. Interesting that Calamity's power doesn't extend out there. We likely only have a few moments before time evens out.

"What are we going to do?" Calamity slightly staggers on his feet, his eyes pinched at the corners as if in pain.

I chuckle and swish my wand. Now the rain stops too. Calamity leans against the bookcase, his face drawn.

"*We* aren't going to do anything. You're confident, but you're out of your depth, Misfortune." I keep my voice steady, devoid of all the emotions swimming in my gut. He can't know that he got to me. He can't know how much I have at stake in this competition. I'm already at a disadvantage—the council might've sent him because they didn't believe in me. Didn't believe that fairies deserve a chance at leadership. That thought causes a riot in my brain. What if they are expecting me to fail?

"Darling—" He says my name breathlessly.

A smirk lifts my lips. "You don't have enough power to keep up with me."

"You just used your magic to expose me—*against* me. Imagine what the MOC would say?"

I shrug. "Fairies don't mind being out in the open."

"Do you really think they'd care about that? Aren't you trying for a spot? Aren't you hoping to fit in?" Calamity straightens. "I won't back down. If you don't want to immediately forfeit, you can't force me to either."

Anger thuds in sync with my heart. I don't want him to back down. Because if this is the best Misfortune the council could send to compete against me, then I should be able to do this easily. I have the power. I have the best intentions. I have the upper hand.

Besides, he's right. I'm not capable of sending him back. Powerful as I may be, I can't harm a celestial. I could expose him, sure, but if I wanted to . . . I don't know . . . make it that when he opened his mouth only crickets fell out (which would be funny), I would be cast out of the Guardians. I'd be even more of a social pariah back in Whimsia.

Maybe that's what everyone wants anyway. While fairies do tend to stay out of celestial and mortal affairs, in our defense, the Mortal Outcome Council never really welcomed us either. I'm not the first or only fairy who wanted to join the celestials to help mortals, I'm just the only one they let in. My audition scores were higher than most celestials. I studied for weeks and proved myself time and time again, and yet I'm still likely just the diversity pick.

My final exam had been higher than anyone else's, my scores a scant point from perfect. The Mortal Outcome Council may appreciate me, but given that Calam is here, they don't expect me to get that spot. They want to keep only celestials in leadership. They can say they tried to be more inclusive while never truly giving me the chance.

"How do *you* want to play this, Calamity?" That's the right question to ask, though I loathe asking it. I loathe that I now have to consider him a part of this assignment. That he could destroy my yet-to-be-planned plans for Lucy.

"You and I need to establish some rules." He narrows his eyes. "We are both working to avoid an Unhappily Ever After for Lucy. Therefore, we should each spend some one-on-one time with her to present both sides."

I nod. That sounds reasonable. "I agree. I'll take tomorrow, you the day after, and so forth till—"

"Definitely not. We can each have a few mortal hours a day. Otherwise, we should be near each other." He cocks a brow. "I don't trust you to not win her over with your razzle-dazzle magic."

I frown. "But—"

"Which is why I must insist on *sustainable* improvements." He holds up a hand as if his thoughts are more important than mine. "I'm aware you're powerful, but if Lucy goes down my path, all your magic will be undone. I see the way you look at this room. You want to wave your wand and make it nice. What happens when you're gone? If you want to make her life better, make it sustainable. Make it fair."

"I can agree to making sustainable changes without magic, however, I'm a fairy." I put my hands on my hips, my voice haughtier than I intend. "We need to use magic, or it builds up. It can be overwhelming." What I don't say is that this is compounded by my illness. He doesn't need to know that. He could be the type to use someone's disability against them. Sometimes celestials—and even fairies—are like that.

"Fine." He takes a deep breath, pushing himself up to standing. He stalks closer, his face inches from mine. "Last rule: We will not, under any circumstance, tell Lucy what we are and why we're here. She may be exposed to our presence already, but let's leave it at that."

My lips mash together. "I'll do my best."

"Which means you and I must act like mortals."

"Yeah, I got that." Annoyance threads my tone.

"Which means we will be sharing that bedroom upstairs and pretending to be friendly with each other." His mouth lifts at the corners.

I furrow my brows. "I know—"

"Which means holding hands and bantering, Darling." The corners of his lips twist. "We're a couple now."

Now I openly stare daggers at him. "I swear if you kiss me . . ."

He outright smiles. "That's the nature of romance."

I glower. "I am exceedingly unfond of you."

"And I hold you in the lowest regard." There's a mischievous sparkle in his gaze.

My fingers bunch up the dress around my hips. "I abhor you."

"Oh no." He faux frowns, hand to his chest. "My precious feelings are hurt."

"I will make you regret coming here." I swish my wand again to make time speed back up. Calam steps back and suddenly I feel like I can breathe again. Oh, how I despise him.

Lucy's voice carries across the store toward us. "Did you hear that Olafsson's new story will be delivered tomorrow? It's about a prince and a woodsman lost in the forest. I can hold a copy for you behind the desk?"

"I'd love that," the girl responds. "Maybe we could get a drink . . . or we could have lunch after? I can bring some—"

"I can't leave the store," Lucy responds with resignation. I expect her to say something, anything, else. She doesn't. But then, I don't know her or the other girl well. Perhaps their faces are emotive?

"Oh right, yes. Well, I'll see you then," the girl says. The bell jingles once more.

Calam's head tilts to the side like he's thinking or plotting. When he leaves the kitchen, I realize I've been staring at him and not thinking or plotting myself. *Sprinkles!*

Okay, I can do this. I can play by his rules. If Calam thinks he's winning because I let him have some control, he won't notice me changing the game. Pride always comes before the fall. That's the reality I tell myself, even as I begin to feel a tinge of weariness mixed with a pinch of apprehension.

❦ ♥ ❦

For a while, I throw myself into helping Lucy clean the store until closing to stop the questions popping into my mind. Yet, the downward spiral gets louder.

Failure.

Fairy.

Don't belong.

Not good enough.

I try to drown it out by chatting with Lucy, but she doesn't open up to either of us. Something shifted the moment that girl came in, and it hasn't shifted back. We'll have to find a way. And I have to get some fresh air if I'm going to be of use to anyone. Otherwise, I'll fall further into self-doubt, which won't help Lucy or me.

"I think I'll take a quick walk outside to grab dinner for the three of us." I pat the pocket where I magicked up some silver.

Lucy looks up from where she's dusting the romance section, which is completely dust-free already. "Are you sure? I can make us oatmeal. There's no need to spend—"

"Don't worry." I wave a hand dismissively toward Calam. He can have his one-on-one time now when she's emotionally closed off and her thoughts elsewhere.

"If you're sure, best to try the inn beside the dressmaker."

She gives me a small smile. "You needn't get me anything though, I do have oats soaking."

With a nod and a deep breath, I meander through the village square in the rain. I wave to shy neighbors who peek through tatty shop windows as shadowy dusk falls around me. Soon, the entire village will be doused in complete darkness. Only the flickering residual glow from the lights inside the shops can guide me to that inn. The slippery cobblestones under my feet try their best to take me down, but my brain's already doing a better job.

Exhaustion creeps through my limbs. It's the nature of my illness. Vacillating disorder, my mother calls it. She has it too, as did my grandmother and her mother. I grew up knowing I could have it. It seemed difficult, required constant introspection. Though I'd expected it, that hope still fizzled the moment my magic started to grow in the center of my chest, only just slightly right of my heart, and my moods began changing.

Since then, I've learned that there's only so much I can control and I would always be susceptible to specific triggers: lack of food, confidence, or control, and the worst, lack of sleep. Though the worry of spiraling preoccupies my mind, I wave at another woman with a head full of white curls in the seamstress shop. Her dark brown skin glows in the light of a candle as she clips brilliant pink fabric. My feet inch closer, seeking comfort in something pretty. While the rain pelts my cold skin, a voice in my head tells me to get to the inn. *Get food. Prepare to fight another day. This doesn't matter.*

The woman smiles and rushes over to open the door. I dart inside, grateful for the warmth that immediately washes over me.

"Come on in, dear, you'll catch a chill out in that weather." Her accented, caring voice is a salve to my many emotional wounds. My shoulders unhunch as her smile widens. She gently places a hand on my back and steers me into the shop. "You're new here? Haven't seen your face around before."

"Yes," I answer through clattering teeth. "I . . . uh . . . began working at the bookshop today. We, my suitor and I, are settling into town. I had planned to get to the inn for food, but I saw your store."

The woman holds up a hand as she crosses the room to grab a thick piece of cloth. "The inn's down that alley beside the shop. It can be a little hidden for people who aren't from the area."

Aren't from the area. Outsider. Like me. The spiral gains steam.

Worthless.

All you do is make mistakes.

See how far that confidence got you? Those thoughts of grandeur are lies.

She hurries over to me, throwing the cloth around my shoulders. "No, please don't cry. It's okay." At first, I'm surprised. I hadn't realized I'd begun to cry. But then hot tears streak down my cheeks and my heart hammers in my chest. A sob breaks free from my suddenly open mouth. And then a yawn.

The woman—I really should ask her name—leads me to a chair laden with fabric. She brushes them aside and pushes my butt onto the thin cushion. The facts of her mortal life pop into my mind at the physical contact. Unlike celestials, I can see the path, not her thoughts or emotions. Which is how I know, as of now, she's on her way to an Ordinary Ever After. I sort through the information quick, not finding anything that led her to that future. No outwardly bad decisions. No crimes or badness in her soul. Just an ordinary life, I guess.

"My name's Minerva Craven," she says. "I'm the town seamstress, though these days it seems everyone would rather buy their garments for cheaper at that new fast-fashion store." She mutters that last part mostly to herself. "Now, I . . . I don't have an inn and I've run out of tea, but you can wait here while the worst of the rain stops, if you like?"

"Thank you, yes," I respond through another sob and this time a hiccup. I really am a mess. "Perhaps I can see some dresses?" My voice sounds muffled through this needless display of emotions. Will I forever be prone to sadness when things aren't going exactly the way I hoped? "I do need a new dress." I know if I focus on something else, I'll feel better.

"Of course, dear. Though I must admit, most of my dresses are rather old and out of fashion. My hands aren't as good as they used to be. Suspect if I don't find an apprentice soon, I might have to close up shop." She tilts her head to the side. "Are you wearing luster powder? It looks like your tears mixed in." Minerva pins me with a puzzled expression.

I smile, dabbing at my eyes quickly. Fairies cry glittery tears; everything we do is colorful. But I tell myself this will be the last time I do. Because I, Darling Sparkleton, am strong. That horrid voice in my head is a liar, I know that. Only the assignment matters. Only Lucy.

My vacillating disorder and malevolent spiral can piss off. I've got work to do.

"I may be able to help with the sewing. If I can come early in the mornings?" I stand unsteadily on my feet. A sudden idea springs to mind; a way to do the ultimate makeover, make everything joyful and pretty. Do the most fairy thing possible where I'll definitely have the upper hand. "Oh, and um . . . the bookshop will be having a party in five days' time. It will be the village event of the season. The villagers will need nice clothes."

"Oh, a party?" Minerva's cheeks look a tint rosier. No doubt she's already wondering how to spend this coin coming her way.

"Yes," I say with my signature certainty. I may not feel it yet, but I will soon. "There's going to be quite a few changes around here. Parties. Celebrations. Music. Food. Joy."

"Well then, I shall see you at dawn." Minerva gives me a slight nod, though I sense a tinge of disbelief. I'll fix that too.

"See you then." I step back out into the rain with renewed hope and a plan. I'll work from the outside in with Lucy. She *will* open up to me. She *will* see how good things can be. She'll be onto the path of Happily Ever After before she knows it.

CHAPTER SIX

Calamity

Mistakes were made. Even I can admit that.

I hear my father's voice in my mind. *A smart Misfortune operates in the shadows. They do not seek the spotlight and they always know their client's deepest, darkest thoughts.*

Well, I'm failing that already. "Lucy, have you always worked at the bookstore?"

"Yes," she answers without embellishment. The same person who threw her head back to laugh at Darling, is now tight-lipped and somewhat standoffish. What changed?

"Do you like working here?" I press on, hoping she will let me in. See, this is why I don't do well when exposed. Unexposed, I can read her thoughts, sift through them, and know exactly what I need. Exposed, I have to actually ask questions like a fairy. While I can read the facts of her life easily, I can't just lean over and plop my hand on her shoulder to know her mind and emotions. It would be awkward. I can imagine her panicking if a new acquaintance suddenly was touching her and seemed to know everything about her. She'd throw me out, assignment failed.

Darling has ruined everything.

"Of course," Lucy says cheerfully as she finishes her display of thin leather-bound stories. On one of the painted covers, there's a pale lady with reddish-brown hair sitting as a pale prince in blue attire kneels to slip a shoe on her foot, a castle off in the distance. Another fairy tale from Whimsia, no doubt. Fairies really are the worst.

I peel my gaze away from the books when Lucy shuffles off to clean something else that isn't dirty. I wonder if she's always like this, adjusting to our presence, or if she just has nothing else better to do.

My hands twitch by my sides. Great.

Lucy has me flip over the sign on the door to say the store is closed just as Darling comes back holding a basket full of *things* and a big wooden pail of something that smells incredible.

She shimmies inside, her cheeks a bit streaky like little pearlescent rainbows. Her clothes look damp, her hair a bit frazzled, but she wears a big smile nonetheless.

Lucy locks the door behind her, and then peers inside the pail. "Are those plates and cups and stew?"

Darling nods. "Some necessities from the inn. There's more in there too. Just you wait." With that, she stalks off toward the kitchen, the smell of a hot meal wafting behind her. She must've bought those "necessities" instead of magicking them, which is startlingly considerate of the local economy. "I know there's no table to eat at—maybe we should make a little picnic? Lucy, do you have a blanket we can drape on the kitchen floor?"

Lucy's brows rise. "Um . . . I don't need any. I don't want to owe anyone—"

"Never you mind about that."

There's a *whoosh* and a clattering of plates in the kitchen. While celestial magic doesn't leave a trace, the room feels warmer when Darling uses hers. There's also a slight glimmer of gold in its wake, which I'm sure only I can see as a celestial.

Once Lucy lays out a blanket and Darling has assembled three bowls full of hot soup, we sit in a triangle. Lucy doesn't protest again about her oats getting wasted. Instead, she quickly eats as if she hasn't had anything hot in ages. She might not have.

"Potato stew used to be my favorite," she says between slurps. "My mom made it all the time." Ah, food makes her chatty. "She would mash extra potatoes in to make it thicker. No one else makes it like that."

Darling grins, eating slowly. Even from here, I can smell sweetness from her bowl as if she added a dollop of honey. "Your mother created this store, right? She bought it and made it what it is?"

Lucy drinks down the rest of the broth before answering. "Yeah, before I was born. She'd always dreamed of owning a bookstore. She loved stories."

"Do you?" I ask, shifting a little as I regard her carefully. She's not what I expected. I mean, she is, and she isn't. I thought she'd be more agreeable. Less guarded. Perhaps it's because I am not in the background working my skills, but confronting them head-on. I suppose I'm not surprised she doesn't seem to want to welcome either of us with open arms. We are strangers, after all. "Like stories, I mean?"

Lucy gives me the side-eye, her thick brows knitting together. I take her in, trying to identify her emotions. Her skin is darker than both mine and Darling's. And while Darling has a fuller figure, Lucy is slight. Almost a wisp. Her face is far more emotive than most mortals I've ever met though. She's annoyed. Or tired, maybe? There's definitely a haze of unease about her.

"I love stories," she finally says.

"What's your favorite one?" Darling ladles more stew from the pail to fill Lucy's bowl. I can already tell that Darling is making her mark. Lucy seems friendlier with her. I must disrupt this.

She takes the bowl from Darling. "I love romances. There's this series about the twelve sisters who are cursed each night to dance through the different realms until their shoes fall apart and they fall down dead." There's no doubt this story was crafted by fairies, considering its grim premise. "And each sister gets a book in the series where True Love's Kiss breaks the curse. My favorite is the third sister, Catarina, who falls in love with a bakery girl named Arabelle. Their story . . ." She doesn't finish the thought. "Anyway, about the room upstairs—it's really just an old mattress, spiders, and the occasional mouse up there. Perhaps you can make something more of it?" Her gaze flits between me and Darling.

"That's great," Darling says quietly as we finish the stew. "Really, Lucy, we appreciate you letting us stay here."

Lucy's pinched expression hints that she's embarrassed she shared as much as she did. Despite the lack of information, I did glean some facts.

1. Lucy loves the stew. It reminds her of her mother. It evokes memories that I would like to know more about—how do I make her remember why this bookstore matters and how she can achieve both her and her mother's dreams? How do I connect the present to the past, so she casts these useless desires like love and romance aside to focus on what she actually needs? Money. Food. Security. No Happily Ever After, just a safe and secure Ordinary Ever After.
2. Lucy is a hopeless romantic. This is something I'll have to nip in the bud.
3. Lucy loves fairy tales, though if she follows them closely, she might be afraid of magic. This could help me yet wouldn't bode well for Darling.
4. I need to somehow find a way to make sure Lucy gets a stove for hot meals consistently, and a cooling box for ingredients. A fed stomach survives.

We put our empty bowls into the equally empty pail. Darling promises to do the washing up tomorrow, which probably means she'll swish her wand again. Lucy folds the blanket, lights a candle that's near its end, and leads us up some rickety stairs to the right of the kitchen. The wood creaks beneath us. Cobwebs stick to my face and I bat them away, loathing for the millionth time that I'm in a mortal form. It's excruciating.

Lucy pushes a thick door open, bringing us into a tiny space with slanted ceilings. The floor's a bit wobbly. There are crates on each side, taking up much of the room. In the center, there's a straw mattress.

She walks over, laying the blanket upon the bed. Dust kicks up, causing me to sneeze. Darling, meanwhile, gapes at the accommodations. She's used to far better. Fairies believe in excess, whether it be magical, material, or menace.

I feel her patience wearing thin. She desperately wants to use that wand. Where I see the mission laid out before me, she sees possibility.

"Are you comfortable sharing the bed? I know it's improper for two people not yet married, but . . ." She trails off again, the sentiment unspoken. She doesn't have anything else for us, and as two people she believes are in love, why should we mind?

This will be interesting.

"No need to worry," Darling says brightly as the dark closes in around us. Dusk gave way to night while we ate, and now we're engulfed in it. There's something calming and terrifying about experiencing it in person, and not being a part of it.

Lucy's shoulders unhunch. "You're both kind. Giving me dinner and offering to help me turn this store around. There's something trustworthy about the two of you that makes me feel safe. I've never felt that before with anyone . . . I don't need to know your pasts, but I imagine the way you look at each other, the way you complement each other, maybe your love wasn't accepted in wherever you called home?" She sniffs. "You'll be accepted here. I can help you; you can help me. But if I'm wrong, if you're here for something else, please don't take advantage. I have nothing to give." She eyes us both over the flickering candle.

I don't respond to the love part. That's the con of this game. "We won't. We need a place to stay. A community to embrace us. We want to help you and we want you to succeed."

"I can tell that about you both." Lucy shakes her head with a slight smile. "That you have good intentions. It's really weird, but I . . . it's as if I can be myself with you."

"You can," Darling affirms. "Thank you for sharing your store and home with us. We will earn our keep, promise. Oh! And . . . hmm . . . I meant to say earlier. Well." Darling clears her throat. Nerves? "I'd like to throw a party at the store on Friday night. Something fun for the villagers. Would that be okay?"

"Uh." Lucy's breath hitches. "Sure, I guess." Then she straightens. "Yeah, that would be nice." Unfortunately, this won't be nice for me. Darling's making plans, which means I need to thwart them.

Lucy lets herself out after another nod. That was likely too much emotion and honesty. She's right that we're emitting vibes of safety. That's what we're taught—we never want a client to be scared or doing things they don't want to already do. Darling and I may go about Lucy's future in different ways, but we both believe we can give her the best this life can offer.

Once her footsteps recede downstairs, Darling takes the wand from the pocket. She swishes it, creating a tiny flicker of light above us. And then she twists around to stare daggers at me.

I take immediate offense. "Don't look at me like that, I'm not the one who decided exposing ourselves to mortals was a good idea. And well done at already scheduling a party. Can fairies even survive without frivolity?"

She sighs, in either defeat or exhaustion. "You can sleep in that corner, there—" She points to a shadowy end of the room that looks to have lost the battle to eight-legged creatures long before Lucy was ever born. "I think it's only fair. And also, imagine the . . . the . . . well, how the mortals will see us? Not even married and sharing a bed!"

I cock a brow her way. "I don't care what mortals think and I will not sleep in a dark alcove. It's *not* fair and it's impractical. And again, why should I be made uncomfortable for your mistake?"

"Fine, then. I'll just . . ." Her gaze flits around the room, searching for something. No idea what exactly.

I pin her with a glare. "You can't just magick another mattress or lamps, can you?"

Her bottom lip curls. "I can't create a hard solid from nothing unless it's food. Food isn't permanent, doesn't have as much magical weight. So I can put meals on a plate, sure. Hot chocolate in a mug, always. Haven't you read 'Cinderella'? That's one of the truest stories of fairy magic. Mice into horses and all that." She huffs. "If I'm making something solid and permanent though, I need solid material to work with." She turns away from me to regard the mattress. "I just don't think—"

"Darling," I say, letting my shoulders drop. My limbs feel weak and my brain a bit mushy. "I'm tired. So are you. Neither of us can make another bed from nothing and this floor isn't conducive to proper rest. We'll share, and if any mortal has thoughts on it, we can tell them to bugger off."

Her expression sours before her voice loses its edge. "You're right."

"Of course I am." I can't help the smirk that's aimed in her direction. "I'm looking forward to you saying that countless times in the following week. But first, we need a bedroom."

She rolls her eyes. "I might be able to . . ." She lifts that wand, nose crinkled, and then through a cloud of gold glitter, the mattress fluffs up, widens . . . and splits into two cushions barely big enough to contain our legs. She coughs. "Let me see, I'm sure I can make these bigger." She swooshes again, lips pursed as the cushions flatten and begin to tear. She stops with a sigh.

"If we want to be able to fit our bodies in this space, it can only be one. Look." She pushes them back together. The blanket stretches across the makeshift bed, plush and a vibrant purple. "This'll have to do. Now, let's find some more materials."

I rush off to fetch her some glass and cloth as requested. Yes, I could probably do my own bit of magic, but I'm already tired, and she has plenty. I hand her two broken wine bottles from one of the crates and an old scrap of cloth. She promptly transforms them into two lamps with her magic light, and then a small but warm rug beneath our feet.

It's mesmerizing to watch.

I've never met a fairy before, never saw what they could do with so little. If you'd have asked me as a child, I would've said that fairies were tiny, mischievous creatures from Whimsia who play tricks on mortals and cause trouble wherever they go. They live to be entertained and help no one. Darling doesn't seem that way.

First, she's in no way small at all, which makes looking at her rather . . . distracting. She's nearly my height, has a pleasing shapely form, and everything about her is loud. As for the tricky trouble, I have no doubt she can do that. Nor does she need to use her wand for it. That one stereotype seems to be true; they do love to be entertained. Yet, she seems like she wants to help too.

Either way, she's pure havoc. She absolutely cannot get that mentorship. What would she even do with more power? Her livelihood isn't dependent on mortals. So why is she here?

What does she genuinely *want*?

"Now for the hard part," she murmurs. "How do I make some sort of heater?" While she ponders that, I look around the room. The crates created a platform for the bed with two side tables holding lamps. There's a rug, pillows, and a basin for washing up filled with water in the corner beside a partition.

"I can make the fire," I finally say. I arrange two more crates in the center of the room and snap my fingers. They change from wood to metal, and I fill them with rocks. Scalding-hot rocks. It'll require magic here and there to keep them warm, but it should suffice for the night.

"Well done, Misfortune." Darling's lips twist into an almost-grin and I admit that tiny compliment does a little something to my pride. "I like this. Do you think we could replicate it downstairs too? I noticed there wasn't a chimney and wood costs money. If I'm to lose, as you think, then is it sustainable?"

I gawk at her. “Why would I tell you that?”

She huffs, head back. “Just when I thought you’d proven yourself useful . . .” She plods over to the basin, washing her face and patting it dry with a magicked towel. “We may be competing, but the least you could do is work with me to help Lucy’s store. She’ll need warmth, she’ll need more resources, she’ll need food. Can we collaborate on that, or would you rather we squabble over doing the same things?”

I unbutton my jacket, fold it, and place it on the chair. “You want to work together on the basics?”

“We can’t magick them, right? She needs it to be sustainable without us around,” she says through the partition. I hear her moving around back there. “So let’s do that. As for the other stuff, we’re still competing for her fate.”

“Fine.” I untuck my shirt and slip into the bed.

I’m aware this could be uncomfortable, but only if she makes it so. The bed is large enough for us not to go anywhere near each other if we stay firmly on our sides. Besides, I don’t get uncomfortable. I’m a celestial. My kind has been around since the beginning of time. Fairies were somehow created from chaos or something, I don’t know. Either way, there’s nothing I haven’t seen and I’m a principled man who doesn’t care about small, insignificant things like sharing a bed with a fairy in a mortal realm.

It’s all very beneath me. It’s a job. A test. A contest I’m going to win.

Darling strides out in a drapey white nightgown cinched at the waist, her hair covered in a pearly bonnet. Her brown skin glimmers in the lamplight.

I gulp and nearly jump out of the bed. "What are you wearing?!"

"A nightgown, Calamity." Her tone is droll, and I just know she wants to roll her eyes. "I'm not going to wear a full, corseted dress to bed and I suspect you'd prefer me not to be naked."

My ears grow hot. "I'd prefer you were never sent here and Lucy was exclusively my client."

"Same." She lifts the blanket on the other side and slips beneath it. "Now if you don't mind, I have a very busy schedule tomorrow. I'm sure you do as well." She turns on her side, away from me.

The lights from the lamps go out, though I don't hear her wand swoosh.

The darkness gives me a reprieve from her. I exhale slowly. My heart calming.

"Goodnight, my little love muffin," I whisper into the dark with a smile.

A pillow swats me in the head as a response.

CHAPTER SEVEN

Darling

At dawn, the first sunbeam bounces through the dusty windowpane and my body screeches with glee. I sit up, rested and hopeful. *Ready.*

Calamity slumbers like the dead on the other side of the bed. He hasn't moved in hours. I can't even hear him breathing. Misfortunes must recharge their power like Guardians.

Back at the academy, instructors didn't teach me about celestial magic. While I was given solitary study in the library, my classmates took more pertinent lessons about their kind. They didn't seem interested in learning about fairies, and in turn, I became disinterested in them as well.

The only thing I know is that celestials rely on mortal realms and they have less magic. Maybe that's why Calamity needs his rest more than me. If we ever get on somewhat friendly terms, I might ask. But then I look at his still form and decide that's unlikely. He's rigid, unbending, and a know-it-all with an arrogance that'll make my task difficult.

So far, I've been rather clever. Giving in to limiting my magic for sustainability was one way to let him think he has me. Little does he know that I have more skills that don't require my wand. I'll prove it.

I change back into yesterday's dress and imagine the courtyard crisply in my mind before poofing outside. My purple boots land on cold stone. Everything is cold in the village of Fulhorn. The wind scratches my cheeks.

My thoughts travel back to Whimsia, to where the trees grow impossibly tall. Paradise Pines. Our homes among the branches, no doors, no walls, just wooden floors and flowing fabrics dancing through the breeze. Community. Laughter. Love. Celebrations.

During the full moons, magic flickered through the leaves, forming teardrop crystals, no two alike. They'd get plumper and plumper until they'd get too heavy and fall into the waiting hands of fairy children. On those nights, we'd celebrate.

Each child would hold their drop in the moonlight and cast their first spell. If they were successful—and most were, though those who weren't had to try again another time—the crystal would shatter into a million glittery pieces the color of their magic's essence. It embellished their wings and coated their skin, and what was left formed a single, pliable strand they could shift into whatever shape they'd like. Their wand.

My drop had been massive, cracked in places as if it wasn't meant to be contained. I nearly dropped it several times. Everyone laughed, saying I needed to choose another. *Oh, Darling*, they muttered. *Always too much.* I didn't heed their words; I was certain the bigger the drop the better.

Instead, I focused on the spell. *Where the leaves are one, the leaves are many. On the ground it does lay, in the air they shall stay.*

The crystal shattered.

The season changed from the end of spring to the beginning of autumn from my one spell alone. A single green leaf became a swath of red, orange, yellow. The crowd gasped when gold painted my skin, my wings, the leaves. I still recall my mother's awe, face bright in the sea of fairies. And I'd been right too—the teardrop couldn't have been carried by anyone else. It was meant for me. Larger than life, sparkly, untamable.

Some part of me knew then that my future might be beyond Paradise Pines with its only two seasons: spring and autumn. Warm air that chills slightly enough to wear a sweater. The scent of sweets always in the air. The spice of tree nuts. The sharp tanginess of sour berries plucked from the vines, staining our fingers a deep shade of purple. Salt that carries on the breeze from the canal where the sprites live just beneath the surface. They'd trade fish for our vegetables and join us for the festivals to celebrate any minor holiday. The parties, twinkling lights, and music. Even the fae from the Aerbor region would visit, carting loads of citrus in their wake.

It was home, it was everything I loved—still love—and yet I wanted more than two seasons and easy pleasures.

I've given up that life for this . . . this place far from home. Here I am in a mortal realm, vying for a mentorship no one wants me to have. As much as I want to flop on the ground, it's not about me. It's about Lucy. It will be for her that I prove everyone wrong.

A candle flickers in Minerva's window. That's how I'll begin my campaign.

Telling my brain to stay on task, I knock. Once she ushers

me inside with a sleepy nod, she brings me to the back of her store. The fireplace crackles in the corner, illuminating a . . . mess. Dresses strewn around a small working desk, cloth scraps littering the floor.

Minerva's still in her bonnet. Her eyes a little watery. "Tea and biscuits?"

I smile. "Oh yes, please."

The moment she's gone, I make good use of my time. First, I grab my wand and swish. In a matter of seconds, the dresses rearrange themselves on the forgotten clothing racks, cloth forms a neat pile on the work desk, and the debris collects itself into an underused waste bin. The air feels clearer.

Then I bend to sort through the scraps. My back begins to ache a little under the weight of my wings. They've been tucked in tight against my back for weeks now. Much as I try to ignore it, it's been giving me a slight headache. Like my magic, if I don't use them, I'll become ill. Perhaps tonight when Calamity sleeps, I'll let them out in my true form for a little while.

For now though, I'm here. I'm present. I'm feeling right. No spirals, no tears. Just excitement. The day holds so much possibility.

After a few moments, I select some periwinkle cloth. I'll ask Minerva to bring me more. Until then, I cross the room to peruse the dresses. My magic is powerful, but I still need a base.

Some of them are gorgeous, with embroidery and rich colors. Others lack boldness. Lack confidence. They're old, out of fashion, and they're the only ones around my size. I shake my head. It seems that in most realms, everyone expects bigger ladies to fade into the background. Hide in neutral colors, swim in pools of fabric so no one can really see their bodies.

Gold glitter shimmers around me as I tap a dreadfully boring A-line and start working wonders. I transform it from beige to a deep green, swoop my wand around to make vines climb up from the hem with gold thread and vibrant flowers in hues of maroon and ocher. With one more flourish, I finish it with a golden sash. There—it's not as rainbow-y as I'd like, and I'll miss my leggings, but it's really quite beautiful. Bolstered by Minerva's fantastic talent.

Perfection. I slip it on, polish a grimy mirror, and pull my refreshed curls into a messy bun dotted with tiny primrose flowers, a favorite among my kind. Yes, that'll do nicely.

Then I return to work, pulling old dresses off the racks and seeing the potential there.

When Minerva enters, her mouth falls open. "I don't recall making that one."

"Hmm. It was tucked all the way in the back and covered in layers of dust," I lie. "I had to pat it down for a good five minutes before I could really even see it. I'd like to earn this dress by modernizing the others, if that's fine?"

Minerva nods, sliding two biscuits and a cup of tea onto the table beside me. "Someone must've paid a fortune for that and never came to get it. Happens more than you'd think. Before the drought ten years ago, this place was prosperous. People had money and threw it around on anything and everything." She holds up a hand before fetching a chair for me to sit. "Crops were thriving—our little village was called the Fruit Basket of

Lumina. The King even named us Fulhorn, you know, like a cornucopia? But then, well . . . the drought. People lost their homes, their money, their livelihoods."

The scent of biscuits entices me, so I sit and gaze up at her while taking polite bites.

"Why did it start? The drought, I mean?" The books I'd studied had told me that the kingdom had been reeling from a long run of bad luck, but it hadn't really given specifics.

"Nature, my dear." Minerva shakes her head. "The fields on the edge of the village remain barren, all these years later. The drought came, then all we got was rain. It's as if we can never have rain and sunshine intermittently. Nothing'll grow in such extremes."

"I see," I say more into my cup of tea than to her. I can't very well bring sunshine to the village. Magic can't do that. However, there must be a way to bring life back to this realm. "Well, we can at least increase sales during these trying times. You'll see. With this dress, I'll be a walking advertisement. Folks'll come in and we'll sell them updated frocks for less money. Better than sitting in this back room, right?"

"You're very confident, aren't you?" Minerva cackles before her tone sobers. "Why would you help me? You're not from here, you've nothing to gain. I can't pay you."

"I don't need money, I need items . . ." I take a deep breath. "First, I need clothes. Second, I have a feeling, Minerva, you might know people who have extra things lying around. Perhaps an old stove, maybe a sink or someone who might do repairs? I need your help if the bookstore will operate in comfort. And lastly, it's the right thing to do. I want everyone to thrive and not just survive."

Minerva pats my shoulder. "You've a good soul, Darling."

"Thank you." I smile, my cheeks burning a little. I hold up the periwinkle swatch. "Could I have more of this and some bright blue thread?"

She looks at it for a long moment. "I know just where that is. I'll be back."

Discreetly, I take a pill from my pocket and swallow it with a sip of tea. It's not that I don't want her or anyone else to know about my illness, it's just that they don't need to. It's personal. And some small part of me worries that if people knew, they'd treat me differently. Or they'd judge me. Or worse, they'd be afraid of me. Best to keep these things close and quiet. It's better for everyone's sakes.

Over the next few hours, I begin a silhouette on a new dress for Lucy and I reconfigure three other dresses that'll be ready for sale later that day using my hands. No magic at all. I can shift my wand's shape into an earring—which I've been loath to do, I really love holding a physical wand—so that if I do need it, I'll only have to tug my ear. By the end, Minerva promises to send over an old, somewhat dinged-up stove that'd been collecting dust in her basement in return for my services. And I promise to come back again before dawn tomorrow.

As I leave her shop and step one purple boot after the other into the sunny morning sun, I keep my head high. It's good to feel useful again.

Across the courtyard, the bookstore's not yet open. That's fine. There's plenty of work to be done around here too.

I pass by a florist who is arranging half-dead flowers in bins out in front of their closet-sized store. After a tug on my ear, some color and life gradually drift back into them. In a few minutes, they'll look freshly picked.

I pay double the asking price for a small yellow flower. The florist—Ember, I learn—nearly hugs me. From the contact, I learn she also is on the path to Ordinary Ever After. Next, I saunter over to the bakery (sorry, "breaderie"), where fresh rolls sit in the windows, steaming up the glass. There are golden loaves with crispy edges, rolls the size of my hand made for butter and cheese, and dark brown pretzels studded with thick specks of salt. Very practical offerings, yet something tells me there is talent in the hands that made these, talent that could be very useful.

An idea pings in my mind, the best idea I may have had yet on this assignment. Oh yes, there's no way I can fail now. I stride into the bakery, sighing at all the heavenly scents before the baker, an older man with olive skin and bouncy black curls, greets me. There's flour crusted on his apron and a smudge of butter on his cheek. "Can I help you, miss?" His voice is gruff from what I suspect is underuse.

"Why, yes. I believe you can." I keep my voice light as I step onto the spotless tile floor. The heat of the multiple ovens washes over my cheeks. "I work at the bookstore across the village square. We would like to create a partnership with you if you'd be interested?"

His brows furrow. "Depends on what yer asking."

I stand taller, emboldened by this beautiful dress, this yellow flower that smells like summer, and the unshakeable belief that I'm going to positively impact Lucy's world. "We would love for you to make a sweet pastry that you'd sell exclusively at the store. Something small and portable . . . maybe a cookie? Yes, that's it. A warm cookie. A smell that draws in the crowds, makes them feel good and . . . and hungry?"

The baker—Baxter, the name tag on his lapel reads—grimaces. "Sounds frivolous. Besides, I don't make cookies."

"Oh, what a shame. A little bit of frivolity, I've found, makes people rather happy and often lines the wallet quite nicely. It's how my family's business became the best in our kingdom." I sigh dramatically. "Well . . . if you're sure . . ." I begin to turn away, patting my pocket with exaggeration, letting the coins clink together as if I have a fortune.

"I didn't say no," he says quickly. "But I'd need insurance. Can't be footing any loss, you understand."

"Of course." I smile, stepping back up to the counter. I reach into my pocket and draw out a thick handful of silver. I feel guilty using it—if I fail, it'll disappear from his till. But I'll find a way to make it right. "Would this be enough?"

Baxter's eyes round. I've got him now. "It'll do for the moment."

"Good. We should like a delivery, say"—I glance at the clock—"just before midday."

Baxter nods, sliding the coins across the counter and into his register. "Do you have any preferences, Miss . . . ?"

"Everyone calls me Darling." I beam at him. "And yes, I think chocolate would do nicely."

"I do have quite a bit o' half-sweetened chocolate in the back." He scrubs his chin in thought, his lips press together tightly for a moment. "Haven't yet found a use for it—townsfolk don't like many indulgences, you see. Might make for some delicious cookies."

"I can't wait to try them." I wink. "And please, hang onto that chocolate, Mr. Baxter. We'll be having a party on Friday night at the bookstore, and we could use an array of sweets to liven it up. Thank you, and I'll be seeing you soon."

With that I flit out of the shop, pep in my step. My plan is falling together nicely. As much as I want to keep connecting with other businesses and set the bookstore up for success, I really ought to get into the store. Do one thing at a time. Get the full measure of the problem.

As the minutes drift past and I stalk past more shops, I sniff something slightly optimistic in the air. I straighten my posture, closing my eyes. Feelings rush through me. Fairies have strong, powerful instincts, and mine are working overtime.

The mood yesterday in the village was that of unhappy resignation. Today, there are the first flickers of hope. It hasn't yet begun raining. The flowers are blooming. Things are happening instead of the same mundane. People want to believe in joy again.

"Darling," Calamity calls, shaking me from my thoughts. At the edge of the square, near the kitchen's entrance, I see him. He looks well—a little too well, to be honest. His headful of dark blond curls seems shinier, his emerald suit tailored and bringing out the color of his eyes, and his cheeks rosier. "Good morning, my sweet." He lifts my hand gently and brings the back of it to his lips. "How I've missed you."

His warm lips brush against my hand slowly, whisper soft. A sudden and very uncomfortable feeling envelops me. My legs shake a little and something flips in the pit of my stomach. Perhaps I'm hungry? Or perhaps this is disdain? What is he doing?

Then I look past him to where a tall white woman with bright red hair, blue eyes, and a scowl stands with her nearly identical son, perhaps no older than me and Calam. There's a wagon full of crates behind them.

"My sweet Calam," I respond quickly with a smile over his shoulders at the others. "I have missed you as well."

"Come meet Mrs. Arconia and her son. Their family works with publishers to distribute books locally." He (ugh) places his hand in mine. He is playing this fake relationship well, and I cannot understand why. What could he possibly gain from this?

A breeze whips through, grabbing the flower from my hand. The son plucks it from the air with ease.

"My lady." He offers it back to me, his frown disappearing into a small grin.

I take it from him, my fingers grazing his. His fate shimmers around him, telling his story and his decisions. I can't read his facts properly—that would be impossible to do while pretending to be present—yet I can see that his path is not yet set. Not inescapable, but teetering on the line of an Unhappily

Ever After. He would be someone I'd be interested in working with in the future. Someone who has the potential to be good, if given the time and compassion. If given more opportunities to make the right choices. "Thank you, Mr. . . . ?"

"Dynnis," he says in a somewhat strangled voice. He shifts on his feet, his complexion turning pink. "That is a very beautiful dress."

"Thank you. It's from Minerva's just there." This I say more to his mother. I fix my posture, letting my outer reality match my inner reality. I want to present as someone who is kind, smart, and thoughtful. Someone who deserves respect, if only so I can aid Lucy the best I can. "She took pity on a stranger in the rain last night and I hope to help her as much as the bookshop. Her work is fantastic, and I do believe there'll be a sale on her newest gowns."

The mother's scowl deepens. "We've our own dressmaker." Then she tugs Dynnis closer to her, away from me. "We only came to drop off the new books for the store and demand payment. It's bad business to accumulate debts and I'd hate to put Lucy out of business."

Somehow, despite only knowing her a few seconds, I doubt she'd hate that.

"Of course." I drop Calam's hand to pull silver from my pocket. "How much do we owe you?"

Her lips lift as she stares into my hands. "That should be a start."

"I think it would be best if you gave us an invoice," Calam counters. His shoulders stiffen while he gently taps my hand.

"We're helping Lucy's shop and I'd like to look at the finances. I need the full picture on how best to organize our payments."

Mrs. Arconia's eyes narrow. "Yes, well, I'll send it over later with my husband, *the mayor* of Fulhorn. He would love to meet you both, find out more about where you're from and who you are—" Her gaze flashes between us. "We are a traditional village, you see. We don't welcome outsiders who don't meet our standards of propriety."

"I assure you, there is no impropriety here." Calam remains rigidly close to me. "I look forward to seeing the invoice later. Thank you both for dropping these crates by. I know many customers are anxious to purchase their copy of *The Prince and the Woodsman.*"

"Many?" Mrs. Arconia snorts. "I'm surprised there are any customers at all, especially ones seeking such drivel. That girl keeps up her mother's bad choices of stocking too much fiction. Would be better if she carried more factual, traditional things—cookbooks or practical arts for the local wives. Things that keep them busy. Gives them purpose." She doesn't wait for any response as she turns and stalks off down the alley.

Calam and Dynnis silently work together to unload the wagon. Once they're done, Dynnis bends low in a bow, one that is entirely silly and requires footwork I've never seen before. His dark red hair becomes disheveled and a child across the square points, giggling loudly. He doesn't seem perturbed by it.

"Nice to meet you, Darling." Then he follows his mother, rolling the wagon along.

I'm about to leave when Calam touches my arm. "That

mortal fancies you. His thoughts are comical. Lots of . . . sensual and, dare I say, *lustful* daydreams. Perhaps you should give up on Lucy and find out what true relationships entail. I promise you, it's more than hand-holding and banter. You might even enjoy it."

I cringe before refusing to let him goad me into an unnecessary reaction. "Speaking of dreams, how did you sleep? Did you have nightmares about realizing you're out of your depth with Lucy?" I drift closer to him. Making sure he knows I won't back down. Making sure he knows not to doubt my power.

"Oh, I find she and you, *Darling*, are very much within my depth." He smiles as a townswoman walks past, eyeing us both cautiously. When she's in the periphery, he continues. "I feel charged and ready, do you?"

"You have no idea." One more step closer and we're nearly nose to nose. "I *will* win."

Calam's lips quirk until he becomes serious. "The mother, Mrs. Arconia? I didn't touch her, but I felt . . ." He pauses, brows furrowing as if he's fighting some internal battle. "Her path is unusual, different than an Unhappily Ever After. We should avoid contact with her, especially in our mortal forms."

I'm surprised he's offering any kind of help or guidance. That he's treating me like an equal.

I nod and just when I think he's done, he smirks again. "I don't *hate* being your intended when you look like this." Then he lowers his mouth a few inches from mine, our noses touching. His warm breath tickles my cheeks. Those big green eyes watching me. Suddenly, the air freezes in my chest and my lips part.

Is he going to . . . ? His smirk becomes crooked, though I notice it's a bit shaky. "See you inside, my little love muffin."

My heart stops as he prances away. Literally *prances*, his curls tumbling in the wind. What was *that*?!

What game are we playing now?

CHAPTER EIGHT

Calamity

Sometimes when you play with fire, you get singed. This is not one of those times. If anything, I'm developing frostbite. Given that I lost the lead this morning, I thought playing on Darling's hesitance of fake dating by fake flirting would rattle her nerves, yet she seems undeterred.

It's frustrating. It's disconcerting. It distracted *me* more than her. It was hard to pull away. Yes, I could say it was because I wanted to see how she'd react, but that would be a lie. The truth is that I wanted to see how *I'd* react. Something about this situation isn't allowing me to keep a level head.

And no, I tell myself, it wasn't because of that mortal boy's disgusting thoughts. Especially not the way he imagined himself together with Darling under a canopy of trees, the sun pouring through branches and bouncing off leaves as he pulled her close, his body hovering over hers, her lips parted in anticipation—

I huff aloud to myself, turning heads my way. A pretend cough racks through me, and I clamp a hand to my mouth. Darling's gaze narrows on mine.

She's sizing me up and has found me wanting. I expected better from myself. I expected to have her reeling with defeat by the second day, but the fairy has been busy. Where was she all morning? And when did she meet a repairman?

"This is an old stove. You can't turn it off, you can only adjust the temperatures. It works well for heating an entire floor, which I think you might need?" The man slides a glance at Lucy, whose mouth hasn't closed since he came in with it. He looks around. "Suspect you might be needing a cooling box too?"

"Oh yes, if you happen to have one lying around?" Darling perks up, her smile wide. She's determined, I'll give her that. By solving the most immediate concerns—all without magic, it would seem—she's proving she's here to win. Which makes her dangerous.

"I have one that might fit in here . . ." He says to Darling, "Minerva told me you're a genius at gowns. My wife's been wanting something new for a while. We could do a trade for it, plus that new book about a woodsman?"

"It's a deal!" Darling thrusts out her hand for him to shake. "Would you be able to arrange delivery today?"

He nods. "I'll be back in a few hours."

After he's gone, Lucy turns to Darling. "How did you—?" Her brows furrow. "Why?"

"For you." Darling loops Lucy's arm through hers. "Now, I want to talk about your vision for the bookstore." She leads Lucy out of the kitchen, leaving me there in the warmth of the stove and engulfed with new knowledge—I need to figure out how to recharge my energy faster. Darling's strength could be my downfall.

It isn't just that I have to be better than her, it's that I need to be better, period. Too much relies on my success.

"And so," Lucy prattles on about business or whatever, "we get shipments every few days with new books approved by the King. Half are informational texts; the other half are stories. The King isn't keen on stories. He believes they addle minds. Same for the press. I'm sure you met Mrs. Arconia." Lucy shrugs. "Though even he can't deny that people need fiction to escape the humdrum."

"Hmm." Darling scribbles something on a piece of parchment with a quill—wait, where did she get that? "What do you see people come in to buy the most?"

"Romance." Lucy grins. "It's our most popular genre by far. My favorite too."

"*Hmm.*" Darling takes in every detail of the store. "And you keep those books hidden in the back?"

"Well—" Lucy frowns and her voice drifts off as a white woman in a beige dress walks through the doors. She nods at Lucy and Darling, but pauses in puzzlement at me. Her hand lifts to her chest and lingers there.

There's a flurry of panic in her expression. Nervousness. Discomfort. Angst? Her attention flits to the corner, then back to me. Without another word, she turns on her heel and leaves the store.

I tilt my head. That was weird, even for a mortal.

Lucy lets out a long sigh, her shoulders sagging. "As I was saying, most men believe romance is a pleasure to be hidden or feel guilty about. Many romance readers often have to sneak in so they won't be seen and be judged."

That thought concerns me. Mortals care exorbitantly about joy, which is why they will do anything to deny it to themselves and others. It's why Unhappily Ever Afters are on the rise. Reading romance has nothing to do with morality. If anything, it should make their short, sad lives more bearable. Yet, in every history book about the mortal realms, it's cyclical: Mortals evolve, they progress, they invent, they form a society that grows and grows . . . and then they stunt their progress with conservative morality politics.

And then in a hundred years, progress will be in favor again. Despite my title, I want to avoid misfortune involving mortals. But at every turn, it seems like my job becomes more difficult. They *want* to be unhappy. They want to make *others* unhappy.

Mrs. Arconia is a prime example. And it would seem the royals are too.

If they're hindering the store's success, we must find a way around it.

I roll my shoulders, take a deep breath, and join them in the store. "You know, I was just thinking . . . What if you started a book club? A weekly romance book club?"

Lucy shakes her head. "If they're too nervous coming in for a book, why would they come in for a book club?"

I lean against the counter. "Who says we have to call it a romance book club? Perhaps we could use something Mrs. Arconia said: a Practical Arts Club for local girls. Though we need not limit it to one gender, that's just what we'll call it."

The idea forms seamlessly in my mind. "It'll be the perfect cover."

Darling sniffs. "It's a good idea."

Lucy pinches her bottom lip, looking at the romance section. "Do you think . . . do you think we can do it?"

"I think *you* can do it," I say with an air of confidence. If she focuses on her store and expands what she has always known into some new direction of what she's willing to learn, then she could have an easier life. An ordinary life. "How about we try to get our first gathering in two days' time? We could discuss that new book that came in. We'll establish an audience of voracious readers."

Lucy smiles, the first genuine one I've seen yet. "Let's do that. When they come in to buy the books, we can invite them discreetly. It's a great idea."

Darling flashes me a glance. "Though, perhaps *you* ought not be there. Your presence already lost a sale today—that customer was too embarrassed to buy her book in front of you."

"I can serve the tea and make sure no story-shamer gets inside." I wink, earning me a glower. I like when she glowers.

Yet again, the bell over the door dings as another customer comes in. I roll my eyes at these incessant interruptions. Yes, it's a business and yes, mortals move freely around their realm, but seriously? I have work to do. And, don't they have somewhere else to be? I could never imagine being burdened with assisting swaths of people shopping all day long. This is absolutely tedious.

Lucy immediately swivels in their direction. It's her.

Today, the hood is down. Her long, braided blond hair, icy blue eyes, pouty lips, and a worn yellow dress that suggests working class, yet is ill-fitting enough for me to think it might not belong to her, are a study in contradictions. She's a mystery to me. An unwanted one at that.

"Andi?" Lucy asks, her tone elated. "I have a copy for you."

Andi, I guess, beams. "Can we talk?"

"Oh, yes. Of course. I'd lo—like that." Lucy darts around the till, almost forgetting we're there. Darling clears her throat and Lucy slows. "Right. Sorry, this is my—this is Andi. She's, uh, a customer. And a friend. Andi, these are new staff members, Darling and Calam. Would you two mind watching the store for a moment?"

She and Andi, who doesn't acknowledge us at all, drift off toward the kitchen, where the crates are still resting. Through the doorway, I hear Lucy opening one, presumably to give her the book.

Darling stares at me, her voice a whisper. "Who is she really?"

I shrug, though I'm asking myself the same question.

"Can't you read minds or feelings? Don't all celestials have empath abilities or telepathy?" She taps her fingers against the counter.

"Very nosy for a fairy," I reply quietly. Try as I might, I can't hear through the walls nor can I read minds properly without touch. We can see their past, the mistakes, the facts, emotions, but there are variables beyond our sight. Only the Mortal Outcome

Council have precognition, the ability to see into the future. They can calculate the fate of realms and power and the balance between. That's why they make the assignments—we're sent to mortals at the precise time their fate will be decided, and we're expected to push them toward one path or another for the sake of the realm. The Mortal Outcome Council can predict that precise moment.

"I'm able to sense someone's feelings and snippets of their thoughts if I focus enough." It also depletes my energy entirely too fast and if I'm not careful, can overwhelm me. Not that I'll admit that to *her*.

Darling waves her hand. "I'll give you a few hours alone with Lucy if you tell me what feelings Andi is emitting. Deal?"

"Sure," I lie. I don't have to tell her anything that isn't necessary. There's no doubt that Darling will have a plan for Andi if this relationship is what I fear it is.

My shoulders droop and I take a deep breath before I focus.

Warm images of her and Lucy stream in our minds. Them laughing. Talking. Reading. Holding hands. Love. Not real. Desired. A palace on the hill. A crown? There's so much happening in her brain that I want to shut it out. It's pure chaos. Madness. Intensity. All-consuming, unending, too much of everything at once.

And then there's fear of . . . something. Family? Home? Before I can dig deeper, her terror begins to overload my senses.

I double over, trying to purge it from my own mind. My vision blurs. Breath comes heavily. Darling places a hand on my arm, her face contorted with care. Which is laughable. I'm her enemy. I've come to ruin her chances, come to beat her. Yet, the thoughts instantly reduce with her contact. I let out a long exhale of relief. When she attempts to pull her touch away, I set my own hand on hers, holding it down.

Please, I try to emote in the gesture, *please don't.*

She doesn't. Instead, her positive energy seeps through my clothes into my skin. My first instinct is to recoil—this really is becoming a roller coaster of emotions—but my second instinct is to embrace it. There's something gentle and welcoming. Something I need. Everything becomes brighter. Better. Complete.

Her voice is beside my ear. "Calam, are you okay?"

I can't answer her. Her presence makes me feel . . . good. Comforted. My breaths come easier. My heart finds its rhythm again. My vision clears. And instead of Andi's thoughts in my mind, I'm feeling Darling. Her . . . everything.

It's unusual, unlike anything I've ever felt. A spectrum. Joy. Anger. Confusion. Determination. Worthlessness. *Worthlessness? Why would Darling feel worthless?* Disappointment. No fear. She isn't afraid. It's nice not to feel afraid.

Unlike me.

Wait . . . am I afraid?

Oh no. Darling is making me feel and think about things I don't want to. I inhale sharply and stand taller. Try to regain my posture and my attitude, as if my world hadn't shifted from Darling's mere touch.

"Mortals can be intense," is all I can think to say. Because in truth, it would seem I, a celestial, am as well. "Sorry, I couldn't get a clear read on her."

Darling takes her hand back and sighs at my unhelpfulness. If she realizes how much she impacted me a moment ago, her face doesn't acknowledge it.

"I think the fields have an irrigation problem." Her lips press into a firm line for a moment, as if she's thinking something serious. "If we find a way to fix that, I suspect there'd be a lot more Happily and Ordinary Ever Afters. Should we check it out?" She wants us to temporarily set our differences aside and talk about irrigation? I want to see where this will go, so I nod.

"We can't fix it with magic, I know, but perhaps there's something we could do . . ." She trails off wistfully and I wonder if she'll continue again or if I'm somehow supposed to know what she means. I'm spared from waiting too long. "Life in Lumina used to be better before the drought came. The economy plummeted and there's a general air of . . ."

"Discontent? I know." That is true. Mrs. Arconia scares me a bit. I've met Unhappily Ever Afters before, but she feels worse.

A line creases between Darling's brows. For some reason, I can't stop gazing at that silly little line that bisects her forehead. Even when she's thinking, she's rather adorable.

No. I didn't think that. *No, Calamity, you are still reeling from the aftereffects of mortal feelings. Get it together, mate.*

"That's not our assignment, Darling. Not that I want to stop you from making the entire village better if it means I'll win. But don't you think you should focus on Lucy?"

"Believe me, I am focused on Lucy. I just think that . . . well, if we can make this store successful at the same time, couldn't we possibly help the village too? In little, teensy, tiny ways?" She flutters her lashes as if imagining a paradise in Fulhorn. Where everyone's smiling and there's glitter on the cobblestones and people are singing. And everyone gets a Happily Ever After. No such place exists. Or should.

"You and I have a different approach to life and living." My hip rests against the counter, my eyes locked on hers. "Our assignment is Lucy. We don't give her everything she wants; we make sure she has everything she *needs*. Fulhorn is the way it is; we cannot change that which doesn't involve Lucy's Ever After. Nor should we. It's not our place to make people happy—they must do that themselves."

She frowns. "But we can change their world, we can—"

"You're thinking like a fairy and not a celestial. We aren't meant to intrude into mortal lives beyond the moment when one of them stands on a precipice. When their fate converges into separate paths. One that has the potential for happiness yet chaos, one that has the potential for stability. And how they'll arrive there will mean making difficult choices that aren't enjoyable, or one that leads to unhappiness and instability that could doom this realm."

Darling scoffs. "What's so wrong about a *little* chaos?"

"Everything," I say a bit louder than I mean to. "Chaos is destruction. It throws our realms, our magic, our lives out of balance. Chaos must always be averted."

She breathes heavily, her chest heaving. And now I'm looking at her chest and my face heats up. "Well, I don't think a little chaos is bad at all," she says.

"That's because your kind thrives on chaos. You encourage it." I run a hand through my loose curls, knowing they might get a bit frizzy. "You're all . . . mischief-making, loud-laughing, merriment-over-practicality. You know nothing about how terrible these mortal realms could be without celestials stepping in. You live in your magic bubble. You don't see beyond it because you don't want to."

"I'm here now because I do want to," she says, head down. Her lower lip wobbles a bit. "I'm not at home. I haven't seen my kin in years. I'm far away, alone. I've not made mischief and . . . and . . . maybe my laugh is loud, and I do love merriment over practicality sometimes, but I want to help too. I just don't think it's sun and moon. Day or night. There's life in between. That's when mortals do most of their living."

"You're a fairy," I reply. If she takes it as an insult, I hope my tone implies otherwise. It's merely a statement of fact. "You may have learned at our academy, but you'll never see the realms the way we do or interact with the realms as we have. If you could, you'd know few mortals can be trusted to make the right choices that'll let them live their best lives without hurting others. There were realms where mortals fought so tirelessly, they ended up ruining their own worlds. They perished. If celestials exist because of mortals, then when they don't, neither can we."

"I know why celestials exist and why your work is imperative, I just think there can be exceptions." Darling still won't look up at me. It's as if I've crushed some sort of fantasy she had with the truth. "We should be able to trust some mortals, or at least give them opportunities to make a better destiny."

"You shouldn't take the mentorship if you don't understand the possible effects of giving large swaths of mortals 'better opportunities.'" She opens her mouth while I press on. "You should be a Guardian. They don't make the hard decisions. They help those who are two steps away from the path of Happily Ever After." I put my hand on her arm, kindly. "I can see that you are good at that. This . . . this is complicated. Not everything's supposed to be pretty or happy. If Fulhorn's fields have an irrigation problem, let them fix that. It's not our job."

Darling lifts her face to mine. "Maybe it isn't, though it seems to me that when mortals aren't given an even footing in life, they make choices that might put them on the path to Ordinary or Unhappily Ever After because it's all set up unfairly. If one of us working for their fate took time to give them the resources they need, I believe they could make decisions about what they want. Regardless of what you celestials think."

I tip my head back to glance at the ceiling briefly. If I allow myself to consider what Darling says, I'll lose. There's no use doing anything beyond helping Lucy. If I interfere with how this realm operates, how this village suffers, then I'll be interfering with more than one fate. And that, in itself, can cause chaos. Darling may not think it's bad, and that's why she can't get the mentorship.

I'm about to respond further when suddenly there's music. Trumpets. The noisy mortal instrument that's made to sound beautiful and yet imitates a stampede of mammoths bouncing around my mind. My lip curls.

"I must go." Andi's voice startles in the back room. "I hope to see you again soon?" She sends a look of longing Lucy's way, which makes Lucy sputter a little.

"Why not come to our book club? Tomorrow night. To discuss the new book. It should be rather quiet and there'll be snacks," Darling calls out, garnering two—no, three—stares.

Andi's gaze darts between Darling and Lucy. "I . . . would love that."

Lucy doesn't respond for a moment, only her lips twist and her eyes widen. "I would like that too."

"Good, see you then!" Darling ushers Andi out before anyone can change their mind.

"Why did you do that?" Lucy frowns, running her hands down her worn dress.

"Because she's a customer and we're having a book club, aren't we?" Darling seems as confused as Lucy. "Did you not want her to come?"

"I did. I do. I just . . . She's—"

The trumpets sound once more, followed by a loud voice that booms through the walls. The three of us amble outside quickly as if summoned. A royal guard, a brown man on a horse wearing a suit of white with gold, stands between two trumpeters. No, not a guard—a royal herald, I think.

"Hear ye, hear ye!"

"Come on," Lucy says, waving us over to get closer.

We hurry out the doorway to listen with the rest of the

townsfolk. The sky is a bright blue, the air smells sweet like baked goods and blooming flowers—Darling was working her magic again, and there's a palpable excitement in the air. Across the town square, an old baker holds a baking tray in one hand and waves at Darling with the other. What has she done now? Honestly, if I'm not in her vicinity the entire time, she'll make this place almost too enjoyable for everyone.

"Hear ye!" The royal herald commands again. All murmurs quiet until the only sound that can be heard is the wind rustling. "Her Royal Highness, Princess Marguerite Lara Olivia Nyissa Andrea Maxima Peggy—"

"*Peggy?*" Darling whispers.

"—Genevieve is giving a costume ball in six days' time. Her Royal Highness is most excited to enter a betrothal. And more news still from the palace: All marriage-eligible citizens are invited. No station is too low! No gender disqualified! Everyone is welcome for a feast and a dance!"

The herald does a bow atop his horse and the crowds cheer. All except me. With this much merriment in the village, there's hope. Foolish hope can lead to chaos. Chaos can ruin my entire assignment if I'm not too careful.

I need to distract Darling—clearly, she made better use of her time than I did this morning and is even more driven than I imagined.

"Hey," I whisper in her ear. "You should check that field tonight while the village sleeps. See if there is an irrigation problem you might be able to fix."

"Nice try," Darling tuts as she chews her bottom lip. "You

made your point earlier. It could . . . well, it's not the assignment. If you want to get rid of me, you'll have to work harder."

I smile. "I don't know, maybe I'm wrong. Perhaps a little magic can make big change. Perhaps that'll trickle down to Lucy too. Everyone will have more hope." I shake my head. It's bait I don't think she'll take. "Besides, I don't want to get rid of you."

She cocks a brow. "You don't?"

"I like having you here." And the worst part is, I mean it.

CHAPTER NINE

After a long day at the shop—we sold seventeen books and all our gooey cookies (which I believe got new customers through the door)—I'm in the kitchen doing the final touches.

The cooling box was delivered while I decorated, thank goodness. With everything where I wanted it, I filled the space with mismatched items from the threadbare rug that lost its colors many moons ago to the cups hanging on the walls. And we have a four-seat table now too. It'll cost me more early mornings at Minerva's, more time and energy than I might have, and it's certainly not perfect. The table needed some propping up and the chairs are a little flimsy . . . but it feels like a home. Smells like a home too.

Steam comes from the bowls on the counter. I inhale the scent greedily before moving toward the table with them. Momentarily, my vision blurs. The headache blares through my senses, making my knees almost buckle. I lose my balance and nearly drop the bowls.

Calam eyes me through the doorway. "Are you well?"

"Fine," I lie with a false smile. "Here we are." I place two bowls on the table while Lucy and Calam shuffle into their seats. Only Calam pauses first.

"You are aware that I can cook as well?" His attention narrows on my shaky feet. "You needn't do everything."

I wave a dismissive hand. "I'm happy to be useful."

"The kitchen looks amazing," Lucy says in a reverent whisper, ignoring us both. "A cooling box, sink, and even a stove. The shelves are full. It's warm . . ."

"I hope you're happy with it?" I ask, taking the heavy frying pan from the stovetop. I add a few bits of crunchy poultry crumbs on top of each bowl of porridge, my mouth salivating. Not too much. Poultry is expensive. And this has got to last us all week. With my back toward everyone as I put the pan away, I dab a bit of honey in my bowl.

My kind does better with sweet than savory. Eventually, I'll need some cakes or hunks of bread drizzled with maple syrup for energy. Or a few bushels of fresh berries. At the absolute least, a glass of sugary milk.

"I love it," Lucy replies quietly, her gaze locked on a painting I'd found stashed in an old closet. It's a bouquet of orange and pink ranunculus on a table tied together with a yellow bow. The colors are so vivid, the picture so vibrant, that I had to hang it up. It brings sunshine and joy to the room. Along with the food, of course.

I'm about to ask Lucy about the painting and if it's acceptable to have hung it, when my stomach rumbles. I want to focus on all the good deeds I'd performed today, but unlike my celestial counterpart, I need to sleep, eat, and rest to get to my next job in the morning at Minerva's. Thankfully, this gingery chicken congee is just what I need. I slide into the third seat with my own bowl and wait until Lucy lifts her spoon to take my first bite.

Silky, savory, delicious. My back falls against the rickety dining chair. Oh, how I love a good meal. It's always the first bite that soothes your soul, so I cherish it until my stomach begs for more.

"Thank you for this warm, delicious meal, *Darling*." Calam takes another big spoonful, watching me carefully. "I had no idea you even knew how to use a stove or make a traditional dish from my homeland." What he means to say is that he didn't know fairies could cook when we use magic for everything or that we can eat non-fanciful meals. And yeah, of course I know traditional celestial meals. That's all there ever was at the academy for lunch.

"There are plenty of things you don't know about me." I quirk a brow. "Do you cook, Lucy?"

"I can make oats," she says after another bite. Then she glances up at us both. "Actually, I want to talk about today." She doesn't wait for us to answer before she launches into everything she learned between sales. Meanwhile, I try not to eat too quickly, fidgeting with the pill in my pocket. I've barely had time to take my medicine today, and I'm a few hours later than I should be.

Calam remains rather mum throughout dinner. Listening. Plotting. Scheming, no doubt.

"Everyone's talking about the ball." Lucy's spoon shakes in her hand from the excitement of it all. "And the book club has at least five people coming tomorrow night."

Though the book club wasn't my idea, I'm confident that I'm making a difference regardless. I'm changing this world and it's been a day. One week may make this a truly special realm.

"Another mother told me she'd like to set up a class to teach everyone how to dance the night before the ball. I volunteered the bookstore." Lucy takes another huge bite of her food before continuing. "I got a little carried away. It might've been too soon."

"You know what, why don't we combine the party I was planning and a dance class?" I smile. It's not ideal—who will buy books if they're busy dancing?—but it could be a good opportunity for Lucy. "Sure, I think that'll be—"

"You and Calam can spend some time together on the dance floor too." Lucy wags her brows, surprising me. This is a very different person than the one we'd met yesterday. She has the beginnings of hope again. She seems healthier. Fed. Warm. Positive.

Though it's easy to stay enthused about her change in demeanor, I'm not entirely keen on the idea of dancing with Calam. That's not to say I don't find him attractive; I do. More than I should, to be honest. But alas, he is my immortal enemy. No matter how good it felt to comfort him today. Or the way he leaned into my touch like he needed me. Or the way he grasped my hand.

It's probably best not to think about all of that.

After polishing off my bowl, setting the dirty dishes in the new (old) sink, I head up to the bedroom, feigning exhaustion, with a cup of valerian tea. Lucy doesn't question it—after all, I've been run off my feet sewing at Minerva's, improving the bookstore, and endearing the village to me. She goes off to her own room, which I've yet to see, while Calam follows up after me.

Immediately, I want to collapse into a puddle. Instead, I pretend to wait until Calam's in loose clothes and on the other side of the bed by reading the new romance book that arrived earlier. When he's out of sight, I take my medicine, exhaling in relief. Any longer and I might have a crisis tomorrow, which simply wouldn't do.

As it is, that's only half the problem solved. I need to set my wings free. I don't think I'll manage another night with them tucked into my back. The headache has escalated from minor to major. The pain from tolerable to unbearable.

Still, I'm not in the mood to be myself with Calam present. Since I left Whimsia, celestials have judged me for my numerous differences. I don't need to give him further proof that I'll never fit in, that I'll never be one of them. In truth, I love my wings; I simply choose not to expose them to others who will attempt to make me feel negative about them. So I lose myself in the story.

Several pages in, my imagination is engaged. A prince meets a peasant in the center of a dark, forbidding forest. Both are lost for different reasons—one because he wished to run away from his palace home, the other because he wished to pick medicinal herbs for his ailing grandmother despite the danger. Instantly, they're attracted to each other. The prince finds the peasant judgmental yet beautiful beyond words, and the peasant finds the spoiled prince rather annoying, yet *also* beautiful beyond words.

My heart begins to race with anticipation for their romance—so I shut the book hastily.

Fairies read stories all the time. It's how we learn about the realms. Kissing, holding hands, ardent gazes, and declarations of love? Yep, we love them. Or at least I remember us loving them. Guardians, not so much. Romances aren't on any of the bookshelves at the library. I assume falling in love and sharing True Love's Kiss is a very private thing for celestials. That said, I'm aware of how love works and some expressions of it, though I'm not well practiced.

When I kissed Virtue that one time, it was because I desperately wanted to. She was pretty and when she touched her hand to my cheek, I felt good. I felt like we had crossed some line we'd been flirting with for a long while. To brush my lips against hers was natural. The world around us fell away and it was just me and her and happiness. When it ended, I was exhilarated.

I smiled big and joyful. I thought I understood love in that moment, even if it wasn't True Love's Kiss.

Virtue, however, did not feel the same. She said it was sloppy. The kind of kiss, she lamented, that only a fairy would give. Unrefined. Uncoordinated. And then she reminded me that celestials and fairies do not date.

Perhaps we could try, if you commit to becoming more like us, she'd said. *Once you fit in, you'll be accepted. It won't be so burdensome to be seen with you.*

If I'm a burden, then let me unburden you. I'd stood up and left. We hadn't spoken since. We became silent rivals . . . and I'd won. Satisfaction spreads through my stomach just thinking of it. Winning feels better than kissing anyway.

Calam's light snoring shakes me from my thoughts. I slide the book under my pillow and quietly push off the bed.

I lower the shoulders of my nightdress. With a flick of my wand—it's been far too long since I've used magic today—my fairy form washes over me. My ears lengthen at the tops into soft points, adorned with golden vine cuffs I've worn since I was little, matching the primrose headband that skims over the top of my head. The colors around me brighten and expand, allowing me to see things I couldn't before. Wings unfurl from my back, lustrous lilac purple with beautiful gauzy centers and delicate gold patterns I've never really seen. I flutter them once, feeling a bit more me. My body loosens a little. The headache is all but gone.

Deep breaths in, deep breaths out. This feels—

"You're beautiful."

I nearly jump out of my skin, the compliment flying over my head. Calam has one eye open. "You were asleep!"

"Was awake the whole time. I could sense you were up to something." When I catch his eyes roving over me, I nearly gasp. I see his true form—luxurious blondish-brown curls, the unblemished, pearly light brown skin of an eternal, long eyelashes attached to expressive emerald green eyes with hues of silky black—who knew black could have so many shades?—traveling from the bottom edge down his nose from thick to thin. It should look like he is a ghost or haunted or terrifying. Instead, it makes him breathtaking.

I swallow down my awe as he rolls across the mattress toward me.

"May I?" He lifts his hand.

"Oh? Yes."

He slowly reaches out to gently trace along the curve of a swirly gold pattern.

I giggle. "They're very ticklish." I flap them away from him. What I don't say is that while yes, they are ticklish, the sensation is more like butterflies swirling and warmth caressing my cool skin.

As are my sudden, unwelcome thoughts. His once-smooth curls are disheveled around his shoulders, and I have an unusual urge to run my fingers through them. Thankfully, I don't. He catches me studying him and winks.

The audacity.

"You're—you look more . . . Even as a mortal, you're very beautiful but in this form . . ." He trails off and my cheeks flame. "I've never seen a fairy with wings," he says quietly, as if in ponderance. "I knew you must have them, only . . . there's not . . . we don't know too much about fairies. We being Misfortunes, I mean." His words trip over the others. His signature snark is gone and his eyes round. "Are they . . . do they hurt when they aren't on your back?"

"Oh, no. Well, a little, yes." Every word he said sorts itself into my brain to be examined later. To clear my head, my wings flap, glitter shaking from their edges. "I don't use them much anymore. They did help when, for instance, a client was in a bad situation and needed some quick rescuing. They're quite weak now, so it's not like I can carry anyone or anything while flying.

Though I suppose with regular exercise they might. Guardians don't *really* allow me to reveal them though."

Calam holds his hand out to touch them again but doesn't. "Did you make them purple?"

"No, I was born with purple wings. Most fairies get white or blue, sometimes green, though some do get red. I suspect mine were because my mother has blue, and my father has red. They're unusual, but then—"

"So are you," he finishes. Still, he stares at them in amazement. "It must be hard to not use them."

"It is." I smile more to myself than to him. "When I've worked with mortals before, I stayed in the shadows, never needing to change form. When I did reveal myself, it was like this." I gesture to how I am now. "This is the longest I've gone without them."

"It's why you were dizzy earlier." He's beginning to read me and I'm not sure this is a good thing. "Well, you needn't hide them from me. Not up here." He reaches out to pat my hand suddenly. Something in the center of my stomach spasms, which I promptly ignore. "We may be competing, but I don't want to make you uncomfortable. I'm aware with the one bed—"

"We're professionals. There's plenty of space for the two of us." I mean it. I've slept on floors and in closets before, and though I prefer it to be plushier, this is acceptable.

I flap my wings one more time to work the muscles. Sleep will be easier with them; they tend to wrap around me like a cocoon. Their weight locks me in and makes me feel safe. Oh, how I've missed them.

"Well, professional to professional, you did an incredible job today." Calam settles himself back on his side after throwing a corner of the blanket open for me to slip into. "You're making me have to recalibrate my strategy."

"You've changed your mind about fairies, have you?" I slide under the covers, glad we have enough space between us. Otherwise, this would feel, as Mrs. Arconia said, *improper.* Even if Calam and I aren't really courting, nor would we share True Love's Kiss. Like Virtue said, celestials and fairies don't date.

He's so quiet, I think he's done with the conversation. I tug my ear, turning off the lights, and close my eyes. My heartbeat returns to normal. The way he called me beautiful rings through my thoughts until he sighs.

"One fairy." His voice is as soft as the wings now swaddling me. "I've changed my mind about one fairy."

CHAPTER TEN

I can't sleep. Though the magic within me needs this rest to recharge, my brain has too many thoughts. Most of them where they don't belong, namely on the other side of the bed. Darling's asleep, purple wings wrapped around her shoulders, a bare brown foot poking out beneath the blanket. Her breaths fall gently, punctuated here and there by sweet little murmurings.

She is ruining me. Why does she have to be so good at this? Why does she have to be so beautiful? Was everything I learned about fairies wrong?

I stare up at the worn rafters. If you ask any celestial, they'll reiterate what we learn in the first years at the academy as well-established facts. Fairies use magic for everything. They are selfish. Incapable and disinclined to work for the greater good. They don't believe in a set morality. Instead, they consider that all creatures make decisions that shift their fate for better or worse, and that's nature. They are convinced we should let it run its course without outside interference. They embrace chaos. Their own realm is chaos.

They are chaos.

Darling has shown me otherwise. She contains not-easily-defined—and certainly unpredictable—multitudes. She's more than what I thought I knew. She's also driven. Also lonely.

I'm not at home. I haven't seen my kin in years. I'm far away, alone.

She must've given up her home, family, friends to be here. She's playing by celestial rules to be here. She's waking early to work, making dinners, using her magic to give us a room in which to rest. All of which begs further questions: How good must she have been to get this opportunity, and why did they send me if she already had the credentials for the mentorship? That's not to say I shouldn't be in the running—my scores were the highest in my year too, but how much higher were her scores before I helped Phred on Barfaris?

I let out a long exhale. There are no answers.

I carefully get up from the bed, snap my fingers to change my outfit, and then tread downstairs in the dead of night. If Darling's doing extra, I should be too. My idea of watch-and-wait isn't working. While the bookstore is in far better shape—mostly because of Darling—Lucy's path hasn't yet been determined.

It's on me to set it for her.

The stair creaks on the bottom step and I snap again, muffling all sounds. Though not the voice in my head. The one telling me to act rationally.

Because despite my changing feelings toward the fairy, if she wins, there's a huge chance that Lucy's life will become uncertain. If what I think is the greatest predicament of her life is true, then Andi is possibly the fork in Lucy's path. When I'd seen her the first time, I knew she might be trouble. The second time only confirmed it.

Andi could be anyone from anywhere. But something tells me she isn't. I suspect she's bigger than that, she could be that Princess hosting that ball. I saw a crown, a palace. She's secretive, emotional . . . She keeps coming to this bookstore for Lucy. Flirting with Lucy. And if Lucy goes to that ball and sees her there, letting herself live the fairy tale . . . they could fall in love. Lucy *could* have a Happily Ever After, but it could be—and likely would be—short-lived. None of this suits her. Lucy is quiet. She's shy. The palace wouldn't be a home. What would happen to the store, her dreams?

Mortals believe that money, power, and prestige are the best anyone could hope for, which is simply not true. Time and time again, those with all three are never happy. They tend to make their realm miserable. They take and take and take and on the other end, someone must give. Everything comes at a cost.

And it's not one Lucy needs to pay. I'll make sure of it.

She's better here. In her store, where we can predict the outcome. Even if it's ordinary. Even if it doesn't have a love component. No one *needs* romantic love to survive. They need food. Money to afford that food. Their home. Clothes to put on their cold backs and heat to warm their hearth.

This is what I came for. Not some purple-winged fairy who makes me question my own education. That's irrelevant and unhelpful. My life is in service to mortals.

I snap my fingers to light the candles, then I get to work in the farthest, darkest corner of the shop. First, I begin weeding through the books. Taking tomes that haven't seen the light in many moons and placing them in a pile on the floor. Next, I begin making more space for the newer stories that I'm sure there's an appetite for in the community. Especially after the romance book club. Copies of *The Prince and the Woodsman* stare up at me as I heave them up onto shelves. I face one out for customers to see the delicate illustrations on the leather.

My gaze roves over the little embellishments, the artistic flourishes. Art in the mortal realms has always been fascinating. How they express their feelings and perspectives in the short lives they lead *should* fascinate all eternals. It tells much about their world, their skills, their minds. Whereas we—who cannot die, age slowly over many, many mortal lifetimes—only have art made by the retired celestials who've thrown their coins into The Dark Mile. Their art, stories, music tend to be too cerebral to understand.

Mortal art, it's direct. I wonder, as I plop another book down, if they make such beautiful art because they live such short lives. They pour everything they have into expression because they are aware that all things must end.

Which leads me on another mental journey into the meaning of life itself. Apparently, I'm in the exhausted, ponderous mood of trying to understand existence. Well, I try. My foot catches on the pile, and I throw my arms out to steady myself. The shelf pushes away, and instead of a messy catastrophe, it reveals a dark, secret room.

After snatching a candle from the counter, I gingerly step

forward. This isn't Lucy's bedroom—that's through a door left of the kitchen. I proceed with apprehension, worried the wood is too worn here to support my weight.

Still, I have to investigate. Everything in me screams that this could be important.

Once I'm inside, I snap my fingers, illuminating the space. There are crates at the back of the room, stacks of paintings on both sides. I set the candle down and begin my perusal, first with the paintings.

They start small in cheap, fake silver frames. Some are of flowers in fields like the one in the kitchen, others are of flower crowns on a woman's head. Her black curls tumble down her back on top of a slate-gray dress, her bare dark brown skin shimmering in the sunshine. The sky is a cerulean blue, the trees farther down a field tilt forward as if they're swaying in the wind or trying to get closer to the woman whose face we cannot see. The colors are radiant, the details numerous. A talented painter created this work. Yet, there are no initials to be found. Nothing to tell me who made them.

Lucy? Or Lucy's mother? What of her father?

I keep moving through them, finding more of the woman. Never facing the artist, always off doing something. Then I come across one that gives me pause. It's in a worn copper frame. I push the others aside before dusting it. A sneeze rips through me as I stare at one of the most beautiful pictures I've ever seen.

It's An Enchanted Story. The bookstore isn't better or worse than it is now. White stone turned gray through endless rain and cold winds. The enticing book displays peek through the glass window. And off to the left, an older brown woman beside a little girl in a flower crown. The woman is smiling, while the girl—no older than seven or eight years old—is staring up at her mother. Her dress is pale pink and dotted with flowers. She has curly braids, big eyes. The mother is older, though nearly identical. Although the metal book sign dangling from the end of the thatched roof is a bit more polished, the scene seems real. Vibrant and full of life.

"It was hard capturing her smile," Lucy says suddenly behind me. I jump, almost knocking over the stack. I'm excessively clumsy in this realm. "It was always so . . . vivid in my head, but I could never get it right. I was too afraid that if I drew her face, I'd get it wrong." She nods in the direction of the other paintings of the woman.

"You painted these." I'm completely taken aback. Lucy paints? "I didn't know . . ."

The lantern in her hand shakes. Her eyes gleam, and for the first time since I arrived, she lets down the wall between us. "I used to."

"But then you stopped." I run my fingertips along the frame, trying to both watch her and sneak a peek at the picture again.

"Paint is expensive," she states without a hint of emotion. This is someone who has accepted her limitations. "I can barely afford oats."

"Do you love it, this art? I mean making it?" It's clear my mouth and brain aren't coordinating well. The exhaustion has gotten to me.

She doesn't answer, her gaze instead drifting back to her mother. "I loved making that one. Took me a long time."

"Lucy . . ." I trail off, shifting on my feet. Art is for the rich. Those who can risk time and money. Lucy can't pursue this if she wants to survive. But I can't tell her that. "You have talent."

"It's just something I do." There's a slight creaking of wood somewhere and the guarded expression slips back onto her face. "It's late. The store will open in a few hours, and I think we both need rest." She ushers me out of the room, closing the bookcase door behind her. "Please don't go in there again. It's . . . private."

"Of course." I nod. "I'll see you in the morning."

She treads back to the doorway to her room, waiting for me to go upstairs. I know that she won't open up to me again. Not about her mother. Not about her art. I'll have to find a new angle that doesn't involve stumbling into her secrets.

Perhaps tomorrow night at the romance book club's first meeting, I'll prove to her she can trust me. I'll prove to her that I have her best interests at heart.

If she lets me.

CHAPTER ELEVEN

After an hour or two of sleep, some inner alarm goes off in my head. I turn over to find Calam gone. And if he's trying to get ahead, so must I.

I dress quickly, dart off through the store, passing by candle-light flickering through the open door—the small storage closet—and head out into the chilly village. Instead of heading to Minerva's, I stalk through the courtyard, down the lanes of sleepy houses, to the edge of the village—all the while pinching my cardigan tighter around me.

Once I reach the end of the road and the beginning of the field, I stop. My breath leaves soft clouds in front of me. The air is crisper here, fresh like morning in Whimsia. The dirt squelches beneath my boots, simultaneously too wet and too lifeless. That's exactly why I'm here, even when I'm not supposed to be. I should leave. Go back to the real assignment.

But in my defense, this *could* be part of the assignment. If I really think about it, if I ask, "What Does Lucy Need?" it goes like this:

1. The bookstore to stay in business—I'm doing well there.

2. Andi, maybe? What more does someone need than love, a home, and a full heart? (Which means I have to research who the girl is and how I can get them together tonight at the book club meeting.)
3. Lastly, for Lucy to truly, absolutely succeed, I'm convinced the rest of Fulhorn should too.

See, following that rationale, it makes perfect sense that I'm here. Right?

So I magick an orb of light and then I promptly ignore the warnings circling in the back of my mind, telling me to do the job I was meant to do, to be more like Calam. Focus on Lucy. *You're doing too much.*

Only, the field has a problem—it *needs* my tender love and care. The right thing to do is help.

I swish my wand—which depletes my energy—to dig holes, and then plant fairy dust, the residue of magic. When a fairy performs a spell, it leaves behind a glittery substance in the air. Normally, that dissipates, but if I take it and add it to something like dirt, something strange happens.

The first time I'd done it was back in Whimsia. My big brother, Favie, and I were competing to win the Paradise Pines piggleberry festival. The winner would be seated at the head of the table at the Primrose Banquet. Favie was desperate to get first place; the Fae Queen's son, Aelvar, had caught his eye a few festivals before and he hadn't yet found a way to make the Prince fall for him. If we were sitting nearby, it'd improve his chances.

Anyway, we planted three bushes of piggleberries months in advance. Tried every trick to get them blossoming. But they never produced a single petal.

Favie became despondent, certain that he would never fall in love. My mother told us these things happen for a reason. My father shook his head and wondered why any of us even bothered.

But I decided to play dirty. I tried all sorts of spells around the stems; nothing worked. After watering it one last time, noticing my fairy dust sink into the soil when I'd done all that magic, I went to bed. The next day, the piggleberry bushes beamed. Grander than anything any of us had ever seen. They were glorious, big purple flowers the size of your head. Bonus, for reasons I still don't understand and could never ask about without revealing that I'd cheated, they held no trace of magic either, so we weren't disqualified.

Favie won a seat beside Aelvar, and his hand too, in time. My mother told us these things happen for a reason. My father shook his head and said he wondered why any of us even bothered.

And I learned that these things do happen for a reason: Because you bother and you care and you try. You interfere. You don't let fate decide for you; you decide your own fate. That was the moment I knew I had to leave home.

I stare down at the soil now, my hands submerged in the dirt. There's a chance that if I do this, that if I use my dust, everything will be undone if I lose. Or, like in Whimsia, my magic could disintegrate into the soil forever, making it something new.

I take the risk.

The water rushes toward the dust as if magnified, redistributing the pools of excess, stagnant rain. I do this over and over again, everywhere I can. Until my body aches and my muscles burn. Until my energy is gone and my head's a little dizzy.

A few minutes pass, and . . . nothing happens. No sprouts. No movement. I may have alleviated the irrigation problems but perhaps that's all. When I did it in Whimsia, it could have been that our realm already had magic in its core. There's no certainty that this would work.

Awareness spreads through me as the first prickles of dawn pierce the darkness. I have precious little time before I'm expected at Minerva's. The cold wind nips at my hair. The dirt and grime cling to me along with the realization that I've seriously messed up.

What was I *thinking*?

The spiral begins as I drop the shovel, backing away from the countryside I spent hours squandering my time in.

Fool. Worthless. A waste. The words whisper through my mind on a loop. Other words join in because misery enjoys company. *Different. Weird. Ugly.* I never even think I'm ugly until the spiral begins and then somehow, that's a thought. Suddenly, I see images of people looking at me with grim expressions. They laugh as I pass. They say cruelties about me behind their hands. Guardians did that. The mortals here too. Maybe even fairies.

This. This is what happens when I take my medicine too

late and don't properly take care of myself. Only a few hours of sleep, not enough food. Work that doesn't yield immediate results. It's the perfect recipe for the spiral of doom.

I *hate* me. I love me and I hate me. *I'm so tired* of all these big thoughts.

Using the last remnants of magic I have left, I poof myself back to the bedroom, where Calam's soundlessly asleep on the other side of the bed. It's the kind of sleep where he knows he's done nothing wrong. He didn't go overboard. He didn't possibly ruin his entire assignment.

Unlike me, he was gone most of the night probably getting an upper hand with Lucy. He's the better opponent. Better at all of this. He knew fixing the field was a distraction. He knew it. I did too. And yet . . . I had to. I needed to. I was so sure . . .

That was likely his plan. I want to believe we're like coworkers on the same mission. Competing while never losing touch of compassion. I want to believe that so bad. Thinking the worst of someone because I disagree with their perspective is wrong.

But *I* could be wrong. He could be playing a wicked game with me. Touching me. Calling me beautiful. Changing moods to test me. Goading me to make a bad decision. He could be manipulating me. Am I that easy of a target? Did I fall for it?

Briefly, I fall asleep standing. When I nearly collapse, I shake myself awake before washing up with warm water from the basin behind the partition, slapping my face a few times. Damn it. I'm making a mess of things again. What will happen with my magic being so tapped out, beyond a difficult day fighting my mental illness? I can't afford to lose sight of what I was sent here to do.

Glittery tears plop onto my undergarments, creating a kaleidoscope of sadness on soft linen. I straighten slowly against the force of my plummeting mood. No more of this. There are five midnights left. Calam no doubt knows what he'll do. It's time I do too.

After cleaning off, I lace up my old dress. I can't use more magic for a little while, so I sneak out of the room, down the stairs, and through the courtyard.

I lift my hand to knock on the dressmaker's door when it whooshes open and Minerva yanks me inside.

"Hurry on in, my dear," she says. "I'll fix you breakfast while you look at some dresses I've taken out. I'll have to leave later this afternoon for a village meeting with all the elders—Mayor Arconia has them every month. I imagine it's about the ball. I'll have to tell you about it later." She retreats down the hall, words still trailing behind her. This is a different Minerva. One with more to say and more energy. "Make yourself at home. The dresses that need to be done first are already on the table."

She takes off before I can even respond. I sniffle one last time. The confidence, the strength, the energy doesn't bounce back the way I hoped it would. My body is tired. My illness has been triggered. I just need to push through and remember that this isn't about me. It's about Lucy.

Not. Me.

I don't need to be anything but useful. Though the negativity continues in my mind, I try to ignore it, crossing the hallway to find another dress. Some part of me wishes to keep it simple, comfortable. Yet I realize it's about Minerva too.

One fine dress brought her better fortune. Two will surely only make her business better. I owe this to her.

I decide to take a gorgeous midnight-blue velvet dress under seven coats of dust from the rack. It doesn't need much tailoring; Minerva is truly talented. If I were smaller, I might not alter it at all. But I'm not small, and I will never feel bad about that. Everything else is a different story. I swish my wand around several times, each time draining my energy more. My magic is nearly spent. The fabric stretches into my size and shape. Silver thread embellishes the seams while climbing from the hem up to the bodice with obscure starry constellations. Not too flashy. Subtle. Understated yet effective. People don't like to stand out in Lumina, so I won't either. I slip out of yesterday's disaster and into the dress, sighing.

I'm not feeling this. But perhaps this one moment of focusing on myself will renew me. Even if I want to go back to sleep and not exist for a few hours. Not think for a few hours. It's not about me. It's not about me—yet the me in this current moment doesn't want to be here. Or anywhere. Not unalive, just not struggling. My fingers thrum against the soft material, anxiety causing them to move erratically. I need to get them busy; idle hands make idle minds.

As I sit down to work, the spiral tightens. It's always there. Always waiting to get my attention and ruin me. Now the spiral is big. I thought it'd pass. I needed it to.

Worthless.

Silly.

No one likes you.

I want to bang my hands on the walls and scream or melt into a puddle and sob till the well inside me runs dry. Some wiser voice in my brain tells me to be resilient. I still have five days to win. I glance in the mirror on the other side of the room, magick my hair better, add a few slashes of powder to make me look less tired, and force a smile. *Let's do this.*

My hands pick up the pace. I redirect my dwindling energy. From down the hall, the first whiffs of something fried and delicious hit my nostrils. *Mmm*, food. It doesn't always work, but sometimes when it's especially yummy, it could be the thing that makes my heart feel a little lighter.

Minerva's footsteps sound closer now. She's carrying a plate. It smells like butter and eggs. Maybe a few slices of cheese? Some fresh vegetables chopped and caramelized perhaps? Saliva collects in my mouth. The spiral quiets a bit, replaced by my rumbling stomach. Oh, what I wouldn't do for a sweet griddle cake too. Or just a glass of honey tea.

She slides a plate in front of me. A nice, big omelet. My brows furrow and I glance up at her.

"You won't believe it." Minerva's exuberant tone drowns out the rumbling. "The farmer says he woke up to an overflowing basket of eggs this morning. He delivered some to everyone in the village, free of charge, though I did give him all the change I could find. Well, some of the change you gave me, to be honest. And he had extra milk and cheese too! And then the florist said when she looked in her old greenhouse for the first time in months, there were rows and rows of perfect vegetables! I offered her a new dress for a box every two weeks for the next few months. What a turn of events!"

"Really?" The sides of my mouth lift. Maybe my efforts were worth it. I'm not completely worthless. I can do something right.

It's that thought that has me picking up my fork and digging in. I still have to see it, really, but this one glimmer of hope might get me through the day. I eat in silence—well, silence besides the scraping of silver on porcelain, and my fuller stomach almost makes me smile.

Once the plate is clear and Minerva scoops it from the table, I get back to work. My spirit's a little brighter. Not all better, but more manageable.

For a while, I work at breakneck speed through the garments. I avoid thinking of anything else—I've already used up all my brainpower on the crisis earlier. I'm so zoned out that I don't notice Minerva standing by my chair until she coughs slightly.

"Darling, did you hear me?"

I shake my head honestly. "I'm sorry, I was, uh—"

Minerva bats a dismissive hand. "I said there's a gathering in the courtyard. We should go see what the hubbub's about. Helps living close to the village square. I'm just glad we ate before the commotion, no matter how good it could end up being."

The moment I stand, she threads her slim arm through

mine, not pausing to let me answer. "That dress is stunning! I don't recall making it and you think I would with all those starry details. And as with yesterday, Darling, it makes you look luminous. Such a beautiful girl."

"Thank you," I lie. Her kind words don't sink in. The spiral won't let them. According to my brain, my inner reality is reflecting my outer reality and it's disgusting. Nice of her to say otherwise. She means well. "I can't take credit for the dress. I bet more clients will come to steal it soon."

We walk outside as villagers gather. The sun is shining. The air smells fresh and floral. People are smiling; some even wave my way. I return the gesture, though voices whisper in the back of my head that they are only doing it to be friendly. They don't want to see me. They don't care about me. I'm nothing to them. Nothing to anyone in this realm. Least of all Lucy.

I'm failing. I'm a failure. Nothing. No one.

"Fulhorn is back," someone yells out in the forming crowd.

More join.

"Our luck has been reversed!"

"It's like magic!"

There are more shouts, too many for me to understand. Then suddenly people clap and embrace one another. There's gaiety in the village. All around me, energy crackles like an electrical storm. The sky is a vibrant blue, the few clouds fluffy white. The florist bolts past me, carrying a bushel of orange ranunculus. When she sways under the weight, one of the flowers leans toward me and . . . winks. My eyes round. A vine reaches out and brushes my cheek.

"*Thank you*," it whispers.

I spin around to see if anyone else notices. They don't. No one seems to have heard it either. A feeling of dread flutters in my gut. It's not reacting to mortals. It's reacting to me. It's thanking me.

My magic did this. What will happen if I lose? Will everything become lifeless again?

The florist yanks it back. "Sorry, Darling. Didn't mean to bump you." Then she lets out a cackle as she saunters off. What amuses her, I have no idea. Before I can even grasp the entirety of the situation, a voice rises above the fray. Everyone stills.

"Good fortune has come back to Fulhorn and the Kingdom of Lumina! Our land bears fruit and vegetables and flowers and . . . and life once again! Ten years we were cursed! Ten!" An older man wearing a lapel pin that says MAYOR ARCONIA stands unevenly atop a stack of wooden crates. Wrinkles line his dark brown skin, especially around his mouth. I suspect from excessive frowning since he's married to Mrs. Arconia. He clutches a very dented wooden cane and waves it around. "The King will be pleased! His beneficence may change our little village into a bustling and prosperous city. Our fate will be altered!"

The crowd cheers around us. I can't help but clap with them. People murmur about all the good things coming their way. That things are finally going to be okay.

Maybe they're right. Maybe it will be.

"Let's celebrate," Minerva says quietly before clearing her throat. Her voice strengthens. "Let's celebrate! Let's open our stores with discounts and food for everyone all day!"

Another cheer. That could be very helpful. Very helpful indeed. That kind of money could boost the bookstore incredibly. For the second time today, I shouldn't feel so worthless. I grin at the joy surrounding us.

And then my gaze locks across the village square on a startlingly beautiful face. Calam stares at me, his lips twisted. His curls are frizzy, and there are dark rings beneath his eyes. He's been busy. From across the cobblestones, the people, the happiness . . . his scowl freezes the hope that was building within me. His scowl tells me I've made a huge mistake. It tells me that it's not going to be okay.

I might've used too much magic, but I'll just have to endeavor to use less going forward. Besides, I did things the slow and right way, and it was taking too long. All of this, it made Fulhorn and Lumina better.

I spot Lucy outside the store, sleepiness and a small, tentative smile on her face. I made this better for her too. For the store. For everyone and everything.

It's too late for me to apologize or feel guilt, even if my illness tells me I should. It's not about me, it's about so much more.

CHAPTER TWELVE

Calam

The bookstore has been nonstop busy thanks to Darling's little escapade using magic she had no business using and therefore leading Fulhorn and Lumina toward chaos. I take a deep breath. This is not my problem.

It really isn't.

My eye twitches and fingers flex.

Except it *is*.

People seem cheerful. Hopeful. Embracing this new change with aplomb.

They feel like all their dreams are possible.

I toss the fairy another dirty look; I should have never trusted her. And I would say as much to her if we hadn't been helping customers all day. They've been coming not only from the village, but from the palace. News travels fast in a tiny kingdom, it would seem. Traders and businesses will wish to restart their relationships with the farms again. There's excitement again. It's a lot of talking. A lot of smiling. A lot of "Can I help you?" and even more of "Of course, let me get your change." I loathe it.

Between this incessant socializing and Darling's betrayal, I'm getting a splitting headache.

As if she can hear my loud and enraged thoughts, she shrugs at my glares. She and I spoke about not saving Fulhorn. While we didn't seem to be on the same page, we were at least in the same book. I thought I made a convincing argument. Sure, I joked about it later, but I thought she'd make the right decision.

I'm half-tempted to contact the Mortal Outcome Council about her flagrantly creating havoc, when merrymakers cackle outside, bringing me back to the present. To Lumina and this assignment slipping away from me.

Through the window, twilight has fallen. The book club is happening in a matter of minutes. I need to get myself together. I shake my head. There's no need to bring the council into this. It could hurt both of us, and there's no need to snitch either; I'm going to win regardless. Today, I've done all the work I could. I've laid the net for the book club and promoting the bookstore; now it's time to catch my fish.

After another glimpse around the shop, I take a deep breath. We're ready.

We've moved aside the shelves to make room for a circle of chairs, made garlands from the dried flowers the florist gave us, and strung them up all over the store. We've set trays of cookies—which Darling exuberantly informed me are oat cardamom drizzled with caramel—pastries, and steamy hot custardy buns on top of any counter space we could find. Personally, I made story displays that should entice everyone to buy a copy or three, and Darling made a sweet lemon punch.

Across the store, Lucy writes questions down about the book's opening chapters to get the conversation started. By the end of the night, surely we'll have enough to pay the debts owed to the Arconias for land tax and the books. Though they still haven't managed to send me an invoice. I'm beginning to suspect they have something nefarious up their sleeves. Why else wouldn't they want to get paid? Why make such a hassle of it?

That's another bridge to cross later.

The bell above the door jingles, causing the three of us to look up. Minerva comes through carrying a cotton garment bag over her shoulder. The sound of laughter carries on the wind before the door bounces shut behind her.

"I have a lovely dress here for you," she says, her smile wide. "Darling ordered it yesterday. 'A dress,' she said, 'that would be your perfect bookstore look.'"

Lucy's eyes widen. Her expression is wonder-struck. The expression of someone who has not received gifts in a very long time. She glances at Darling. "You did this?"

"Of course," she says, setting down a book from another romance display and swooping over to her behind the counter. "You deserve to feel your best in *your* store."

Minerva shuffles Lucy into the back to get her ready for the evening. Zeal flitters through Darling's expression, which I promptly dissipate when her gaze meets mine. I snap my fingers, causing our voices to be muffled as I use this temporary time alone to scold her.

"What did you *do*?"

"I did what I thought was right," she hisses across the counter from me.

"You're just like every other fairy—"

"Colorful and delightful?" She puts a hand on her hip, her lips pressed into a flat line. Daring me to say otherwise. I accept.

"Troublesome and maddening," I reply.

"Lucy's happiness depends on us making this realm better for her!"

I cross the room, hovering above the countertop separating us. "I don't care about Lucy's happiness. *Happiness* is not the objective!"

She leans closer, her face inches from mine. "Happiness is *always* the objective."

I huff. "You're exasperating."

"You're overbearing." She cocks her head to the side.

I smirk. "You're reckless."

Her nostrils flare. "You're dull."

I jab my finger at her collarbone. Just to remind her that I'm as solid as she is, as present as she is, and as powerful as she is. "Better to be dull than an irresponsible, meddling, mischievous, candy-coated, magic-misusing disaster of a—"

My voice cuts off when her eyes suddenly brim with pastel, glittery tears.

She swallows, her lower lip wobbling.

She's going to cry? The fairy who just upended everything with a swish of her wand is going to cry?

"Disaster of a what?" Her voice cracks.

"Never mind," I say through a sigh. Name-calling is beneath me. I'm an enlightened, well-meaning Misfortune. All of this is unnecessary. We may be children in the universe of our kin, but we're two budding professionals.

"You don't think I know that I'm a disaster? Or ridiculous? Celestials have been telling me that since I showed up begging for a job. I'm well aware that I'm . . . too much. You think you're annoyed—imagine how I feel. I have to live with me and all my flaws every day." Her tone shifts melancholic and I'm not sure what to make of it. "I didn't mean to cause so much uncertainty in the village. I just wanted to help."

"That's your problem," I reply gently. "You still haven't learned the difference between what mortals want, and what they need."

"I have." A tear slips down her cheek, streaking it with gold sparkles. "I just believe they deserve both. Mortals, celestials, fairies, we"—she flaps a hand between us, tapping my chest—"deserve both. Forget about need; don't you ever *want*?"

I stare at her. My gaze drifts from her big brown eyes to her button nose and pillowy lips. For a moment, I get lost in her and her nearness. My hand acts on its own volition, cupping her jaw and swiping the tear with my thumb. The store, Lucy, everything, drifts away in my periphery until only her face remains. It takes all my energy to answer. "Darling, I don't—"

"Save it for the wedding, you two!" Minerva crows, stomping through the back door. "When is the date, by the way? Should we begin the preparations?"

Darling and I jump apart, the hand that went rogue smacking the hard wood counter. Whatever nonsense I was about to admit is thankfully unsaid. I almost drag in a breath, relieved. *Almost.* If it weren't for the sudden heat climbing up my neck and this tickly feeling in my hand that impertinently disobeyed my mind. That can be the only reason I did what I did. Temporary lack of bodily autonomy. I'm sure that's a thing and I read it somewhere. No need to investigate further.

We're spared from any response to Minerva's unwelcome question as Lucy slowly leaves the kitchen, shining like the sun lives within her. The dress is a light mint, with rows and rows of golden embroidery depicting full bookshelves. It's a bookstore in thread. *Her* bookstore. It's perfect. It makes her skin glow. Her braids have been pulled back into one big braid that drapes over her shoulder. Her eyelids have been lined with kohl, her lips daubed with beet paste.

"Lucy," I exclaim as I regain my composure. "You look lovely."

Lucy smiles even wider. "Thank you, Calam." Then she twists toward Darling. "Thank you for this, Darling. It's truly . . ." Her smile falters and I try to read her thoughts, see if she's as wowed by material things as she is by the bookstore's potential success. Only, her thoughts are flashes of her mother. The twirls in the grass and around the books here that made their skirts flare. The little moments. The dresses like this one. If I were closer, I could read more. This is all I can get now. "It's amazing."

Darling sniffs, and I'll grant her this, her magic seems to have positively impacted Lucy's mood. It's just not sustainable or reasonable or predictable. "Anything for you, Lucy."

"Well, best be off," Minerva says. "The celebrations will begin soon, and I've got to get customers in the door. Hope you all have a great book club tonight. And you two"—she gestures to me and Darling—"try not to get too swept up in your romance, huh?"

"We won't," I respond quickly. "Have a good night."

I watch her scuttle through the door and into the candlelit courtyard, which is already beginning to fill with villagers in their finest garments. They're colorful and jubilant. They drink and tell stories by the fountain that still hasn't flourished to watery life. The dwindling light bounces off their various skin tones and smiles.

Guests—namely feminine-presenting mortals with a few unsure-looking men who seem either nervous or embarrassed to be there—tiptoe inside, whispering to ask if the book club meeting is still happening.

We quickly usher them to where the seats are arranged in a circle, drawing the curtains on the window we'd installed earlier to ease their discomfort. Once they've filled their porcelain plates with pastries, they all take their copies of the story from their belongings. There seems to be a shameful pervasiveness about these books that I can't quite figure out. Why hide books? Why be ashamed about loving stories?

The door jingles one last time and Andi slips inside. Lucy's eyes flash excitedly as everyone begins to chat passionately. She locks the door, assuming everyone who wants to be here is here, and then takes her seat again, hands fidgeting. Darling and I give the mortals ample space. Enough to be present, not enough to draw attention.

"Always loved this store," one woman in a pale green dress says as she takes a bite of cookie.

"My father forbade me from coming inside. He's off at the pub now, so he won't know." A young man, about the same age as Darling and me, rubs his hand over the leather cover. "I know we're only supposed to read a few chapters since we'd only got it yesterday, but I'm halfway through. I just love it."

"Me too," another young man says on the other side of the circle. They share a timid smile.

They switch seats to sit next to each other while conversation swirls around us.

Andi shifts so close to Lucy that their elbows touch. Though they don't speak, I can't imagine their thoughts are anywhere but that point of contact. Andi doesn't look the least bit shy. If anything, she's bold. Too bold for me to see into her mind again. Otherwise, I'd have to find relief with Darling, and that's simply not happening.

"Loved your mother, dear." An older woman sips from a fancy teacup Darling, no doubt, magicked earlier. "She was so enchanting."

"She was," Lucy agrees with a nod, her voice heavy. Andi leans in, patting Lucy's arm. They exchange a long glance—which I don't like the look of. Darling clears her throat, gesturing for Lucy to begin while topping off teacups and offering custard buns. I see her shove a tiny scrap of parchment toward Andi while Lucy takes a deep breath. I'll have to figure out what that was about later. "Like you, Bruno, I love this book. I also found it hard to stop reading last night in bed."

What follows is a lively—if boring to me—conversation about the story that eventually gives way to romance in general.

If I weren't so concerned about how Lucy and Andi are interacting and what that could mean for the future, I'd have already left for some more useful way to spend my time. Likely sleep. I'm tired and . . . uneasy.

"I adore when one character is very serious and the other very lighthearted. They balance each other so well." Mrs. Lanigan clutches a hand to her chest.

Ms. Chambers shakes her head. "Oh no, my absolute favorite is when they loathe each other only for them to realize they're deeply in love."

"When they have to share a horse! Forced closeness!" Bruno nudges the boy beside him, Matti, with his shoulder.

"When one of them falls first," Andi adds, earning a quirk of Lucy's lips.

"There's only one bed!" Mrs. Howe shouts out, causing a raucous of giggles around the room. "That always evolves into something . . ." She wags her eyebrows suggestively.

Darling hacks a cough, her cheeks pinkening. That makes me smirk in her direction. Everyone turns, concern threading through the group.

"Are you okay?" Lucy pushes off her seat, only for Darling to raise a dismissive hand.

"Sorry, just sipped my tea wrong," she lies. Now I'm outright smiling. She's not a romance reader, and clearly has never heard of what the "there's only one bed" trope might lead to. I wonder how that'll impact *us* later, if she knows we're like characters in one of those books. If she considers us loathers-to-lovers, or one-serious-one-light or . . . "I'm rather keen on meant-to-be."

Huh. I wasn't expecting that.

"That one's great too—almost as good as those custardy pastries." Ms. Chambers laughs. "I daresay there's not a single bad romantic concept if you're a fan of romance."

Mrs. Lanigan opens her mouth to respond when there's a knock outside, causing a quick panic. People shove their copies under their chairs, into their skirts, and into their pockets. I rush over to answer it, unlocking it and opening the door just slightly.

"Can I help you?" I say for the millionth time today. Mrs. Arconia attempts to poke her head in, but I hold the door fast. "Ah, Mrs. Arconia. Good to see you."

Her thick reddish-brown brows furrow. "Mr. Calam—I never did catch your last name." I only stare at her until she gets the hint that I won't be sharing it now either. "I came by to check in on the store and to accept payment on its debts. If An Enchanted Story is doing half as well as the rest of the small businesses tonight, then surely, she should be able to—"

"You will receive payment as soon as I can look over the invoice, Mrs. Arconia." I frown. "Do you happen to have it with you, or should I pick it up at your home tomorrow? I'd like to have financial clarity."

"I don't believe that it's your business." Her lips pinch. "Lucy Addlesberg is the sole proprietor."

"Proprietor, meaning she owns the store, right?" Her face contorts even further. "I'm her bookkeeper, as it were." My hand squeezes the wood door hard. She makes me . . . uncomfortable. There's something malignant simmering beneath her surface. The last time I encountered her, I knew she was something different than an Unhappily Ever After. Now I'm beginning to understand that she's worse than that. A Miserably Ever After. I've heard of them, Blight even mentioned them, but I don't know how to handle one. "Now, if you'll excuse us—"

At that, she bristles and shoves her way inside the store, nearly knocking me into a bookcase. "What's this, then? A meeting of some sort?" She tries to peek around for some clue about why there's a circle of chairs, empty trays and teacups, and several villagers in one place. I can't say if she's hoping to find us doing something illegal or if she's offended to not have been invited. "What is the meaning of this?"

"Um . . ." Lucy slides off her chair now, Andi following. "We—"

"I thought it'd be great fun to meet some of our regular patrons. Since we're new here, after all," Darling says brightly. "We wanted to discuss our favorite books."

Mrs. Arconia huffs. She smooths her hands down her green dress. "I see."

"The get-together is over anyway," Lucy concludes. "I hope we can see each other again soon."

"Oh yes, definitely." Mrs. Lanigan glances between Lucy and Mrs. Arconia. "Let's discuss another time tomorrow."

Ms. Chambers sends a small smile Lucy's way, her voice falling to a whisper as I hand her a leftover custard pastry. "Lucy, dear, I do adore that dress. I'm an amateur seamstress myself and I've never seen such beautiful embroidery."

Lucy's eyes light up. "Thank you."

Meanwhile, a rather put-out Mrs. Arconia huffs. "Well, I suppose we *all* ought to be going, then."

The guests reluctantly filter into the courtyard. Matti and Bruno purchase a few books before leaving together. Lucy and Andi begin cleaning up while the Arconia son, Dynnis, stays behind. I hadn't even seen him enter the store. The way he gazes at Darling stirs a strange sourness in the pit of my stomach.

Forget about need; don't you ever want*?* Darling's words flick through my mind.

I didn't answer then. Standing here now, even I can admit that I do want things. Worse, I know what I don't want. And that's this mortal boy's attention on her.

I *want* to say something along the lines of "Please leave" when the open door invites more villagers inside. They're loud and obnoxious. They take sweets and laugh with Darling. They grab books off the shelves. They're too changed from the folk I'd seen when I first arrived. Darling has had three midnights here, and this place has flourished.

Not good.

"Excuse me." Lucy gently pushes past me to sell at least fifteen books in the span of moments. I stand there uselessly, watching the Arconia offspring and Darling and the people and the books and the silver that fills the till inexplicably fast. Darling's laugh travels through the milieu. It's all very lovely and luscious and delightful. It needs to end now. Andi even offers suggestions to customers. I should do something. *Anything.*

"Hey." Lucy places a hand on my shoulder. "Can you grab me another crate of books from the back? We'll be out of stock on the new bestsellers if the pace of sales continues." I nod and I turn just in time to notice Dynnis bowing before Darling. My feet root farther in place.

"You look resplendent tonight, Darling." His ruddy cheeks blush. His red hair seems to sparkle like it was spun with the same glitter as Darling's magic. His suit, a matching midnight blue to Darling's dress, is a bit stiff, though it makes him look dashing. He's strapping and observant. Attractive, if you're interested in that sort of thing. I can't imagine Darling falling for his charm.

Yet she encourages him with a smile of her own. "As do you, Dynnis."

"Would you like to take a turn about the courtyard? You must be ravenous. The store has never looked so enticing before, and I've no doubt it's your handiwork." The hobgoblin has the nerve to step closer to her, his lips tugging upward as if to say, *See? I'm kind and doting, unlike your betrothed. I could make you happy.*

"Oh, I assure you, all three of us have played an equal hand in making tonight possible." She taps his arm playfully. "Lucy especially. She is a wonder."

"Is she?" Dynnis hazards a glance at Lucy while she sells books. "I'm ashamed to admit that I never took the time to know her. My mother wasn't very welcoming to her or her mother. We weren't allowed to play together. And I doubt it'll change with my mother's—"

Lucy's voice cuts in beside me. "Calam, would you please get that box? We're out of stock on the floor, and I could really use the help."

"Yes, yes. Of course." My feet seemingly unroot of their own accord. Despite how much I want to hear the rest of the conversation, the rational part of my brain pushes me into the closet to find the crate of new books. I heft it up, somewhat annoyed by how weak my physical form is, how slight I am compared to Dynnis. Part of me questions if Darling likes the burlier type. If she wants someone muscly with more prowess. If she wants someone who tells her repeatedly how beautiful she is and worships her as if she is a goddess . . .

What a silly thought.

I bring the crate back in to find Dynnis and Darling gone. After setting it down on the counter, I search for them. In a corner perhaps? In the kitchen? I'm at the threshold of the door when Andi sidles up to me.

"Don't worry. She's taking a walk with Dynnis. He told her more sellers wish to speak to her about a partnership with the store. They'll be back soon." Andi's gaze flicks to Lucy, who is finishing up with the last customer and opening the crate to restock the depleted display. The romance one, naturally. I roll my eyes. I've had enough romance for the day. And anyway, I'm quite displeased. Darling leaving is bad form. She should be here. How does she know I won't shove Lucy even farther down the path of Ordinary Ever After?

It's not professional is what it is. She should be here. Dynnis doesn't deserve a moment of her time and beauty. She can't be serious. Between this and fixing the field, she's completely ruining her assignment. It's not really my place to sit her down and tell her to adjust her behavior but . . . well . . .

"You have no competition," Lucy says right behind me. How and when did she get there? My shoulders tense. "Believe me, Darling wouldn't be with anyone else. If I know anything from these books"—she lifts *The Prince and the Woodsman*—"then she's very in love with you. She angles her body toward yours. She looks at you with admiration. She hangs on your every word."

I snort. "You're wrong. Darling is my . . ." And then I correct myself. She doesn't need to know all of this, especially the truth. What am I doing? "Darling, I'm afraid, is . . . we're different people. I'm not sure such different people can or should work out."

Lucy and Andi cringe. Huh, I could use this to my advantage after all. Darling will regret leaving me alone with them.

"Sometimes different people work out *because* of their differences," Andi says, her head held high. She's a tough one.

"I suspect that depends on the nature of their differences, don't you think?" My eyes meet hers. Time to test my theory. "For instance, if one wanted a quiet life full of stories and one wanted a . . . a palace full of parties and gowns and rules . . ."

Andi steps back, silent, fiddling with the bracelet on her wrist. I'm right. She is the Princess, and Lucy has no idea.

"Not everything has to be one thing or another. I think . . . I'm sure that love requires compromise." Lucy's mouth lifts with hope. "As for Darling, you just need to tell her how you feel about her."

Andi drops her arm, her face lighting up. "Do you really think so?"

"Of course," Lucy says with more confidence than I've seen in the days since we met. Darling gave that to her with the dress and food and everything. This is not the Lucy who will be just okay with her status in life. I need to bring her back down. Remind her that hope is futile. Better to go with what you know than what you feel. *Forget about want; don't you ever* need*?*

"I have to go," Andi cuts in. "But tomorrow night? Darling suggested we could all have dinner together. A bit like a . . . a double date?"

Of course Darling did.

"I'd—" Lucy turns her back on me to answer. "I'd . . . Yes. We could—"

Though I'm invested in what she says and how I can ruin this, I can't for the life of me do anything about it. I can't even listen. I'm so . . . so . . . I let out a groan of frustration. I'm angry. Furious. But why? At what?

"You should find Darling." Lucy's voice is soft, caring. Compassionate. I haven't done enough to earn that.

I shift on my feet, acting nonchalant. Like I'm not interested in Darling at all. She can walk with whomever she wants. She left Lucy with me. It would appear she wants to lose. That's on her. In fact, good for me.

Lucy smirks, illuminating the hazel in her eyes. Facts skitter through my mind. She's closer to an Ordinary Ever After already, but there's still a chance of Unhappily too. Perhaps her nearness to Andi? "Find her and dance with her," she tells me. "She seems the type to like dancing. Make her heart race. She's *good*, Calam. She deserves good."

I begin to shake my head, even as my stomach roils. Everything in me wants to go find Darling. It's foolhardy nonsense. Darling and her fairy ways are rubbing off on me. That loss of bodily autonomy I thought was temporary has its hooks in me again. Maybe if I go see her, I'll get this all out of my system. That's what I tell myself. I'll be reminded why I must beat her. Why Lucy needs to have an ordinary life.

I bolt out the door without any further acknowledgment of Lucy. I do not want to be perceived, least of all by mortals.

The night air warms my cheeks and the flickering lights around the courtyard add an ambience of allure. Stalls selling hot foods, mead, and sweets line the area. Each smell pulls me in a different direction. An unwelcome hunger roars in my gut. I haven't eaten since breakfast. But I don't have time now. This is too important.

Music, cheerful and rhythmic, flits into my ears. Flutes and violins glide on the breeze, and my own body sways in response. People laugh, and behind the fountain in front of Minerva's store, there's disorganized dancing. The warmth increases. They stamp their feet, bat away sweat, and get lost in the movement. It's all very polite. Close but not too close. They touch tepidly. This is a fairy tale realm, after all. No indecency. Nothing to cause a scandal.

When my eyes find Darling in the center of the fray, I can't help but wonder if we could change that. Be impolite. Wild. Fun. I'd bet that's how fairies are in Whimsia, free of rules. I meander her way. Her hair's frizzy, her makeup smudged around her eyes. Her dress sticks to her while she twirls around.

Dynnis holds her close, watching her every move. Captivated by her energy, her smiles, her laugh, her everything. Insipid mortal. Entitled too. How could he possibly think he could be her match in any way?

I walk up to him and tap his large shoulder. "Go."

"Do you know who I am?" He sizes me up. Likely he would win in a fight, but I doubt brawling would endear Darling to either of us. I don't need to shove my masculinity into arguments to prove it exists.

Unlike Dynnis, it would seem. He steps closer. "My family runs this town and the people in it."

I laugh before leaning down near his ear, adding a bit of menace and Misfortune to my tone. "I said *go*."

CHAPTER THIRTEEN

I'm not a good dancer.

Unlike most creatures in Whimsia, my body can be uncoordinated and my balance off-center. Swaying to the beat is the extent of my abilities. And sometimes, if I'm doggedly focused, I might even get a step right. Tonight, though, in this dark courtyard surrounded by mortals, no one can see my movements or my lack of talent. The melody is beautiful enough to get lost in anyway.

My eyes are closed, my body loose, my mind *somewhat* quiet. Of course, important information is steadily replaying in the back of my head. Like how Dynnis told me his mother's grand plans for the bookshop, which was the only reason I even came out with him—well, that and sugary almonds. And then there's the matter of Lucy's budding romance. I may have slipped a note to Andi suggesting dinner tomorrow night, but how do I make this work in the remaining three midnights? Then there's Lucy herself. We haven't spent much time together and I need to rectify that.

Still, my body rocks slowly to the music. Exhausted as I am, I feel like I've achieved so much in such a short time. Yes, I made the mistake with my magic, but it doesn't seem to be too big a deal. I'll just have to do my best—and less—going forward. And sleep better tonight. And—

A hand wraps around my hip and my eyes snap open as I'm twirled around. Several facts pop into my mind then. First, this isn't Dynnis because my skin burns on contact—a delicious sort of heat. The kind that makes my mouth dry. Second, when I'm met face-to-face with him, I know I'm in trouble. My legs quake and I stumble forward, only to be caught in his embrace.

"Careful, my betrothed." His voice comes out deeper than I expect. "Shall we dance?"

I glance around at the revelers, wondering if this is necessary. No one cares about our little betrothal act here. Not in the dark. "Why?"

"Because I want to," he says quickly, shock flooding my senses. Calam *wants* things? I can't begin to unwrap that thought when he pulls me close, resisting a smile when air whooshes from my lips. Despite my surprise, I don't run away. Emotions flutter like pixies in the middle of my stomach. A strange feeling, one I don't quite understand, washes over me. As if all the thoughts and noise taper down until it's just him and me.

His expression mellows like he can feel me, read me and my mind. Like when he became overwhelmed by Andi that first time and only my presence helped.

Or . . . what if that's just how he acts when he touches me? If so, then why? Does he hate or admire me?

"I'm having a hard time with your oscillating moods, Misfortune." My lips sink into a frown. "I know why mine do, so what's your reason?"

"It's not in my nature to enjoy," he admits over the thrum of the song.

"Enjoy what?" My eyes widen as his hand on my back steers me away from another wayward couple. I like the way he does that. The way he moves me. *Oh sprinkles*, I loathe myself for thinking that.

"Anything." He gives me a lopsided smile. "Why do your moods change?"

There's this moment when I think, *No, don't do it.* It's not for him to know. If he does, he could try to use it against me. He could hurt me. Deem me incapable of this assignment and the mentorship on the Mortal Outcome Council. But . . . I shouldn't be made to feel ashamed about my illness. Just as I'm not ashamed of my thick body or my purple wings or love of sweets.

"Vacillating disorder." I stare up at him in defiance. How he responds will let me know what the rest of our time together will look like. How he responds will tell me how I should treat him too. Though I've trained like a Guardian, I am, and always will be, a fairy. And we can not only be petty, we can hold grudges for centuries.

"I'm sorry," he says softly above the music. "I didn't know . . . I've heard it is a difficult illness. An isolating one."

"Well . . ." I jut my head away, unsure of what to say to that. Unsure what I wanted him to say. Most celestials haven't heard of it. At least they didn't when I mentioned it before. Virtue thought I was merely dramatizing a bad mood. "It doesn't make me worse at my job."

"No." He carefully places his fingers on my jaw, turning me back to look at him. "It makes you extraordinary at it. I had wondered . . ." I try to shimmy a little back, give us space—give myself space—but he holds me there. And I let him. He doesn't finish the thought, instead moving the conversation on. "Your illness, from what I've read of it, it's not measured by worse or better, it's measured by highs and lows. Is that true?"

I take a moment to breathe. No one ever asks me about this. No one ever seems to care about it enough. There's no curiosity or compassion. It's a side note. It's usual to get an oh-goodness-this-is-too-personal response from people. And worse, there's no consideration either. If I ask for accommodations, I'm met with the assumption that once granted, I'll be normal like everyone else or I'm asking for too much.

"It is," I admit. "The lows are easier to control than the highs. But the lows can get worse if I'm not careful. If I'm tired, or hungry, or if I . . ." My voice trails off as I realize what I forgot. I'd been so busy it hadn't crossed my mind. *Again.* "I have to go." I step away from his embrace. As I maneuver through the crowd back to the store, I notice Calam tagging along behind me. "Go back and enjoy a party for once."

He doesn't respond, only trudges with me. We spot Lucy with Minerva standing at a food stall, and while I wish I could join them, I don't have the time. I wave with a smile that I'm sure doesn't reach my eyes as the bookstore beckons me near. Inside there'll be stability against the looming storm.

I'm grateful that the sign on the door says CLOSED even though it's unlocked. Small villages do tend to trust that their community won't steal from them. That gives me hope about the future of Lumina.

I dash to the kitchen, fill a glass of water, and take a pill from my pocket. Two days in a row is . . . not good. Normally, I'd care that Calam—or anyone—is watching me, only my mind is whirring with too many thoughts. I've been late before. I even missed one day once, but it comes with a cost.

After a big sip to swallow the pill, I stand against the warm stove. My eyes close, torn between relief and alarm. I should be fine, right? I have to be.

"You seem worried," Calam states, watching me closely. "Should you be worried?"

I consider his question. No one needs to know how I handle my illness. While his response earlier was kind and measured, how am I to know he truly means it?

I answer without hesitation. "If I'm late taking my medicine, my mood can get . . . a little unpredictable. I've been late two days now, missed my morning dose, and I'm not sleeping properly. I'm not sure . . . how my brain will react."

His expression turns pensive as he leans beside me. His shoulder brushes mine. "Would you tell me more?"

My lips twitch. Admittedly, I'm not displeased that we're touching. "It's best to think about it this way. If I throw an apple, the apple will go one direction. My illness is like five different apples being thrown at the same time, some going in one direction, some bouncing off the others, some falling to the ground . . . When I take medicine, the apples all go where they ought to—mostly. When I'm late with my medicine, the apples aren't entirely sure where to go. When I'm late twice, the apples might all fall. They might all go in different directions, and I won't know how to collect them for a while."

He nods. "Is there anything I can do?"

"No, it's my problem." I can't help appreciating how attentive he is with me.

"It's not *anyone's* problem. It's just a part of you and your life," he murmurs, flattening his thigh against mine. "When do you take this medicine?"

An answer momentarily eludes me. My brain lingers on our bodies touching. The warmth of him seeps through my gown. His scent swirls around me. The feeling from earlier stomps into my thoughts. An unusual feeling. I don't dislike it. I enjoy it. I want more of it. That's disastrous.

He waits patiently as I focus and find my words. "Once in the morning, once in the evening. I'll just have to—"

"Thank you for telling me," he says, still close. Still touching. "I would hate to beat you when you aren't feeling your best." His mouth slips into a sly smirk. His favorite, I think. "Are you hungry?"

Courage surges in my core and some other emotion I'm not sure I want to identify. "Why are you being nice to me? You loathe fairies . . . You're here to take the mentorship that I was sure would be mine. Why care about me? Is it a game? I don't operate like that. I don't . . ." I trail off as he turns, his face only inches from mine while his hip rests against the counter.

"Because I like you." His voice drops a little, as if he's

lacking confidence for the first time since I met him. "Despite your excessive nonsense and overused magic, I like you more than anyone else."

"You like me? *You?*" My skin heats and those pixies in my stomach are tap-dancing now. I gulp. "More than anyone else?"

"Yes," he says simply as if that's the most sensible thing he's ever admitted. "I have a job and I do it. The joy I derive is from knowing I'm making good decisions for people who are prone to making bad ones. I know *about* these mortals; I don't *know* them. I don't particularly like them—at best I feel nothing for them. But being here, being exposed, spending longer than a few hours in a mortal realm . . . It's changing things for me. *You* are changing things for me."

A response rises to the tip of my tongue, but nothing comes out.

"Don't let that go to your head, fairy. Just because I like you doesn't mean I'll let you win. I'm still walking away with that mentorship." He holds my gaze steady, his lips impossibly close to my own. "I'll merely feel a little bad about it when I do." He straightens, realizing he's nearly crossing a line with me. One I might not mind. "Has this realm changed anything for you?"

I think about that, my eyes still on those lips. "I don't . . . I'm not sure yet."

"I hope it does." Then his tone snaps back to normal. Confident. Careful. Assessing. "Fairies prefer sweets, don't they? I saw a stall that sells honey cakes. We should get some before bed."

I swallow down that unidentifiable emotion, confused by how quickly he can go from Calam to Calamity. "Y-yes, that would be nice."

❦ ♥ ❦

Rain pelts the windowpane, startling me awake. I lay there quietly, listening, breathing. Letting a calmness settle over me. Calam's dead asleep, and while I want nothing more than to replay what he said to me earlier, it'll likely be drowned out by the spiral slowly picking up steam. But it's not so loud yet. It's almost nice. Almost peaceful. Which I'll need if I'm ever to accept coexisting with it today.

I tiptoe from my bed, dress quickly, and leave the store. Minerva's door is unlocked when I arrive, so I let myself in and go to the back room, where fabric awaits transforming.

It's barely been a few moments perusing the racks when a peachy color peeks from an old garment bag. Immediately, my attention engages. I untie it, inhaling softly at the fine tulle and silky bodice. The luxurious materials slide through my fingers. My spirit perks up further when I don't have to magick it to my size. It fits flawlessly. Though it's perhaps not my style, it's too stunning not to wear.

I arrange my curls into another high bun, and I decide to be easy on myself today. I'll do something I love. Something that inspires me.

To thank Minerva for her generosity, I'll surprise her. I stalk down the hallway as her snores carry down the stairs. I smile. She must've had a lovely night, and far too much fun. I reach the kitchen and let out a sigh. It's cozy in here. My favorite room in any house. I open the cupboards and the cooling box, grabbing everything I need to prep my mother's favorite meal. Well, what used to be her favorite when I was a child . . . back when I was feeling particularly awful with my illness.

My mother would tell me that creating something will help you fight the battle. My mother was always right then. Though she wasn't a particularly good cook herself, she'd learned from her mother to make this one meal. And she taught me.

I wonder what she's doing at this very moment and if the first snow has fallen near the fae border of Whimsia. It looks so idyllic then that the fairies throw the "winter" ball. Using our collective magic, we make Paradise Pines into a winter wonderland. Everyone travels from all over to dance in the snow. We drink hot drinks—I've won the hot chocolate competition four times running, obviously—eat comforting food like wild legumes braided into buttery buns or apple bread pudding with hot vanilla sauce, or my favorite, sweet potato waffles dripped with spicy melted cheese, shaped like a rainbow.

Just thinking about it makes me homesick. Still, cooking for Minerva will be like coming home too. Or sharing home with her.

Once peaches—I chose them to match the dress—have cooked down in a molasses and cinnamon sauce, I add a few good handfuls of thick oats. With a swish of my wand, I make it bubbly perfect as if it's been cooking slowly overnight. Using a spatula, I spread a light custard on top of the oats, brûlée it with my wand, and top with more fresh, thinly sliced peaches—glad that Minerva went to the market recently. I remind myself to buy her more later.

Soon, her footsteps sound and I hurry to spoon the hot oats

into bowls for us. Her brows rise when she sees me there. First at the bowls, second at the dress.

"It's beautiful on you," she murmurs from the doorway. Her eyes get misty, and moments pass before she speaks again. "It was her dress. My daughter, Emelia. She was your age when she . . . when she passed. She was ill for years, but we'd thought . . . I made that dress for her to wear to the royal wedding. Only the best for my baby. She never got to wear it."

My hand flutters to my chest. "I'm so sorry, Minerva. Do you wish for me to take it off? I didn't mean—"

"No, it truly is beautiful on you, Darling. There's no fairer heart than yours, none who deserve it more." Minerva swipes at a wayward tear. "She would have loved you."

"And I her, no doubt." I meet her gaze with my most sincere smile. It means a lot that she's sharing this with me, and I don't want it to end. Talking about feelings can be cathartic. "Would you tell me about her?"

Minerva's smile is warm enough to dry up her tears. "Where do I start?"

Over breakfast I learn all about Emelia and Minerva. I realize how deeply people carry loss. How that loss twists over time until a person must make impossible choices to survive. How someone might one day grieve something (or someone) so pivotal to their being that they might not give their all to living anymore. How that one choice of withdrawing from the world could turn your Happily Ever After into Ordinary or even Unhappily Ever After.

Calam was right. Being here can change our perspectives *or* strengthen them.

There's something wrong with the system of fate and destiny and deciding who deserves happiness. It isn't fair. We aren't giving everyone an equal chance. We aren't doing right by the mortals. I've been here four midnights now, and Minerva's fate is drifting to a Happily Ever After, despite her path looking set before. Not because I've done anything especially grand; I only gave her company. Worked for her. Wore her dresses. Gave her a reason to go out into the world once again.

Could it be that simple?

How can I use this knowledge to improve the realms? How can I use this to help Lucy? Perhaps the loss of her mother is what's making her life so uncertain . . .

"This is spectacular, Darling. I've never had anything like this." Minerva's eyes brighten. It's not from the promise of more business, it's from being seen. Heard. Appreciated. "Thank you."

"It's the least I could do," I respond quickly, washing out our bowls. "I've always believed that giving food is like giving love. I hope you know how very loved you made me feel these past days. I can never thank you enough."

"You have many times now." She sniffs. "You are—" There's a sudden knock on the door down the hall. Minerva pushes to her feet, confusion furrowing her brow. "I wonder who that could be. The store's not even open yet."

I follow her to the front, where Ms. Chambers and Calam

stand in the drizzling rain outside the window. Ms. Chambers is wearing a vivid blue cloak, her dark blond hair streaked with gray and brown. She beams at us both.

Minerva quickly opens the door. "Come in, come in."

"Oh, thank you." Ms. Chambers yanks Calam in beside her. "We know it's early."

"But—" Calam interjects, his gaze meeting mine. "I had realized yesterday that you, Ms. Minerva, are in need of a seamstress."

"Oh?" Minerva's glance darts between Calam and Ms. Chambers.

"Well, yes. I need a job, you see, and I've been told my skills are quite exemplary." Ms. Chambers stands taller, unbuttoning her cloak. Now that I look over it, I see it's perfectly tailored, and superior work to mine in every way. "And I've always loved your shop. I've admired you for many years."

"I've admired *you*, Hannah, for many years." Minerva's voice takes a higher pitch.

Hannah's fair skin blushes a rosy shade of pink as she laughs. "If Calam hadn't told me about the work Darling has been doing, I wouldn't have known you might be looking for help. And I would really, very much, like to help."

Minerva asks her a few questions, and there's an instantaneous zing between them. What has started as admiration is already on its way to something like a budding friendship. I'm happy for them both, though I'll miss our early mornings together.

"We just created a Happily Ever After." Calam's suddenly near me, his voice low.

"Really?" My head whips in his direction. Hope suddenly surges in my chest. "Did you—"

"Sometimes I can be bold and do the 'right' thing." There's a hint of amusement in the quirk of his lips. "With this sorted for now, I'd like you to come to the Arconia house with me, *my dearest.*"

"You seem to be up to something, *my betrothed,*" I say loudly enough to be overheard.

"I am slightly concerned to be around a Miserably Ever After, *my love muffin.*" He grimaces while taking my hand, and instead of kissing the back of it, he leans down, turns it over and kisses the inside of my wrist. Minerva and Ms. Chambers—Hannah, I guess—smile our way before continuing their conversation. He murmurs against the sensitive skin. "Are you ready? I need you at your strongest if we have any chance of getting Lucy from under Mrs. Arconia's thumb and saving the bookstore."

"Almost." I slip the white pill from my pocket, and since there's no tea or water in sight, dry-swallow it as he stands. "You need me?" I cock an eyebrow.

"Yes, my *Darling.*"

CHAPTER FOURTEEN

We take an umbrella from Minerva's and dart out into the rain-soaked square, where the village folk talk animatedly.

While I can appreciate Fulhorn's rise in joviality, there's an unpredictable element in the air that concerns me. Excitement. Hope. Ambitions that'll either lead to dreams coming true or a descent into Unhappily Ever After. The one thing I'm meant to help mortals avoid.

I suck in a deep breath as Darling's arm threads through mine. People glance our way, giving us small, sly grins.

Darling waves before she shivers from a sudden chill. I pull her closer under the umbrella until we're both covered. "Have you ever done this before?"

Faces mere inches apart, I slide her a glance. Her cheeks are a little pink while she clutches her coat tightly with her other arm. "Done what, exactly?"

Darling's lips purse as we turn onto a cobblestoned road lined with perfectly trimmed trees and bright pink flowers. Eventually, she answers. "A relationship?"

"N-no," I nearly choke out. "I'm never in Malespero, and I was never interested in that anyway."

"Oh," she says quietly.

"You?" Why am I so interested in her answer? I'm certain she's never been in a relationship—if anything, she seems somewhat terrified at the prospect of it.

"Never." Her voice is soft, her gaze following the long, grand road to the Arconias' mansion. "Not because I'm, you know, not interested. I just . . . I'm a fairy. Celestials aren't keen on me."

"Celestials can be—"

"Traditional?" she offers.

I shake my head. "Xenophobic." Her arm stiffens, her mouth drops. I take in her expression, surprise lifting her brows. "We lack curiosity beyond the bare minimum about mortals or fairies. Misfortunes and Guardians hardly mingle either. There are so many of us across the realms, and yet we're a lonely species."

"Is that why you want the mentorship?" She bites the inside of her cheek. "To create more of a community? Is that what you'll do if you get it?"

"No," is all I can say. I wasn't thinking about community when I decided to try for the mentorship. Yes, I was hoping to implement new tools to make the realms more stable, but also because I need to get out of my house. I've been counting down the days till I could finally be free from the man who raised me and the memory of the woman who abandoned me. While community would be a great objective, I have many, better reasons.

When I have too much time to think, I still hear them arguing. Her saying that he didn't know how to have fun or be spontaneous. He wouldn't bring her flowers or even kiss her. All he did was complain, work, and complain some more.

Blight, I can't live like this. We stop Unhappily Ever Afters for mortals, but don't we eternals deserve happiness ourselves? Can't we be happy? She cried while he said it was nonsense.

Misfortunes live to serve the mortal realms. We're entitled to nothing. Happiness is folly.

She turned to me then as she stood by the door. *He can give you opportunities I can't, Calamity. Just don't become like him.* And then she left.

Screams tore up my throat like jagged glass. *Take me with you! Please, Mama!*

She never came back. Never even stopped in to see me. Her reputation was ruined—how could a Misfortune dole out Ordinary Ever Afters but not accept one for themselves? She abandoned me to Blight and his loathing. She broke my heart so thoroughly that I questioned its existence.

Blight has been wrong about many things, but he was right about one: Misfortunes live a life in service to these realms and the continued survival of the realms. Our own personal paths don't matter.

Though, since meeting Darling, I wonder if happiness is possible. It's not about entitlement or about what we deserve, only what we want. We're taught not to want.

My fingers squeeze Darling's arm and I consider she was taught that want is just as important as need. She's been very honest, even now, but hypocritical too. She may want love one day, countless laughs, smiles, and someone to hold her in the nights and the mornings . . . except she left her home. Left her family behind to be here. She gave up her creature comforts and path to Happily Ever After to work with mortals.

We're different sides of the same coin.

Two eternals walking in a mortal realm, arm in arm, both likely never having futures outside of our jobs. We put them above everything else. Why should we want anything else?

"Okay," Darling says, looking away, and I know in that moment that I should've said more. "Well, we can pretend now. To be in a relationship, I mean. When we're here. In this realm. I don't want to make you uncomfortable."

Emotions swirl around us, the inner turmoil she must be having soaking into me through the contact. Like before, I can't hear her thoughts but I can *feel* her.

Embarrassment.

Worthlessness.

Exhaustion.

Self-loathing.

Something unidentifiable that flashes across her features.

"Darling." I stop, keeping her close. "You aren't making me uncomfortable. There's no one else I'd rather pretend with."

A shy blush creeps onto her brown cheeks, almost unnoticeable with her skin tone. Almost.

The feelings persist within her, yet they're less intense. Less outward. I hope she's going to be okay—it's important to me that she's okay. If that means making sure she doesn't bog herself down in working for the greater good at the expense of her health, then I'll do that. She's a do-gooder with plentiful empathy, power, and an arguable sense of justice. Someone must keep her on track.

We continue onward in companionable silence as I can't help wondering if I'd rather not pretend, or if I want to pretend so much because I know this will be the only chance I'll have to be close to someone I admire.

All those ridiculous thoughts flee the moment we're up the long drive at the Arconia mansion and its printing press somewhere on the grounds. It's grand. Three stories of pastel green cladding, big open stained-glass windows, and architectural flourishes that catch the eye. They have an immaculate lawn that has clearly never had an irrigation problem, dotted with patches of organized flowers. It screams money and authority.

And misery.

Darling's footsteps halt, her face is pinched. "I don't like this."

"Neither do I." That dislike doesn't keep me from taking the silver knocker in my grip and tapping it into the door. For a few moments, nothing happens. The floral scent carries on the wind, and Darling chews her bottom lip. That crease between her brows is back, and I try not to smile at her.

The truth of my words last night hits me like an arrow. I like her. More than I've ever liked anyone else.

She's my competition.

A fairy.

Recklessly good, with a potential for chaos.

And I like her.

I run a hand through my curls, hoping I don't make them

messy. This is the absolute worst time for me to develop any sort of feelings for a person.

The door opens and I stumble back.

A servant girl, likely no older than twelve, bows before us. "How—how may I h-help you?" Her tiny voice trembles, her eyes are averted down to the marble floor.

"We're here to see Mr. and Mrs. Arconia. I believe they're expecting us." I keep my head up high, my tone direct; these people will step all over us if we don't appear strong.

Her gaze lifts to us. "I will—"

"It's quite all right, Mariam. You're excused." Mrs. Arconia stands as still and proper as a statue. A rich statue. Her gown's a sharp red, her shoes polished, hair meticulously styled without a single strand out of place. She stares daggers at us with her piercing blue eyes. "Mr. Calam and Darling, was it?"

Since Darling cannot read cues or thoughts, she vibrates beside me. "Hello, Mrs. Arconia. So good to see you again."

Mrs. Arconia only cocks an eyebrow. Kind words mean nothing to her.

"We would like to assess the invoice for An Enchanted Story and set up an organized payment system going forward that can be notarized by the village lawyer." I nod in propriety. She's a big fan of that as I recall. "Lucy's shop may have fallen on tough times, but it would seem that with new events, a village that has seen a rise in revenue"—a truth I'm reluctant to admit since it was Darling's doing—"and new books, this could bring the shop back to good standing and stability."

Mrs. Arconia's brow never lowers. She scans Darling and

me for weaknesses. Her mouth pinches like she found several—and doesn't want to let us into her home. "You may come in," she says through a tight-lipped grimace. "Though we are quite busy and haven't the time to dilly-dally." With that, she stalks off leading us to trail after her.

Once I flatten the umbrella and place it by the door, I tug Darling with me, hanging on to her closely. Despite being a highly successful Misfortune, this situation is new to me. When I'm touching Darling, nothing seems overwhelming. Mortal thoughts are quieter, less invasive, and I feel solid. Besides, it helps us look like a real couple. I can be good at pretending.

In the foyer, we take a right into—I'm guessing—her less formal sitting room. An oversized stone fireplace is the centerpiece. Painted portraits hang along the walls, old and elegant. There are more of those flowers in delicate vases sitting on every available space. The walls are red, embellished with gold ornamentation. Everything looks spotless, from the gold sofas to the finely woven rug spread along the floor.

"Sit," she commands, lowering herself onto an expensive-looking armchair. "If we could get this all ironed out before my husband arrives, it would be better." Darling and I gingerly sit as far away as possible from the woman. "I'd offer you tea, but I don't think you'll be staying all that long." She gives us a placid smile. "I'm sure the store will be open soon and Ms. Addlesberg needs your services now that frivolity is fashionable again."

The words drip from her lips like venom. She loathes frivolity. I mean, I guess I do too, but if I were a mortal, I'd enjoy it.

Darling stiffens beside me. "I'd hardly say that reading is

frivolous. It's not only good for literacy, it's good for developing compassion for your fellow mor—man. Stories are good for the soul. They bring people together."

"Stories are nonsense that make moronic dreamers of those who read them, while the books themselves steal pennies from your purse best used on supper." She sniffs, smoothing down her dress. "Which is why I expect few will be too displeased when—"

"An unusual stance considering your family owns the village press," I interject. If she's going to do business, she'll have to respect it.

"If our villagers don't mind losing their senses and giving their pennies away, why shouldn't I be the one benefiting?" Her gaze scrapes over us, her frustration evident. "That color is very unbecoming on you, girl. You look like a peach."

Darling's laughter flits through the room, adding a new layer of tension. "That's exactly what I was hoping for, Mrs. Arconia."

"You are round like one, I'll grant you that."

Darling falls silent. And I know, I know, that I should be unemotional. Focused. Diplomatic.

But *no one* body-shames Darling.

"Now listen here, you foul, iniquitous, awful woman—" I jump to my feet, back straight. My fingers press together, ready to be snapped for something. Bad-intentioned magic springs to my mind, something, anything to make this mortal rue the day I came to this realm. Perhaps all her socks will have holes. Maybe her cooling box will malfunction. Or I could wither every flower on this estate.

"Ah, Mr. Calam and Ms. Darling," a deep voice calls through the foyer, delaying my need to exact revenge. "I was hoping you'd both stop by. We haven't had the chance to properly say hello." Mr. Arconia walks slowly into the room with assistance from his cane. His smile is huge, dark brown skin crinkling on the laughter lines etched at the corners of his eyes, a genuine vibrance in spirit. What on earth is he doing with Mrs. Arconia? "Dorette told me all about you. Two young upstarts betrothed and full of energy. And working with poor Lucy too. A welcome addition to our village."

"Really?" Darling lifts off the sofa too, her shoulders sagging. "I was under the impression we weren't welcome at all."

"Couldn't be further from the truth." He grins our way. "Sometimes people aren't good with change. But not me. And not Fulhorn!" His voice booms and he takes the armchair across from his wife, close to me and Darling. He waves for me to sit again. "Would you like tea? Bread? I think our housekeeper, Ms. Bales, made some cinnamon cake earlier. The whole house smelled enticing."

"No, thank you." I shift on the uncomfortable cushion. "We really came to discuss the invoice for the store and what the payments might look like. Mrs. Arconia had informed us the debts are dire."

"Oh pish!" Mr. Arconia says after asking the servant for the cake. "Lucy's father was a good friend of mine—shame he died before she ever got a chance to meet him. It's true we do charge for the books—authors have the stories all written up and sent to us, then we copy them with the press and print as needed. It can be pricey, and Lucy may be behind there, but not too much. Certainly not enough to be deemed dire, right, Dorette?"

Dorette doesn't reply, glaring at her husband. I suddenly realize this is why she didn't want us talking to him. Either she's lying or he's ignorant of her plans.

"Don't mind her sour mood. Since the Princess announced her ball, Dorette's been stressed. She's sure our Dynnis will win the royals' hearts, but she's worried we don't have enough money to impress them."

The mayor *is* oblivious it would seem, either by choice or because he's too busy running the village.

"Dynnis *will* catch the eye of Princess Marguerite at the ball. Our son was born to be royalty," Dorette says as if it's a forgone conclusion.

"I wish him the best." And I truly mean that. Dynnis, however much I dislike him for his interest in Darling, would be better off at the palace than here.

There's a strange dynamic at play. Dorette's been hassling Lucy for debts Mr. Arconia assures me she doesn't owe. No one has given me the invoice. Mr. Arconia is lovely, if a bit too jovial, and Dorette is a locked-in Miserably Ever After. Even from my seat, I feel the abyss circling her and everyone in her path.

"He doesn't need your wishes." Dorette gives me the side-eye, my insults lingering between us though she doesn't reply to them, before turning back to her husband. "And as you and I have agreed, Josiah, it should be time for raising the cost of the books and encouraging Lucy to pay rent on the store."

"Rent? I thought you said that Lucy is the proprietor just

yesterday. Does she not own the deed passed to her from her mother?" I cock a brow. "Or am I mistaken?"

"Yes, the store is hers, however, she owes enough debt and land tax that she would have to sell it as repayment." Dorette raises her head, splaying her fingers across her lap. "That's the nature of busin—"

It takes all the control within me to not stand again and snap my fingers. "When you accosted me twice about payment, you suggested that we could easily hand you everything in the till and that would be sufficient. And now you're saying she owes enough to lose the store?"

"Mrs. Arconia, I really think there's another way to solve this, don't you?" Darling tries empathy like it'll work. She's never encountered a Miserably Ever After either. She doesn't know that there is no reasoning with them.

"I'm afraid not," she says without a glance in Darling's direction. "Neither An Enchanted Story nor you have a future in my village." Now she eyes us with withering disdain, her bottom lip curling. "It is one thing to live in impropriety and flaunt it around Fulhorn, it is quite another to encourage others to do the same. To flagrantly disregard our . . . our social order! You've come here, ingratiated yourselves into our society, and . . . and . . . you've made a mockery of me. Hold meetings without me! I'm a valued member of this community and gathering behind my back—"

"Dorette, my dear—" Josiah's head tilts to the side as wrath washes over his wife, her skin a vibrant shade of red to match her gown and hair. His expression transforms from affable to terrified with alarming celerity. His lips pull into a frown, his hands shake on his lap, and if I listen closely, I'm sure his heart is racing.

Before Dorette can answer, I snap my fingers. Time stills. Everything's quiet save the rain outside that my magic cannot extend to.

Darling looks at me, her brows creeping up to her scalp. "That was . . ."

"I need a moment," is all I can say through a deep breath in. I grip her arm, letting her soothing energy seep into me before I speak. "They are a problem."

"She is a problem." Darling juts her chin in Dorette's direction. "That mortal has it out for everyone, especially Lucy."

"I can change a mortal's luck, make difficult choices for them to survive their own actions. But I cannot change a Miserably Ever After. I don't know a single Misfortune who could. And if I can't get her to back off Lucy, neither of us will be successful." I let out a long huff, my head falling back against the stiff sofa.

"So what you're saying is, *I* should?" Darling sneaks a smirk in my direction. "If you wanted a fairy to help, all you had to do is ask."

I shake my head, appreciating her offer. "Miserably Ever Afters can't be saved, Darling. They won't stop till—"

Darling takes the wand from her pocket and swishes. Dorette's body sparkles for a moment as if she's engulfed in gold glitter.

A startled gasp whooshes out of me. "What did you do?!"

Dorette's perfectly coiffed red hair, fair skin, piercing blue gaze, and gown that could've cost a fortune disappear in a cloud of white smoke.

Sudden nausea forces me to clasp my stomach. My mouth is dry. "Darling! Did you just—did you just *kill* her?!"

"No, don't be silly." Darling pushes off the sofa, stalks over to the armchair where Dorette once sat, and clears the air by waving her hands. "I turned her into a housecat. See?"

I look at the orange-striped cat, staring back at me. It blinks. I blink.

Darling bends to scratch behind the cat's ear. "Not so scary anymore, right?"

CHAPTER FIFTEEN

Darling

"I don't know what you're so mad about." I rearrange the books to be more appealing, shooting Calam a look over my shoulder. "It's the best possible solution, really. My spell worked: His own mind supplied a reason for her sudden absence and he didn't seem all that shaken up. Nor did he bat an eye when we left with an orange cat either. You should be thanking me."

"*You cannot*," he harshly whispers across the aisle, "*turn mortals into pets*."

"But you kept going on about how miserable she is and how she makes everyone else miserable too. She was keen on booting us and the shop out of town. I thought this was a great solution." I nibble on my bottom lip. What else was I supposed to do? I've trapped her in a tinier vessel. I'm the only one she can talk to—a lesson I learned after spreading fairy dust in the field and that flower said thank you. "She has less opportunity to be needlessly cruel to Lucy in this form. She understands the dynamics of our relationship, she knows how we have the power for once. How if she causes trouble and further strife, she'll remain a cat. She knows only I can change her back. Considering her docile nature now, she understood."

Calam's gaze narrows while mine pans to Mrs. Arconia. In

the front window, she sits on a swath of blankets while Lucy and a bunch of schoolchildren pet her. Given that she's a cat and likely still volatile, she could've gouged our eyes out or scratched us—I half suspected she would just because. Instead, she seems rather pleased to be getting pampered, loads of attention, and endless snuggles.

I have hope that this experience will teach her to be a better person.

Lucy's voice pierces through the argument far down the aisle. "Where did you find her?"

"Oh, she was wandering the streets, poor thing. People will love to pet a fluffy creature while buying books," I answer loudly. "People *love* bookstore cats."

Calam slams a book down, his voice low. "When you lose, she'll be back and then she'll attack Lucy even more. Have you thought about that?"

We glower at each other, the air heavy between us.

"I have a plan." I nod with a tight smile. Well, it's more of an idea than a plan—which I won't admit to him. "Now that she has no recourse, we'll appeal to her better nature. You'll see. We just have to make sure she's receptive."

"You fairies," he mutters angrily. "I should have never trusted you."

I lean closer, my eyes on him as I try to keep us from being overheard. "She was going to take the store and put Lucy out on the street. Dynnis told me last night and she confirmed it not an hour ago. Believe me, I can take a few barbs about my body without losing my composure, but this was too much. She was too unreasonable. Too entitled. Her voice was too loud. We had to do something."

He stares at me, chest heaving. "You. Cannot. Turn. Mortals. Into. Animals."

"But. I. Did. It. For. A. Good. Reason," I say back. "She was lonely. You remember last night when you said you—"

"Liked you? I've changed my mind on that real fast!" He scowls, and the words sting.

"No, when you said you were seeing new perspectives." I hold his gaze. "Well, so am I. Mortals may turn down the wrong path because they're sad. Angry. Lonely. They have no one to listen to them, no one who cares or sees them. Mrs. Arconia is lonely. You saw it! Her prickly nature has turned people off her, and she doesn't know how to change. So we're giving her that opportunity."

"She's not our assignment." He shakes his head. "For the millionth time, you've done too much. *You* are too much."

"That's what you fail to realize, Misfortune. To truly help Lucy, we have to help those around her, who impact her. When we leave, we need to know there are people who care about her and want to make sure she is happy like we do." I take a deep breath. "We need to provide a warm place for her to open up and feel safe. Feel loved."

He rolls his eyes. "Love is not the objective."

I huff, drawing his focus back to me. "Love is *always* the objective."

We stare at each other for what seems like eternity, neither of us backing down. Neither of us willing to admit we're wrong.

This is where the battle line has been drawn. I know I made some drastic decisions these last few days, but I stand by them. There's only one thing I've failed to do, and I will rectify it very soon.

"What do you even know about love?" Calam's question nags at me. "You've never experienced anything like it."

"Have you?" I ask pointedly.

He drags a hand through his curls. "I know what it is. It's not holding hands and bantering. Calling each other *love muffin*. It's the knowledge that there is someone else carrying a piece of your heart."

"That's romantic," I admit before regaining my composure. "If you know so much about it, why haven't you done it, then? Why hasn't it interested you?" My hands flatten on the back of the bookshelf as he hovers above me.

"Because I never met anyone worth ruining my life for." He stares down at me, his voice gruff. He studies my mouth, my lips, his breath a whisper against my skin. "And if I'm lucky, I never will."

He turns abruptly and stalks off.

My heart pounds in my ears. The pixies in my stomach are throwing a party with all my nerves. My thoughts whir with uncertainty. About him. Myself. This assignment.

Silly. Fairy. Fool. Too much. What do you even know about love?

Nothing, I think. Nothing at all.

∾ ♥ ∾

The rain picks up after lunch, keeping most customers away. Mrs. Arconia is taking a nap by the windows on a plush little pillow I "found" in storage. Lucy sits beside her while Calam works on another display. It's calm. Quiet. Perfect to work my magic.

I plop down next to Lucy, smiling. "Are you going to the ball?"

"I don't see why I should." She pats Mrs. Arconia. "I don't have a dress and with everyone gone, I should have some hours to rest. Maybe work on the store, instead of in it."

She's right, Mrs. Arconia says to me only, while Lucy hears a meow. *Balls are not meant for people of her stature. Besides, it would be a waste of time and money for her when my Dynnis is going.*

"Hmm," I say, glancing at the dress I bought her and ignoring Mrs. Arconia completely. If there's one thing a fairy loves, it's a makeover before an event and the True Love's Kiss that follows. The moment that ball was announced, I worked on a few ideas for Lucy's gown. Something that suits her gorgeous dark brown skin and sharp cheekbones. Maybe ocher? "I think you ought to. It could be good for business. People from all over the kingdom will be there, including Andi. I doubt there are many bookshops in all of Lumina, and there are readers desperate for stories—not only the news."

She slides a lopsided grin my way. "Even if I wanted to, I still don't have a dress."

"I'm sure I can find one," I say with a wink. "Would your mom have wanted you to go?"

Lucy's hand pauses on Mrs. Arconia's soft tummy. I bet that

grumpy woman's tension is all but melting away. "She . . ." Her voice trails off. We sit in silence for a few moments. "She would want me to be happy," she says finally.

"*What* would make you happy?" I try to sound nonchalant, yet I'm desperate to know. Truth is, I've been working from the outside in with Lucy. Fixing the village. Fixing her home. Fixing the shop. Giving her a dress and something to look forward to is all good, though it's not enough. Minerva taught me that.

Waving a wand helps, listening is better. I've been so busy transforming Fulhorn, I never stopped to ask Lucy what it is she wants. I never really tried to connect to her before, not in a meaningful way. My fear has been holding me back. But right now, I'm starting to believe that this assignment is meant to teach me to push through that. Listen. Help. Care. Be curious.

"Sometimes, I'm not sure." Her words fall quietly, directed more to herself than to me.

Happiness only comes from security, Mrs. Arconia interjects through half-lidded eyes. *I was born a servant. When I married for money, I found happiness.*

I want to say a number of things to Mrs. Arconia regarding that, only I don't. Lucy is more important. I need to press her about her disquiet, but something in me tells me to back off. Lucy is guarded. She's slow to share herself with anyone else, especially strangers who showed up days ago and have made huge changes to her life. Still, it's time for me to get her comfortable enough to let me try.

She's not like other mortals I've worked with. First, I never had a whole week to work with them, I had precious hours.

I also had an instructor standing over my shoulder. In realms with magic, I exposed myself as their fairy guardian. In realms without it, I stood off in the shadows for a while before meeting them.

All of this is new to both of us. So I need to get us back on level ground, where I can be more confident, and she can be less . . . reactive.

A sudden thought pops into my mind then, and I roll with it. "The painting, in the kitchen, of the flower? Did you paint that or was it your mother?"

Lucy's eyes widen and she purses her lips. Her shoulders tighten and tense. Whatever I expected from this exchange, it wasn't abject terror. She slow-blinks before gulping and responding. "Me."

Be cool, Darling.

Don't blow this.

Tamper your excitement.

I take a deep breath.

"*Ohmygoodness*, I love it so much. You are so talented. You know what we should do? We should close the store in the morning and then paint a mural on the wall and we can unveil it at the party tomorrow night!" It all leaves my mouth in a wild flurry and Lucy's face goes on an emotional journey with each new sentence.

Her mouth opens. Nothing comes out.

"Leave her be, Darling." Calam's eyes flash in warning on the other side of the shop.

"I—I . . ." I flinch, my hands fisting together. "I'm sorry. I didn't mean to upset you." I move a little on the seat, careful to give her space. "I just thought because I saw all those paintings in that small closet when I found the flower one for the kitchen, you could incorporate them into the store more. You can feel the joy in them. I can tell painting them—well, they might've made you happy. They're beautiful and personal and thoughtful, especially of you and your mother. I—"

"You had no business going in there." Lucy stands. "You don't know me. You don't know my mother. You don't know anything!" Her voice grows cold and sharp, her nostrils flare. "All you do is push and push. You're here to work. We aren't friends." Then she tears off through the store, out of sight.

And I'm left sitting there, contemplating my mistake. Was I too much again? I'm always too much. *We aren't friends.* I just thought . . . But then, no. I wasn't thinking. My instincts told me to stay cool and I didn't. Sometimes I get so excited that my mouth runs away from me. I get anxious and I keep talking and I ruin everything.

I see Calam place a book on the counter and slowly take off after her.

While I . . . do nothing.

Mrs. Arconia meows and I just know she has thoughts to share.

"I really messed up," I say, the words clawing their way up my throat. "I'm not good at this, am I?"

Not at all, Mrs. Arconia agrees. *You're truly the worst.*

"Of course you would think that, I turned you into a cat," I reply through rising panic as the argument replays in my mind.

I used magic to fix her and everything else because I don't know another way.

Calam's right. Lucy's right. I don't know anything.

I've hurt Lucy. I've hurt her. And I don't even know how or why.

Too much. *Push and push and push.*

The spiral uncoils, waking up when I'm at my weakest. Its whispers gain traction. They become loud, drowning out everything else.

You should leave here and never come back. No one wants you in Fulhorn. All you've done is make a mess and turn me into a domestic animal. Mrs. Arconia heaps onto my negative thoughts.

"You're right. I have to go. I have to go away now. I shouldn't be here. I only make trouble for everyone. I ruin everything." All the rambles leave me in a haze of crushing sadness. I smack my face with my own hands. The sting of it makes my skin smart. "I don't belong here. I don't belong anywhere. I'm nothing. No one. I'm no one. I'm no one. I can't do this. Worthless."

All the poison drips from my lips. I know it's happening and there's nothing I can do to stop it. I'm tired. I'm hungry. I'm sad. I haven't been taking my medicine like I should have. My fists pound against my legs. And it hurts. It hurts. Hurt is a manifestation of my turmoil. That's what I did to Lucy, right?

I deserve it.

My outer reality is now reflecting my inner and it's not meant to be beautiful.

It's not even about me. I'm making it about me. I'm selfish. Whiny.

One mistake and everything's crumbling down.

I slide off the seat onto the floor. Wrapping my arms around my knees. Crinkling the peach dress.

If you're going, turn me back! I need—

I tune her out as my mother's voice filters through it all. *Don't do this, Darling. You have no business there. They will never understand you. They will never love you. Not like us. You aren't strong enough.*

If you go there . . . you shouldn't come back, my father said. *No daughter of mine will spend her hours toiling with the celestials. You dishonor us.*

And I left.

And I leave now too.

I was never going to win. I never deserved to. Lucy never deserved the likes of me either.

CHAPTER SIXTEEN

The bell above the front door rings, only I'm too busy sitting by Lucy in the closet to go help a customer. Darling's there, she'll handle it. I know she's reeling from Lucy's temper, but this is her assignment. Change comes with emotions. Sometimes it isn't easy, working with someone's fears and insecurities, especially when you don't know them.

I could've told her about what I found in the closet. About Lucy's reactions. We may be on opposing sides, but Darling's been open this entire time.

I'll apologize later. She'll understand. She's good. Waiting like I am for this storm to pass. And it will pass. They always do.

Lucy's shoulders shake. "It wasn't supposed to be like this."

I say nothing. Either she'll continue or she won't. I've nothing to add. I'm not the right person for all this. My job has never been about this. Darling would be better. But I'm here and I'll try.

So I sit tight. My back presses against the paintings. After all that anger about murals and art, that's where Lucy went. To be near them, I guess. A past she struggles to remember and dreams she struggles to forget.

"She wasn't supposed to die. She was supposed to be here,"

Lucy sobs through a hiccup. "We had all these plans. She would make this the best bookshop in all of Lumina, and I would travel the world, paint the world, grow tired of the world, and come back home. But then . . ." She died. It goes without saying. "Nothing worked out."

My leg brushes against hers, only to remind her that I'm here. I'm listening. I care. That's what Darling said. Lucy wants people around her who care. I oblige.

Mrs. Arconia slinks in through the door, pausing to look around. I watch her closely, hoping she doesn't sink her claws into the paintings or us. Surprisingly, she doesn't. She paws through them like a mortal trapped in a cat and somehow, I know she's listening too.

"My mother loved me so much and there's no one else now. *No one.* I wanted that. I want love and painting and traveling and the store. I want all of it." Lucy's rambles flit around the room. "I want to go to the ball. I want to dance in a beautiful gown. I want friends."

Do you need *them, though?* I want to ask. I know the answer—no one *needs* those things. But telling her that will not help her now.

She needs her shop. She needs food. Clothes. Customers. She needs a little bit of hope to sustain her through the hard days. A little bit of humility to keep her from reaching too far without losing her balance. She needs her community to keep selling books.

She needs the town to have some modicum of success so that they can afford those books.

She needs people to come in for the book club.

She needs those people to have the time and disposable income to come in for that book club.

She needs the baker's pastries.

She needs warmth.

She needs Minerva's dresses.

She needs . . .

Fuck. Darling was right again.

I was being shortsighted. Lucy is not a singular assignment—Fulhorn *must* be part of it. I want to pinch myself for being too narrow-minded. Perhaps she does need friends. Perhaps she does need more people who care like me and Darling.

Mrs. Arconia tentatively stops in front of Lucy, peering up at her. I reach out, touching her fur. Despite Dorette's form, if I focus, I can hear her thoughts.

She's alone. She's sad. She yelled at that magical monster. My mother died too when I was young. I wish someone had been there for me. I wish . . .

"What do you want now, Lucy?" I ask, unsure if she'll lose her temper on me as she had with Darling. It's a question I've been worried about asking, because it implies she has a choice in her future. And if that's true, then why would I be here?

She sniffs, petting Mrs. Arconia. "I don't know. I don't want to close the shop. I just don't know if I'm the one to run it either. I see my mother in these walls and I want to be close. I love the books. But before you came, I never thought about book clubs or offering cookies or changing things around. I don't have a mind for this business."

I take a deep breath. The backbone of my plan was for Lucy to get this store stable so she'd have an Ordinary Ever After.

Now what am I supposed to do? Any other option could lead to any other path. Good or bad. Happy or Miserable. Without me steering her, I can't predict where she'll end up.

And that's unsettling.

I cross and then uncross my arms, and then decide to slip my hands into my pockets.

"I shouldn't have yelled at Darling like that. I know she only meant well." Lucy smiles shyly as Mrs. Arconia lets out a little purr. "I should go apologize."

I nod. "There's no rush. Darling will understand. Take the time you need to sit with how you feel."

"Well, not that much time. I still have dinner with Andi tonight. And I need Darling's help." She exhales slowly as if she understands the breakthrough she just had. As if her world has shifted and she's ready for the changes to come. She's learning what she wants, she's seeing beyond what she needs.

This is the last thing *I* need.

"Do you care for her? Andi, I mean?" I really hope not. That would ruin my plans even further. And hers, even if she doesn't know it.

"She's been coming here for two years. Always buying my favorite romance books. I know she likes me. Or at least, I think she does. She's . . ." Her voice tapers. "I want to care for her. When she's around, I don't know. I like the way she makes me feel. I like the way she lights up the room. Every time she comes in, my day is brighter."

"I see."

And I do see. This I can work with. This I can end easily.

The attachment isn't strong enough for me to completely recalibrate my assignment. I came here to make sure Lucy doesn't have an Unhappily Ever After. As of now, she doesn't seem to be on that path anymore. All of that could change though if she were to fall for Andi. Love can enhance one's life or doom it.

Isn't that what I learned from my parents? Isn't that what Misfortunes learned through our training and every time we bounced to a new realm, fixing fate for the mortals?

Love is disruption. It's a fork in the road that leads to an unknown destination.

Andi, I'm certain, is a princess. She's the girl everyone's vying to marry in two days' time. On the last midnight.

If she and Lucy were to become more than a flirtation, I can't say that they would be happy together. I can't say if Lucy would survive. She has been living a quiet existence and being with Andi would put her in the spotlight, for better or worse. The store may not be a concern, they'd have plenty of silver; it's her dreams. Travel. Painting . . .

I cannot let this happen.

Ordinary is better than Unhappy.

"Let's find Darling." Lucy stands and then scoops Mrs. Arconia into her arms. The cat is startled, eyeing me in the process, but accepts it. "You know, I really love cats and this one's good. We should name her something."

"What about Dori?" I offer, stifling a laugh. I wonder if the woman would hate that.

"You know what, I think that suits her. Right, Dori?" Lucy scratches Mrs. Arconia behind the ears, earning another purr.

"Come on." I follow behind her into the shop, expecting to see Darling in the window seat. Only she's not there. Nothing is. Not a note. Nothing. "She left?" Lucy looks around the shop, peers out the glass into the pouring rain. "Maybe Minerva's?"

She puts Mrs. Arconia on the pillow, her brows furrowed.

"I'll go find her." I keep my tone light and nonchalant, yet inside, I'm slightly panicked. Why would Darling leave? Was she okay?

Then it hits me. This morning.

What if I upset her when I told her I'd never let love ruin me? I disparaged her too. I was so mad about what she did, I didn't once stop to ask if she was okay. What if that, combined with Lucy yelling at her, made it worse? Did she feel like no one wanted her here? Would she . . . leave us? Leave this realm?

I think about her emotions. Worthlessness. Self-loathing. Joy. Sadness. Hopelessness. Excitement. Ambitious, yet compassionate. Sensitive. Her moods are like apples, she said. What if this day caused them all to fall on the ground and she didn't know how to collect them?

Would she take her golden coin and concede?

I don't spare Lucy another glance and dart out of the shop into the rain.

I can't let Darling lose, not like this. I can't let her think that she's anything other than perfect—flawed like all of us, but still perfect. She's perfect.

And I lied.

If I could love anyone, if I could let love ruin me for one single person, I'd want it to be her someday. She's brilliant. I want to know her. Dance with her again. Bring my lips close to hers again and not hold them back. Would she want that?

I hate that I made this worse for her. I hate myself for giving her illness fuel. She doesn't need that. She needs someone to care, just like Lucy.

The rain splatters down on me, washing away any hesitation I'd felt before. It's not a question about me caring about her; that happened after watching her drink hot chocolate and calling Lucy her "little love muffin." She has a kind heart, too much hope yet not enough.

It's a question of giving in to it. If I'm honest with her now, how could I stop myself from being honest about my intentions? How could I stop myself from following where my feelings might lead, which could be utter chaos?

Does a Misfortune even deserve to pursue happiness? I've seen what that thought did to my family. Is that really what I want?

Yet, if those are the questions, then the answer is that I'd confront my own ideals of the future for her. She could ruin me if she wanted to.

If it's not too late.

CHAPTER SEVENTEEN

I walk without aim. People wave at me, but I know they're only being nice. They don't really care about me. I should've never left home.

This is why the Mortal Outcome Council sent Calam. They knew I couldn't do this. They saw the weakness I'd been denying. Good grades, ambitions, determination, and confidence, every flaw I tried to hide, the wings I folded into myself to fit in . . . none of it was good enough.

I'm not good enough for Lucy or the mentorship.

I'm not good enough to be a Guardian.

My head falls back and I stare up at the sky that cracks with thunder. Another warm tear slips down my face. I swipe it away yet it's no use. Soon, another tumbles down after it. And more. My eyes fill to the brim and I can't breathe.

The rain plops onto my cheeks, blending with my glitter. So silly. How was I ever going to make a difference when I can't stop being selfish and annoying? How could I ever help Lucy when I make everything about me?

After shaking my head, I drift to the edge of the woods between Fulhorn and the palace far up on the hill. It's colder here. Gloomy too. Matches my egotistical mood.

The gold coin burns in my pocket. I could leave. Give up now. Everyone expects me to; *I* expect me to. If I lose, it's not like I can't still be a Guardian. Only the mentorship will be gone.

My mind can't let Lucy's words go, no matter my dithering resolve to quit.

We aren't friends.

I thought we were. I thought we could be. I haven't had friends since I left home. I'm not friend material. A burden. That's what I am.

One more step into the woods, and my boot plunges into a puddle. I look down to see my reflection, a mess of pastels. The pretty peach dress that belonged to Minerva's daughter is downtrodden and nearly destroyed.

I know I can wave my wand and fix it, but it's further proof that I ruin everything. Selfish. Ridiculous. Catastrophe.

You push and push.

I let out a scream. The biggest yet. All the anger unleashes within it. Birds scatter in the sky, and I wonder if the trees sway from the pressure of it. If the sky turns another shade of gray and the rain pelts harder. The scream ends when I finally need to take a breath.

"Darling!"

My posture stiffens as I throw my hand on my chest. I glance up at my name and the familiar voice.

"Hello?" I peer around at nothing other than trees. There's no one out here.

"Down here."

My gaze swoops in the direction of the puddle that's still only reflecting my face.

"Not there, the mushroom," a small voice says.

"The mushroom?" I tiptoe forward, spotting a cluster of mushrooms sprouting from a tiny blanket of moss and a scattering of small primrose petals. I bend, my knees squishing into the muck. I set my hands into the damp earth. On top of the small brown mushrooms, a tiny fairy sits. I squint. "*Favie?!*" I nearly scream again. "You look like a pixie! What are you doing here?"

"How dare you!" he exclaims. In truth, although there's nothing quite wrong with pixies, we simply don't enjoy being compared to them. And them us. "Hold on."

Magic whooshes around in a cloud of blue glitter. I sneeze and then see Favie standing in front of me at full size. He's dressed like the fae. All midnight blue with shiny green thread. His light-tan skin shimmers like it's been touched by fresh morning dew on the orb pines back home. His green wings flap behind him, intricate and opaque, which indicates age. Mine aren't nearly as detailed yet and they'll remain translucent for another few hundred years.

"You look excessively untidy," he remarks with his usual matter-of-fact attitude, hand on hip. He's only a few inches taller than me, but he's always seemed bigger in my mind. "Shall I?" He taps his silver-pierced nose twice, first to create a bubble around us to stop the rain, and second to transform my dress from the peach into a soft, baby-blue gown with silver drops on the neckline and a frothy skirt made of oversized, glimmering dragonfly wings. Matching flowers and leaves lace through my once unkempt hair. Everything's coated in Favie's signature blue magic. "That's better."

I smile down, swinging my hips a little to watch the wings catch the air. This is more me than anything I've worn in this realm. This is more me in every way. Then I remember the peach dress.

"I need it back, it's important to Minerva. Please."

Favie rolls his eyes, plucks a flower from the grass, taps his nose, and then holds out a little crochet bag stuffed with the dress. I take him in, my heart beating a little faster. His power is so much stronger than mine. "Why are you here?"

"I could sense you truly needed me, little sister." He cocks a brow my way. "And given the state of you, I was correct."

"I thought you wouldn't talk to me again." My lips wobble, holding back another silly, emotional outburst. "I thought you hated me. It's been years, Favie."

"You're young enough that years feel long. We often forget that, Mother and I." Favie shakes his long, silver-haired head. "And don't be ridiculous. Just because Father says it, doesn't make it so. We've been with you all along. We popped in to check on you throughout the realms—we wanted to give you space and time to chase your dreams. Well, not in the celestial places, our kind aren't welcome in them. We did send you packages though. Not Father—Mother banished him for a hundred years after the way he treated you."

"She did?" Mother and Father had been inseparable my

entire childhood. She was the lighthearted to his serious. They argued here and there, never intensely. That she would banish him on my behalf is . . . unexpected. "But—"

"His attitude needed adjusting, and you're her daughter. She loves you. She misses you. And she told me to remind you that it's imperative you eat more sweets. Your skin's almost pale, and your eyes are sagging. When's the last time you had honey or a cup of sugar? You're deprived." He picks up a rock from the ground and magicks it into a mug of steaming hot cocoa for me. "Drink."

"I didn't—I didn't know. I didn't get the packages." I take it from his hands, gulping down half before I can even respond. Instantly, my spirit feels a little lighter. "Thank you."

He huffs. "We were worried the packages would be 'lost.' The Mortal Outcome Council has made it nearly impossible for us to communicate with you in any traditional way. The all-powerful bigots sit in their shiny offices, deciding fate against the natural order of the universe, while excluding anyone who thinks and acts differently." Favie's fists ball beside him. "You would think they'd be grateful we stay out of their business, considering we're far more powerful." He takes a long breath before changing the subject. "And never thank us for taking care of you," he says, as if me doing so would be offensive.

"Now, why are you crying? Is it because the mortal realms are despondent? Did a mortal make you feel poorly? Shall I turn them into a toad? This place could use more toads. It certainly has the right climate for it."

"Apparently, we aren't supposed to turn mortals into small

creatures even out of good intentions," I say with a little smile. "I've missed you."

"I've missed you too—you're my favorite sibling."

"I'm your only sibling," I counter.

"Which is why you're my favorite." He winks. "Aelvar says hello, and hopes you'll visit the fae kingdom soon. You know how he loves your effervescence, namely your laugh."

"My laugh is too much." The words come fast, the spiral still spiraling. "*I'm* too much. No one likes me. I've been so alone, Favie."

He pulls me into a hug, my hot chocolate sloshing a little. "You're never too much. You're just enough."

"I want to come home," I whimper, like a young sister to her older brother. I don't need to withhold my feelings with him. I don't need to consider my youth, maturity, or ignorance with him. The dam breaks loose once more. My nose begins to run and dread sinks into the pit of my stomach along with the cocoa. "All of this was a mistake."

His voice is gentle, kind. "You can always come home, Darling, but I don't think you really want to." Favie bends back and swipes a tear from my cheek. "You never give up. And if you did now, you'd regret it."

I sit with that for a long moment. "You could be right."

"I'm always right."

"You're right about forty-five percent of the time."

He chuckles. "We knew you were meant for bigger and greater things than Paradise Pines. You've always wanted to change the realms, use your magic for the betterment of everyone. Make people happy. We struggled with letting you go and there are times we still do." Favie's quiet a beat, his radiant yellow eyes on mine. He looks serious, which is unusual for him. "But if we knew *you* weren't happy, we'd have come for you sooner. Are you . . . Are you happy, Darling? Truly?"

The question brings me back to Lucy. What really is happiness? Laughter? Hope? Friendship? Feeling settled in your life?

Is it love?

Or perhaps love is not the objective, like Calam said.

"Sometimes," I answer honestly. "This is all a lot more difficult than I thought, and my illness . . ." I trail off. "I want to do more than the celestials. I'm not—I don't think I'm a good Guardian."

"How could you be? They're so very boring, and you're so very not. I wonder if you're even capable of being dull." Favie's shoulders jiggle from a barely contained laugh that lights up his face and my senses. I love his laugh. I love that he has always been undeniably himself, even in the fae court, where they're more reserved and serious. "The celestials don't know about us because they never wanted to. We can be just as good as them, better in most ways, and we can change. *You* can change. Them, the realms, everything."

I take a few deep breaths, letting the negativity out with each exhale. It'll remain, as will the spiral, yet I feel stronger. More solid. More seen too. "I love you, Favie."

"I love you more." He kisses my forehead. "Oh, and one last thing." He steps back toward the primrose petals we use to travel through realms unofficially. "If every day is a battle, wear your best armor. You will not accommodate these celestials—*they* will accommodate *you*. Powerful and all-mighty as they may be, they're lucky you chose to lend your talents to their mission. Remember that." He gestures to my hidden wings and my tear-streaked skin. "All of Whimsia is proud of you. Whether you continue or not. You will always have a home there."

I smile as he disappears into a cloud of blue glitter.

The bubble bursts, letting the rain patter on me again. I don't mind.

My spirit is still a little broken and also a little renewed. My wings unfurl from my back, breaking free of their constraints. The tension in my head eases as they flap. If I wished, they could carry me up into the air, through the trees, above the rain clouds, where I could feel the sun on my face again.

Instead, I'll stay down here and give Lucy my best. Win or lose.

Favie is right—I don't give up. I never have before, and I won't start now.

So I shimmy my wings back into place to not shock the other villagers, but I refuse to change Favie's clothes. I refuse to keep trying to be like a celestial and be shamed for thinking differently. If Lucy doesn't like my first approach, I'll try another. If it doesn't work, I'll lose.

And losing isn't the end of the world. I have a home to go back to, after all, and I'll find other ways to change these realms, even unofficially. Mortals deserve that.

"No more spiraling. Let's do this," I say aloud, hoping the command is followed. "My outer reality reflects my inner reality." Deep breaths. I shut out the world. The mud. The sadness and the warring anger that wants to lash out at me and everything else. Shut out my feelings. Shut out Calam and Lumina. Deep breaths.

I listen to each droplet of water falling from the sky. Imagining I'm the cloud and the rain is all the negativity I'm carrying.

Deep breaths.

I nod. Okay.

Okay.

My feet turn back toward Fulhorn. Toward the source of my despair and toward my dwindling chance to give Lucy a Happily Ever After. This time I'll do it better. I won't let myself become so selfish and hurt again. I'll be honest with myself and with Lucy.

The least I can do is try.

CHAPTER EIGHTEEN

Minerva hasn't seen her, not that she recalls ever looking up from Ms. Chambers. The florist says that Darling walked toward the pub. The pub keeper said they saw Darling walking toward the baker. And the baker swears he saw her walk into the woods.

By the time I begin trekking in that direction, Darling strides by me into the village square carrying a bag strapped across her chest and a look of resignation on her face. She spares me only a glance as she continues to the bookstore.

"Darling!" I shout after her. Either she doesn't hear me or she doesn't care. That's not like her. But that dress . . . that is.

She's walking art. The blue primroses threaded through her updo of voluminous curls make her ethereal. Her skirt is luminescent, gauzy, and intricate enough to pick up every spark of light in the realm. The pastel glitter from her tears streaks her cheeks, her eyelids the palest of shimmery blue.

It makes me long to see her lilac wings again. Touch them.

A moment later, I regain my senses and head back to the bookstore too. Lucy and Darling are already talking when I push the door open.

"I know, it's—I'm so sorry, Darling. I didn't mean to say any of that to you. I know you're just trying to help." Lucy gives her a hopeful smile.

"No, you're right. I do push too much and I don't listen enough." Darling meets my gaze briefly before staring back at Lucy. "Now, I have to be honest with you too. I'm not like you. Or him." She points in my direction. "I'm a fairy, from the realm of Whimsia. And I'm here to make sure you're happy."

My stomach sours. We agreed not to do this. Everything's going to change. Everything's going to get more complicated, more difficult.

"You're . . . what?" Lucy's eyes widen, her words flustered with disbelief. "From where? *What?* Is this a joke?"

"I'm from Whimsia," Darling answers. Her tone lacks her signature lilt, the little inflections of joy. She has a plan and I'm not sure what it is. "I'm a fairy, like in all those books you love. I've been doing magic since I came here to make your life better. I really do want to help you."

"A fairy?" Lucy swallows, her hands pressed on the counter. "But those are just stories. Magic's not real."

For a few moments, Darling explains everything about her species through Lucy's shock to surprise to delight. She gives a demonstration with her wand, moving books and making orbs of light. She answers each question factually and patiently. She's poised.

Once Lucy understands, she looks my way. "Are you one too?"

"I'm not a fairy." I'm not prepared to tell her exactly what I am either. Only fairies are open about their identities. I'm already exposed, pretending to be a mortal. Exposing my race is a step too far. Not to mention, telling Lucy I'm here to make sure she has an ordinary life isn't the most endearing truth I'd like to share.

"I don't understand." Lucy's brows furrow. Her head tilts to the side. "Why?"

Darling ignores my entire existence. She lifts her chin. "Because I believe in helping people like you live your best life."

Lucy stands there a minute or two or ten, slowly blinking. When she finally reacts, a strange smile lights up her face. Her eyes mist with unshed tears. "You're really here to help me?"

Darling nods, giving her a slight quirk of the lips. "I am. Like in 'The Cinder Girl,' which was written by fairies, by the way."

"And Calam?" Her gaze swivels in my direction as she considers me.

"I'm also here to help." It's not a lie. But inwardly, I'm cringing.

"So you two aren't really in love or betrothed?" Lucy's shoulders sag as if this one fact detracts from the revelation that there are magical creatures in the world working toward making her happy. As if this is a real source of disappointment.

Darling answers before I can. "We aren't." She runs her palms over her skirt. "I'm sorry we lied."

Lucy doesn't respond to that, only dashes out from behind the counter and pulls Darling into a hug. "The way I—I didn't know. I wish I knew. I wish you had told me the truth in the beginning."

"So do I," Darling mumbles into Lucy's shoulder. Then she disengages with a wink. "Now I believe there's a dinner to be had tonight, and I'd love to help you woo the mysteriously pretty Andi, if you'd like?"

"Yeah—yes. I would like you to. Please." Lucy stares at Darling like she's a savior. And at that moment, everything I thought before didn't matter. I've lost Darling. She's back in this without knowing what I do: that Andi is a princess, soon to be betrothed to another. That a life with Andi would never be right for Lucy. That a match between them could lead to an Unhappily Ever After.

So despite my growing feelings toward Darling, I will have to be in complete opposition.

"Oh, and for the dancing class tomorrow night, perhaps we should do something special?" Darling asks tentatively. "I'm not talking about the mural again, but—"

"I want to do the mural." Lucy's voice is small yet decisive. "We can start after dinner and close the shop tomorrow morning to work on it."

"Really?" I blurt, watching this all from the front of the shop, slowly losing my grip on the situation. It's not like me to be a passive participant in an assignment. Darling has thoroughly thrown me off.

"It'd make the store feel like . . . I don't know, I'm a part of it and not just running it for my mom." Lucy takes a deep breath. "That was hard to say."

Darling nods. "I'm proud of you for it."

"Thank you, Darling—and Calam. Thank you for trying

to help me. I still can't believe you're a fairy; I've only ever read about them in stories. I love them. I've always wished for one of my own." Lucy purses her lips. "Wait, do you have wings?"

Darling throws her head back and laughs, the most welcoming sound I've heard today. A warm feeling blooms in the pit of my stomach.

"I do!" Then her face turns serious. "But, Lucy, I need you to keep this between us, okay? I don't think the villagers should know about me. In a few days, I'll be going back home. It's best if no one were to know that creatures like me exist."

"You're leaving?" Lucy's smile fades and she stares at Darling for a long moment. "Yeah . . . Of course. If Mrs. Arconia knew, she'd have you imprisoned in the village jail for the rest of your life. I won't tell anyone."

"Oh, don't worry about Mrs. Arconia. She's in no position to cause any trouble. Now"—Darling slides her wand from her pocket, eyeing the cat from the floor—"let's make this shop romantic."

∾ ⚡ ∾

Thwarting this date will require talent.

Darling's been half-magicking, half-cooking a feast for us all while Lucy and I have been moving the bookcases around for the picnic and subsequent mural painting. The bookstore looks magical, inviting, the atmosphere laden with hope. Candles placed as far away from flammable objects as possible, some of Lucy's paintings sit around the room, and the air smells like freshly picked flowers. The exact kind of place where fools could fall in love and I could lose this mentorship for good.

Lucy's been peppering me with questions meant to suss out my own magical gifts and how I actually met Darling—with no success.

"But I can tell you like her. It's all over your face," she whispers sharply. "I saw the way you got jealous when she took off with Dynnis."

"All part of an act," I respond. "We're just friends." The lie sits uneasily within me. Are we even friends? I don't know. She hasn't spoken to me since this morning. She barely looks my way.

I made myself too standoffish and now I'm surprised when she stops trying? I said I changed my mind about liking her. I said I couldn't believe I trusted her. I said she is too much. I said I couldn't ever love someone like her. Well, I didn't say that specifically, but it was inferred.

Now she thinks I hate her. And now she likely hates me.

I *am* a calamity, finally living up to my name.

"Friends don't look at friends the way you look at Darling." Lucy's brows furrow. "You care about her."

"You read too many romances." I smirk nonchalantly. Can anyone smirk nonchalantly? "It has addled your mind."

Lucy chuckles. "And maybe you haven't read enough. Maybe you need your mind to be a little addled."

That doesn't warrant a reply. Instead, I switch subjects. "What are you going to paint?"

Lucy regards me slowly, finally accepting the new direction of the conversation. "I haven't decided yet."

"Perhaps a larger version of the bookstore with your mother again? That's beautiful."

And it is. That would create nostalgia for the customers who remembered the early aughts of the store, while including Lucy in it. People love art, feel drawn to it. It would be good for business.

"No, but I'm going to hang that one up somewhere special." Lucy lets out a long breath as Mrs. Arconia rubs against her legs. "I should go get ready."

Without another word, she drifts to the back of the store, through the kitchen and into her bedroom.

She passes Darling, who comes out with several platters of a veritable feast. She maneuvers around me as if I'm a wall, not a person. Either she's ignoring me, or she has determined I have nothing to say to her anymore.

"Darling," I try. "Can we talk?"

She doesn't glance up at me. "What do you want to talk about?" Well, at least she's not ignoring me.

"Us." I blow out a long exhale. "I want to . . . talk about us."

"There is no 'us.' We're here to compete, you've made that very clear. One of us will lose, the other will win, and I very much doubt our paths will cross after the next two midnights." She arranges a plate of cheese, a basket of hot corn cakes drizzled with honey, and a bowl of fruit on a soft blanket. She goes back to the kitchen for a pot of something that smells spicy and rich, a tray of steaming meat pastries, and a pan of seared green vegetables. "That's probably enough," she says more to herself than to me.

"How did you learn to cook like this?" I'm trying to break the ice that has formed between us, yet the way she glowers at me, I don't think I'll succeed.

"The celestials forgot to feed me. Since they only served lunch to the students, there was nothing for breakfast and dinner. As the only person living at the academy, I had to learn to cook for myself." She goes back to arranging the cushions, one of which the cat plops onto.

"I'm sorry, I didn't know." Why would I? Most celestials can pop into the academy from home. Whereas travel between Whimsia and the Mortal Outcome Academy is verboten. I'm still somewhat surprised they even let Darling into our ranks. We tend to eschew anyone who isn't us.

"Don't feel sorry for me. I learned to be a very accomplished cook," she says dismissively. The cat meows in her direction and she shakes her head. "I don't care if you 'highly doubt that.' You would taste the proof if you weren't so odious all the time." Mrs. Arconia doesn't retort to that, instead turns around, showing us her back. Darling lifts her gaze to mine. "How are we going to play this tonight? I believe we should give them space to connect."

"I will not give them space. I disagree with them connecting." Unfortunately, her somewhat cordial mood dissipates with a scowl. "I don't want to fight you on this, but our approaches deviate here."

"I see." She stands, meeting my gaze head-on. "Enemies at last."

That statement makes me wince. "We don't have to be enemies, Darling. We're only coworkers with different objectives at this moment."

"No, we've been enemies from the beginning." Her posture and voice are calm. Too calm. So very unlike the Darling I was getting to know. "I was a fool for not seeing it earlier. We are from realms too far apart. I want Lucy to have a Happily Ever After more than I want to win this mentorship. You want her to be ordinary because that'll win you the mentorship. We were never going to be friends. We should keep this professional. Besides, there's not much time left. We'll be busy enough to avoid each other."

With that, she leaves, her dragonfly skirt swishing in her wake. My eyes track every movement with confusion.

I don't *want* to be enemies. What I want with Darling I can't define. But it's more than what we have, and I'd give anything to see her smile. To watch her do a little mischievous magic again. To wrap my hand around her waist and lead her on the dance floor. To let my lips lower onto hers—

There's a sudden knock on the door, pulling me from my needless fantasies. Everything's changing within me, and none of it good.

Andi stands outside, the rain bucketing down on her. She's in a red cape like something out of a fairy tale. Wisps of blond hair stick to her forehead, and she looks somewhat bedraggled. As I continue unhelpfully staring at her, a question arises.

How do I stop this from happening?

Darling darts past me, ushering Andi inside. "Sorry about that, we've been preparing dinner all night. Lucy has been terribly excited."

"Has she?" Andi's face flushes a rosy pink. Darling assists in taking her cape off to dry and offers use of the bathroom.

When Andi's out of sight, she narrows her gaze on mine. "Do your Misfortune all you wish, but don't hurt Lucy."

"You misunderstand what it is I do. I didn't come here to hurt Lucy; I came here to make sure she doesn't hurt *herself*." I shake my head. "I don't want to hurt anyone."

Darling huffs and stalks off to dim the lanterns and fusses over things that are already perfectly fine. As both Lucy and Andi take a seat on the floor, that's when I realize my plan.

CHAPTER NINETEEN

Darling

I did a little magic on Lucy. Her dress hugs her form, her braids are without a single strand of frizz, her lips a bit pink, and a little slash of kohl on her lids makes her eyes pop in a very natural way.

Andi can't keep her eyes off her.

Unfortunately, neither can Calam. He's plotting. He's going to ruin this, and I'll have to head him off at every turn.

"So how did you and Darling meet?" Andi pops a berry in her mouth, settling closer to Lucy on the fluffy blankets. Since it's raining outside, we couldn't very well have a picnic out there, this had to do in a pinch. I'm proud of it too; it's not just magical, it's got an air of possibility. I'm giving Lucy the tools to be bold.

Before I can answer, Calam jumps in. "I wish there was a better story. It's very simple: The moment I saw Darling, I just knew we were meant to be together no matter how opposite we are." I frown. There's absolutely no reason to entertain the idea of us being together anymore. Lucy knows the truth and Lucy is the assignment. There's a spark in his eyes as he glances at me. "Andi, when did you meet Lucy for the first time?"

"Oh, I've been coming in for years to buy books. We have

a library at home—it's just all old and boring." Andi laughs. "Nothing like the stories Lucy has here."

Lucy's mouth opens to reply, but Calam cuts her off.

"Wow, you must be affluent to have a library in your home. Where do you live?" Calam's on the prowl here and I'm not sure what he's getting at.

Andi plucks the braid off her shoulder, unconsciously smoothing it while she chooses her words. "We are comfortable—"

"No offense, but in my experience, people with generational wealth never think of themselves as privileged or rich, only comfortable." Calam even offers a look of sympathy as if he really doesn't mean offense. Such a liar.

Lucy coughs. "Do you want a drink, Andi? Darling made some lemonade."

"I would love some." Andi nearly bursts off the floor with Lucy, trying to run away as fast as she can. "Let me come with you."

I could say any number of things to Calam. Namely, *If I could do bad-intentioned magic on you, I would turn you into a mouse for Mrs. Arconia to chase*, yet I don't. He's setting a tone that I have to match.

So I do the most mature thing possible and shove a honey corn cake into my mouth, letting the sweetness pick me up. Goodness, I haven't had nearly enough sweets. All these vegetables and meats are going to be the death of me.

When Andi and Lucy return with their mugs full, sharing some small joke between them, I've had five more honey corn cakes. The evening isn't lost. Good.

Now it's my turn.

"Andi, what do you want to do with your life? Do you want to run a store like Lucy, or travel the world? I know Lucy wants to see the other kingdoms." I ask it in my most friendly of voices. The kind that puts mortals at ease.

"I would love to travel and I think running a store could be really hard—though rewarding—work." Andi smiles over at Lucy. "I'm less interested in finding my purpose in life and more interested in finding a love to spend my life with . . ." She becomes wistful. She's said enough already. Love truly is in the air.

"That's so romantic," I blurt, my own cheeks heating. "I've always felt that love makes even the most mundane things like washing the dishes more interesting—and sometimes *that* is the purpose of life. Existing, breathing, enjoying, being together while doing the extraordinary or the most boring of tasks. Don't you think, Lucy?"

Lucy gulps down her drink before answering. "I wouldn't know much about that," she admits, putting her mug on the floor and fidgeting. "I want to believe you're right though."

Andi's hand pats Lucy's knee. "Me too—"

"That's all very optimistic," Calam interjects. "But I believe no love can exist without a solid foundation of honesty. Don't *you* think, Andi?" He gives her a pointed look.

Does he know more about Andi than I do?

She yanks her hair a little harder. "Sometimes the truth has a way of getting in the way of happiness."

Now my own eyes narrow. What does *that* mean?

Lucy tilts her head, as confused as I am. "Are you going to

the ball, Andi? Have you got your dress all ready?" She wags her brows, trying to steer the conversation away from all these little mysteries Calam's desperately trying to uncover. "Will you be vying for the Princess's hand?"

"Uh, no." Andi's smile is tight. "I mean I'll be there, but not vying for her hand. I don't—that's not really for me."

"What *is* for you?" Calam takes a meat pie from the platter, his gaze boring into hers. "Would you say a quiet life or a loud one full of ballrooms and important meetings?"

"If I had my choice, I'd prefer a quiet life." Andi works her jaw back and forth, letting her braid go. In a split second, she goes from being a gentle girl with a keen interest in Lucy to defiant, almost angry. "Not everyone gets to choose how they live."

"You know, I think you ought to try the spicy sweet potato stew I made." I grab a bowl and begin ladling some into it. In moments of high stress, my illness flares to life. I tend to talk incessantly and far too fast. All sorts of things come out of my mouth. There's no stopping it until either the mood shifts or someone else takes over. "My brother-in-law, Aelvar, loves sweet potatoes. He's from a different village than my kin, and they tend to enjoy more savory foods than sweet. I remember this one time, his mother said that he really must eat more traditional meals befitting a prince—he's a prince."

I'm rambling. I know it. I'm tired. I want this to work out for Lucy. *Shut up, mouth! There isn't any stress!* "And so in front of his mother, he ate two full pots of this. Admittedly it was delicious, which is why I made it for you both tonight. You add a bit of cream to roasted sweet potatoes, all different types of seasonings from cinnabark to spicy peppers pounded into powder. It's just . . . it's luscious, really. You have to try it. You'll want more, I know it!" I nearly shout that at her.

Both Lucy and Andi stare at me, unsure of how to proceed with all that information I spewed at them. Even Calam's mouth parts as if he can't figure out what to say to that.

"Anyway." My lips stretch into an uneasy, unwarranted smile. *Sprinkles*, I hope someone stops me. "Aelvar's mother, the Queen, demanded to try it. She took one bite and declared my stew acceptable. I nearly fell out of my seat! And then she invited me to the royal modiste because she said my clothes were 'too high-spirited' for the court and—"

"Your clothes are always perfect," Calam adds, his brows raised.

Lucy chuckles. "She probably was jealous of your style."

"Wait—your brother-in-law is a prince?" Andi's eyes flash, ignoring the rest of my babbles. "So you're related to royalty?"

"Well, very far away, yes." I shove the bowl at her, hoping she takes it and no one asks me anything else. Thankfully, Andi does. I begin to get Lucy's ready too. "My brother, Favie, and Prince Aelvar married when I was young. Maybe nine years old. It was a big wedding. I got to be the flower girl."

Lucy holds her bowl, though she doesn't eat it. "Was this in Whim—I mean did you spend much time with him at their palace?"

"Oh, um, no. I went to the academy not too long after." I shove another bowl at a confounded Calam. "Anyway, Lucy, why don't you tell us about—"

"Do you know any royals, Andi?" Calam seems to have come back to his senses. "I always imagined them to be rather stuffy and entitled. Rich beyond means and uncaring of their subjects as long as they pay their taxes to overflow the royal coffers."

Andi's nostrils flare. "That's not true at all."

"Have you met the royals?" Lucy inquires innocently. There seems to be a conversation going on that neither she nor I understand. She slips a braid behind her ear, her face turned up to Andi flirtatiously.

At that precise moment, Mrs. Arconia knocks over a bowl of stew she's apparently trying to taste. Its contents spill over her paws and she lets out a walloping yell.

Bollocks, that's hot! she shouts. *I don't want to be a cat anymore! Turn me back!*

Since I really can't reply in this company, I give another fake smile. I scoop her up as she continues yowling. "I'll go wash her off. Be right back!" And I hope to all that is good that I will be. Somehow leaving the two girls in the room with Calam makes my blood feel like it's on fire. I need to get in there before it all goes sour. The stress of this evening is enough to make me rip out my hair.

I've done my best to listen and help, but this is really too much now! Mrs. Arconia caterwauls as I set her in the sink and clean her off with warm water. *I can agree that I was being unfair to Lucy, but having her date the Princess is too far! That girl is intended for my Dynnis!*

"The *Princess*?" I gasp. "She's not—her name is Andi. She can't be—"

Oh yes she is! Mrs. Arconia continues her wailing. *I met her at my husband's swearing-in ceremony. She will not be a part of your illegal magical schemes!*

Loud voices drift from the front of the store. I leave Mrs. Arconia in the sink and follow the sound.

"Are you happy now?!" Andi seethes. "*Yes*, I'm Princess Marguerite. *Yes*, I didn't tell Lucy because I didn't want to lose her. My life isn't my own but *Lucy* is my choice. I've been coming in for years hoping she would notice me. Hoping she would . . . date me." She gulps, her face red. "I—I never meant to not tell you the truth, Lucy. I just didn't want you to hate me for it."

Lucy bats away a tear. "Andi—I mean, Marguerite. I mean—" She bows slightly, her entire posture closing off. "Your Highness." She looks away from Andi then. "I always noticed you. I would have never hated you for the truth. I hate that I'm finding out about it now when you're about to throw a ball where you're supposed to get engaged."

Andi's eyes glisten. "I've been sneaking out of the palace this week to see you. To take a chance and tell you. Convince you to come to the ball and dance with me under the eyes of everyone. Then we could—"

"We could what?" Lucy barks. "I'm a peasant with a bookstore. What could I possibly do with a princess? I have my shop to run and there's nowhere to go. I want to travel, but I've already accepted that I cannot afford it. I don't own pretty gowns and no one wants my opinion. I'm not right for you or your life."

"That's not true—" Andi reaches out for Lucy. "If we spend more time together, you'd see that we could—"

"We could be nothing." Lucy's voice drops. "This was a mistake. We shouldn't have done this. I'm not for you."

Andi shakes her head. "You don't even want to try?"

"What's the point in trying?" Lucy turns her back on Andi, who lets out a sob. "You're—you're—you're not for me."

A second later, Andi runs out the door into the rain, under the cover of a falling night. A wet Mrs. Arconia slinks out, shaking her paws to rid them of the water. Meanwhile, Calam has won, even if he looks less triumphant than I expected.

I take a deep breath and bolt out after Andi. Lucy didn't mean that. She doesn't see her own worth or value. She's never been given the opportunity to explore her different options. She's self-conscious. She's afraid. She doesn't know that she deserves every good thing in the world.

If she knew, she'd be out here with Andi. The Princess, the girl who would willingly give Lucy her heart if only she would let her.

Once I'm outside in the courtyard, I can barely see Andi through the rain. Thunder booms and lightning follows it. The sky darkens as if it too knows that Happily Ever After is going to be so much more difficult for Lucy now.

My dragonfly wings stick to my legs and I let out a long exhale. I don't know where Andi has gone and I'm not sure I can chase after her either.

Every step forward we make, we take another two steps back.

I shut my eyes, the cold of the rain seeping into my skin, raising goose bumps up my arms. What a terrible day.

For once, *I* didn't ruin it. Only, I don't know how to fix it either.

"You should come in," Calam says behind me. "You'll catch a cold."

"Fairies don't get colds," I retort without looking back at him. "You ruined tonight."

"I made the hard decision that best benefits Lucy." I know he thinks that argument is sound, but it's really not.

"Because you think she and Andi aren't predictable, right? They could be chaotic and there's a risk of Unhappily Ever After if they don't work out." Calam may think I don't understand Misfortunes, but I do. I just don't always agree with them. "Happiness is a gamble, Calamity. It can be chaotic. That doesn't mean it isn't worth trying for."

He steps up in front of me, the rain matting his curls. "If she tries, I can't guarantee an Ordinary Ever After either. Is gambling for a chance of happiness a better choice than stability?"

"It's not our choice to make!" I stare up at him. "It's hers. She should make it."

"You can't trust a mortal to make the right decision. They don't see the big picture!" He treads closer, his face inches from mine. "Their stability impacts ours. We were created to keep the realms safe. Keep the mortals from destruction."

"All of that may be true." I shake my head. "But we don't get to decide their fate, Calam. We can present their options. Help them make their choice. And yes, I would say a chance at happiness is better than stability. Lucy wants love. She wants happiness. Who are we to tell her that she can't have either?

We'll be gone in two midnights and she'll have to live with the choices we've imposed on her for the rest of her life. It's not fair."

Calam's hand cups my jaw. I don't move. I don't flinch. We're enemies. We're coworkers. We both think we're doing the right thing and going about it in different ways. I loathe him. I like him. I have no idea why he vexes and enchants me.

"Fairness is subjective, Darling." His thumb rubs against my cheek, lighting my skin on fire despite the cold. "You're so passionate about everything. You're all or nothing. You want the best for everyone—even strangers. You are infuriating—" I pull away, but his other arm wraps around my back, pushing me into his chest. The rain washes down between us. "I was wrong before. About not liking you. I like you immensely. I like you more than I've ever liked anyone or anything. All I do is think about how much I like you. All I want is for you to like me too."

For a long moment we stand there like that, his eyes meeting mine. Waiting for me to say something, anything. "I . . . I don't hate you."

He smirks. "Would you call that liking me?"

"I would say I almost like you." I avoid looking at his lips now as if one glimpse will make me melt into a puddle with the rain. He's close. Too close. I want to be closer.

"And how would I make you like me?"

"I'm not sure," I answer.

"Hmm." He rests his forehead on mine, shutting his eyes briefly. I'm left watching his beauty, admiring him. Losing a little bit of my dwindling sanity in the moment. This day has been entirely too long, my mood entirely too jumbled. The walls I've built between him and me are crumbling down because he's holding me like I'm precious.

"I understand why you want this mentorship, why you want Lucy to be happy. I know why I want it—because I never had love like you had with your family. I never had love like Lucy had with her mother. I've had the opposite, I—"

"What did they do to you? How did they hurt you, Calamity?" I can't help asking even as the wind pecks at my cool skin. "Please tell me why you need this."

"I—It's . . . After my mother . . ." He gives me a small sigh before starting again. "When I was a child, my father looked down at me when I failed to goad a mortal into a bad decision. I was ten years old. I was still learning. And it was something silly too; like selling his prize horse to invest in a conman so that he would learn consequences. Anyway, my father said, 'Calamity, do you know how much hinges on you succeeding? How much I've given? Keep disappointing me and you'll never be free. If you imagine me cruel now, imagine how much worse I'll be if you fail.'" He lets out a long breath. "I'm failing. And I . . . getting this mentorship means I won't have to be unhappy with him anymore. But that doesn't mean we have to be enemies. Win or lose." His hand clutches mine as if he needs me to know this. He gazes deeply into my soul. For some nebulous reason, I don't want to look away. I like being seen. "Whatever happens, I'm always going to like you."

"Really?" I nearly choke out. Calam's doing this for

freedom. Not for power. For choice. That shifts my already shifting perceptions of him. I imagined he did it for glory and proving how much better he is than everyone else, how good he is at being a Misfortune. Now I know that he's unhappy, I wish I could help him. And yet, my mind can't think of a solution while he's touching me. Being near him makes me excited and nervous and some other mysterious third thing.

He doesn't hesitate. "Yes."

"And Lucy too?" I counter. "Will you give her the chance to be happy? Will you break free by imprisoning her in mediocrity? Doesn't she deserve the same chance?"

"If that's Lucy's choice, I can do my best to respect it." His lips quirk. "Causing that argument . . . I didn't like the way it made any of us feel. I wish I hadn't done it. All I can do is try to fix it."

My skin blazes then and I try to act like I'm not at a loss for words.

He keeps staring at me, his gaze falling to my mouth. "Can I kiss your cheek?"

"What?" The question sends banshees wailing through my brain, each of them for different reasons.

Calam doesn't seem to care about my reaction. He gives my cheek a gentle whisper of a touch with his finger. "Just here."

"I . . . um. Yes?" I'm just as surprised as he is by what my mouth says. "That would be okay."

"Thank you," he murmurs. He hovers fully over me now as the tip of his nose touches mine. It's warm. Affectionate. He smells like fruit and bread and I kind of love that. He's so soft, so careful, so gentle. His breath sends a trail of heat everywhere it caresses. I stifle a groan. I do like being close to him. More than I knew until this moment.

When his lips flatten against my cheek, the air in my lungs disappears. My body nearly falls over from swaying with electrified nerves. The kiss is nothing like Virtue's.

It's realm-shattering. It makes my heart sing and light up from within. Everything drops away around us. The rain and cold—nothing else matters but this. My breaths are shallow. My head swims with the sensations of his smell, his warmth, his everything. I close my eyes, imagining what it'd be like if his lips were on mine. If we hugged at the same time and I felt him all around me.

Would I burst into flames?

Would I ever be able to kiss someone else after that? How could it compare? Because as small as this one gesture is, it'll become my obsession for a long time to come. It is everything I wanted but never knew existed.

And then, to my dismay, it's over.

Calam pulls back, a frenzy in his gaze. "I don't want to be enemies, Darling."

"Then let's not be, Calamity." I inhale shakily. "We could be friends. Friends at last."

CHAPTER TWENTY

Friends? She wants to be friends? Friends don't kiss friends. Especially not in the way I did.

That didn't feel *friendly* at all. It was as if everything in me came alive when I inhaled her flowery scent, the sweetness of her, touched the softness of her. When my lips found her perfect cheek, my nose grazed her perfect nose. It was like seeing colors after only black and white my entire life. It should've been overwhelming. It wasn't. If anything, it was revealing. Feelings fluttered around my center, singing little songs of contentment.

I don't want to be friends. I want to know everything about her until I know her as well as I do myself. I want to watch her wings flutter in the sky and her eyes sparkle when she smiles. I want more kisses and touches. I'll always want it to be like that.

I'll never be the same.

We cannot be friends. My life would be a failure if we don't become an *us*.

I flap *The Prince and the Woodsman* shut, letting it rest against my chest. Morning is beginning to break outside the windows.

After the whole kiss thing, cleaning up the store, and eating some of the abandoned feast, we went to bed. She constructed a pillow barrier—for her benefit or mine, no idea. It was a smart choice.

Now that I know what kissing her is like, why wouldn't I want to do it again? It was only a kiss on the cheek. It was too short, too small. My first kiss. The best kiss.

I glare down at the romance book. "How did you become more than friends, huh? What's the secret, you ridiculous fictitious mortals?"

"Calamity!" The sound scrapes in my ears, and the book drops to the floor. Darling doesn't stir. My stomach seizes. "Calamity!" The coin on the bedside table glows. I take it in my palm, ease out of the bed, and head downstairs. At first my skin sizzles from contact, then it gives way to a slight thrum. I swallow my growing apprehension.

Once I'm down in the store, I close my eyes. Waiting for the inevitable unpleasantness to ruin my day. Darkness swirls around me; the air becomes thick and hazy with ill-intent. My father's voice pierces through the silence, his tone impatient.

"You have two days left, child. Do not disappoint me."

"I will not," I utter it automatically, though it's likely I will. Anything less than perfection would disappoint him. I'd basically agreed to let Lucy decide her own fate last night. After watching her slink off in tears to her room, I knew it was time to back off. A necessary decision to help her stay on the path of least unhappiness.

And now I'm reconsidering my role in it.

Worse, I'm falling for a fairy. I'd rather spend time with

her—kissing her, holding her hand—than anywhere else. I've well and truly lost my mind, and I've never felt better. I have no idea what will happen next, but if it's around Darling, it'll be an adventure.

"Have you found a way to defeat the fairy?" He seems to cut to the heart of me with one question. He must sense a divided loyalty, a change that would disgust him more than he already is. "Need I remind you that everything I've done, every sacrifice I've made, can be undermined by that fairy succeeding? If you want that mentorship, prove it by winning."

"Thank you," I snap, "for putting that onus on me. Of course I remember what's at stake." I want to be free of him. I want to shape our realms and have real impact.

I thought I needed it. Some part of me is realizing that I haven't been following my own advice: knowing the difference between want and need. I want to be free of him. If I fail, I'll find another way.

"Don't be petulant. You're better than that." I feel his annoyance through the coin. "Secure an Ordinary Ever After. Honor our family name."

And just like that, the coin cools. He's gone. I shove it back into my pocket, my thoughts narrowing.

Mrs. Arconia stretches and meows on her fluffy bed beneath the romance section. She eyes me wearily. To be honest, I'm happier knowing she's a cat. If her mortal form was still in charge, we'd have a slew of issues. Not that I'd ever admit it to Darling.

Lucy comes through the kitchen door carrying a box of books. She glances my way as she slides it onto the counter.

"New books for tonight's party," she says. There's not an ounce of happiness in her tone. It would seem that last night's dinner had as profound an effect on her as it has on me.

This assignment is ruining my perception of Misfortunes. I used to be able to goad a mortal into making a bad choice to save themselves, yet they'd still be the one making it. I've never pushed too hard. I never needed to. Mortals *want* to make decisions that worsen their lives—it's just those decisions ultimately could make them better too.

Fundamentally, I believed mortals to be flawed. That's the easiest conclusion to draw. Having spent several days here though, I'm understanding that's only half true. Some mortals make choices because they have no other options. Some mortals are in a state of mental anguish, which can't be their fault. Some mortals need attention, need a purpose.

I was certain that only the wrong can lead them to the right. Now I'm beginning to think that the wrong can lead them to more wrong too. Mortals are more nuanced than I ever imagined.

This experience is gnawing at my reality. Not all mortals deserve Unhappily or even Ordinary Ever Afters. Yet if I agree with that sentiment, then I'm forfeiting the mentorship. I'm losing my freedom from Blight and the future I thought I needed.

A decent Misfortune would tell me not to pursue Darling. Though I know they would be doing it for my benefit, I can't stop myself. All so Darling can call me her friend. *Ugh.*

Lucy disappears into the kitchen briefly before stalking back with several canisters of paint.

"You still want to paint the mural?" I ask, surprised. I would think after the argument with Andi, she would've stepped further away from her art. Some part of me thought she would've given up on happiness altogether. If she had, I would've had an easy win.

I was wrong, and that gives me a strange—extremely unhelpful—sliver of hope.

"I do, and I think I know just what I want to paint." The corner of her lip lifts, which I suspect is the closest we're going to get to any expression of happiness today. But it's better than nothing.

Soon, Darling joins us in another signature fairy outfit, this one a pale green with intricate, shimmery silver thread, strewn with wildflowers. Beautiful as always.

Whereas I've just been wearing plain suits in various shades of blue.

I do the one thing I never thought I'd do just to see her smile: "Darling, will you make me an outfit?"

Her brows lift. "Really?"

"Please." I give her a small grin. "Perhaps not as bold as yours."

Darling takes out her wand and taps it against her chin. "Hmm . . . something for Calam." Then she swishes. My suit transforms from basic into a casual shirt with white sleeves, a navy-blue vest embroidered with gold thread reminiscent of the night sky, complete with slim, matching trousers.

"I'm appalled by this, Darling. Appalled. And pleased at its splendor." I chuckle, and she joins in. Fairies love beautiful things, and if her changing my clothes . . . best not to finish that thought.

Lucy watches us both, wide-eyed. "It must be amazing having a wand."

"It is." Darling shrugs, though obviously pleased. "Every fairy has one. Normally, I keep it in its original form, though sometimes I change it into an earring or brooch. See?" Her wand poofs into a small golden stud in her right ear. She tugs the lobe, and a candle flickers to life.

"You're incredible," I blurt like a lovestruck fool. One kiss and I've lost all my senses.

"Thank you." Darling's face lights up, her cheeks blushing slightly. "Now, Lucy, what did you want to paint?"

"It's a surprise for later." She waves us away as Minerva knocks on the door.

Darling hurries over to answer it, her skirt swaying with the movement. I'm enraptured and I need to snap out of it. This is an assignment that will end. I need to stay on task.

Minerva stands in the doorway. "Darling, the village is talking about your gowns, especially that pretty dragonfly one you wore yesterday. Everyone wants a signature look for tomorrow night. Would you mind coming over and helping us plan some?"

Darling spares me a glance. "Sure, of course."

"And you," Minerva says in my direction, a glint in her eyes. "I have a special task for you. Since the store's closed, I've got plenty of things to keep you busy."

For the next few hours, I hardly have a spare moment with Darling or Lucy. Darling ends up helping Minerva *and* the grumpy baker somehow while I get roped into making flower crowns and corsages. I don't enjoy it. My lips freeze into a curl by the fifteenth crown. I'd magick some if I could, but I'm never alone.

By the time we're back to the shop, there's a tarp covering the left wall.

"It's still a bit wet. Darling, can you wave your wand again?"

Darling nods. "Sure thing." Gold glitter bursts in the air and, presumably, the paint dries. At any rate, Lucy looks almost proud of herself, though there's still a sadness clinging to her. Andi. And . . . I understand. I felt the same way when Darling left yesterday.

She has a choice to make now, and I'll respect that.

The door swings open, jingling the bell again. It's all very annoying. A line of villagers walks in carrying bushels of flowers, cakes, decorations. In seconds, the racks of books are pushed to the side, and in the chaos, I miss the mortal's approach.

Dynnis suddenly stands in front of me, his eyebrows arched, smile mysteriously smug. "If you would, I need to help clean up for the dance tonight." He gestures for me to get out of the way, I guess.

"*Darling*," he says like an endearment, "where should I put this? You have my muscles all day long. I'm here for your every need."

Which is promptly when I roll my eyes. I snap my fingers and untie his boot laces and send one shiny lock of red hair up into the air in an inexplicable cowlick he'll not be able to tame. I have nothing to be jealous of—he's a mortal. A temporary hindrance. She may look at him with kind eyes now, yet I'm the one who kissed her. Once I earn her affection, her trust, I could have her kind eyes forever.

I've lost my mind, haven't I?

"Watch the store?" Lucy asks before darting off to find the recluse of a dance teacher. She doesn't wait for me to answer.

This day is my nightmare.

⁂

Come early evening, the bookstore resembles a tiny ballroom. It smells floral. Darling has added more twinkling lights, flowers are everywhere. I'm uncomfortable. That feeling only grows when more and more of the local youth gather inside, hands by their sides, staring across the store at each other. The tension could be cut with a spoon.

The dance teacher, an older woman with a high bouffant of gray hair dotted with faux rubies, drinks her sixth or seventh glass of punch. It would seem they bribed her to come with the free libations and not the actual dancing.

Darling stalks into the center like a beam of starlight, her hair in a curly bun. She freshened up and looks even more enchanting. Obviously, I'm trying to calculate when I can kiss her again.

"Shall we dance?" She stands there under the lights, holding her hand out to me. This one moment is going to live in my mind for the rest of my eternal life.

Minerva squeals with glee, clapping her hands together behind her. Lucy smiles. I step forward only for Dynnis to saunter onto the floor. He scoops up Darling into a quick hug, followed by a twirl. Her dress flares out, sending sparkles all around us. There's a frown tugging on her lips, a wrinkle between her brows.

Something flips in my gut. For the first time since we met, I know Darling prefers me above others. My heart pounds like a stomping mammoth. The grin that finds my face surprises me. I meander slowly toward her, catching her gaze. When her eyes meet mine, they flash, emoting: *Are you going to dance with me or am I stuck with this mortal?*

When she nearly loses her footing, sliding on the polished wood, I reach out and tug her into me. Her head tucks into the crook of my neck, her hair tickling my chin. Briefly, we stay like this despite the crowd around us. No doubt this is improper.

Dynnis's hand plops on my shoulder. His envy streams through his mind and threatens to enter mine.

"I'll take over from here," I tell him with a smirk.

He storms off and I block him out. Block out everyone. Darling's heart races. She smells like chocolate and sunshine. I try not to sigh. That would really be embarrassing. If a mortal acted like this, I would be concerned about their proximity to an Unhappily Ever After. I'd concoct a seven-step plan to get them back to Ordinary Ever After.

Minerva coughs pointedly. Darling pulls back and places

her hands on my waist and shoulder like the other couples, who all seem to be properly stepping in a coordinated routine.

We try . . . poorly.

It's at that moment we both realize we have no idea how to dance like mortals. And as Darling winces, I'm guessing fairies don't do this kind of thing either.

I attempt the twirl Dynnis did and her hand slips from mine. My foot skids on the wood, and I yank her back to steady both of us. She inhales sharply before cackling. I join in, my head thrown back. Darling rocks forward, giggling with tears streaming from her eyes.

Around us, I see other dancers join us. But I couldn't care less. We attempt the whole affair again while we can't stop laughing.

"You two are doing it all wrong!" The dance teacher sets down her cup and marches toward us. "Who taught you how to dance? Aren't you betrothed? How will you entertain at your wedding?"

I snort and Darling tries to wrangle herself into a serious person although there's a jubilance in her spirit.

"We weren't really thinking about the wedding, more about after." The words leave her mouth in a rush. To her, they're innocent. To anyone else, she just said the most inappropriate thing. *Oh* fairies.

Now I can't help but throw a hand over my chest and chuckle earnestly.

Darling's face drops, her eyes widen. "I mean, like . . . er, when you say *I do*. We were thinking about the . . . uh, the thing where people pray to a mighty deity. That white place with the high tower? We were thinking about how we'd, er . . ." Then she explodes into giggles because she very clearly does not know how to continue with this reasoning. Minerva swoops in, her lips pursed before she tells us we should go outside to cool off.

We maneuver calmly through the dancers until we're engulfed in the fresh air. I breathe a little easier. And then we bust out into fits of more laughter.

"It's. Called. A. Chapel," I say through chortles.

Darling wipes away tears. "How would I know? Mortal customs are weird!"

"You basically told her you were thinking about having intimate relations with me." I double over at that.

"Kissing? That's not scandalous!" She roars with glee, and that makes it even more funny.

"Not *just* kissing. You know . . ." I wave my hands around trying to gesture the act of consummation. The entire thing takes more breath out of me. She's got her hand over her mouth, shaking her head. She doesn't understand at all. "Intercourse?"

And then I watch as her hand falls and her jaw unhinges. "Wait a minute. Wait! The thing that uses your . . . anatomical bits?! I didn't know the name of it in this language."

I bite my lip, trying to stop tittering. "It has several names. Sex. Lovemaking, more traditionally."

"It's called *lovemaking* here?" She steps closer, her face lit up. "That's splendid! In Whimsia, our undeniable desire is called *elfhaeme sidhe*, coined from the fae, because, you know . . ."

I absolutely do not know. "Celestials are required to study

this—well, maybe not Guardians. It's huge for Misfortunes. It affects their love life, friendships, all kinds of things. We just try to make certain it doesn't lead to Unhappily Ever Afters."

Darling shakes her head. "Guardians only taught me that pretty dresses, good decisions, and a positive, can-do outlook lead to Happily Ever After. I assumed that Guardians didn't talk about sex because it offends their conservative, extremely narrow concepts of morality." She tilts her head in thought. "Fairies engage in all the *elfhaeme sidhe* they want, especially if they share True Love's Kiss."

Now my shoulders shake with silent delight. I clear my throat before continuing. Fairies are so cute. "Mortals don't believe in True Love's Kiss. Neither do celestials."

"Wow, really?" Darling claps her hands in excitement. "Well, now that I know it's not against the rules with you all, we should do the lovemaking!"

"*What?!*" The question nearly gets lost in my throat as my lungs stop functioning.

"It could be fun." Darling says it so seriously. "You kissed my cheek yesterday and I enjoyed it immensely. I'd imagine lovemaking with you would be even more enjoyable." At my puzzlement, she rambles on, her cheeks flushed. "We already share a bed, and like Mrs. Howe implied—"

"I don't know," I cut in. My heart thuds loudly. The laughter has shriveled, and I'm struck with too many emotions at once.

She points her finger at me. "Have you done it?"

"No—" I can't even tell her she was my first kiss, that she

was the only person I've ever wanted to kiss. This conversation has taken a strange turn entirely too fast.

"Well, let's try it together. And"—she gestures to her chest—"I may be biased, but I have great anatomical bits. They are very ample."

"Your bits are indeed lovely." I try not to look away; the tips of my ears are hot. "I like your figure very much. I would, uh . . . Um . . ." She glances at me through her long, dark eyelashes, which glint in the flickering light of the village square. All the words get trapped somewhere between us. My bold hand reaches out, pulling her hip until she's flush against my chest.

Suddenly, I'm very warm, and all those emotions whittle down into something I never experienced before, never knew I'd feel before. I wait for panic to flood my senses at the prospect of where my mind goes. Only, instead, *she* floods my senses. The scent of vanilla and chocolate. Images flick behind my eyes. Her hair down. Kissing her. Touching her. Losing myself to *want* with her instead of my endless pursuit of *need*.

She lifts her head to mine, her lips close. "Can we kiss?"

"Please." I lean down, my lips skimming hers. My heart's racing. I want. I want. I want.

"Hey," Lucy calls out, causing me and Darling to jump apart. "Darling, Calam, come back inside for the unveiling of the painting. I can't wait for you all to see it!"

CHAPTER TWENTY-ONE

Darling

With everyone gathered around, under the flickering lights and in the general atmosphere of hope, joy, and wonder, Lucy unveils her mural.

Admittedly, it takes me a moment to swallow down the desire that overwhelmed my body and mind before I can adjust to where I am. What we're doing. When I peek through the crowd—when I see it all laid out in front of me—I gasp.

There, in vibrant colors, are Lucy, Calam, and me standing in front of the bookshop. Lucy looks the same as she does now, in the mint dress with golden embroidery of books. Her braids flow down her shoulders, her eyes are bright. She seems more . . . peaceful. Less sad. She's the person breaking through the walls erected when her mother died and she had nothing but the store and oats. She has dreams. And she's beautiful.

In the painting, I stand next to her. I'm wearing the timeless peach dress Minerva made. It makes my brown skin more vibrant. It honors the past.

Minerva sniffles beside me. "It's like Emelia is with you in that gown."

"It is," I agree, though I'm still admiring Lucy's talent. My smile's wide. There's a gold wand in one hand, just like mine.

I'm magical. She made me a fairy. I almost laugh when my eyes catch on Calam.

He's painted to my right in his signature blue suit, his curls fluffy on his head and down past his ears. There's a pile of books in his arms. He's looking . . . He's looking at me, his lips twisted up in a smile. Not a smirk.

Virtue never looked at me the way Calam does in that painting. Venom dripped from her lips instead of soft kisses like the one he gave me last night. It confused my heart then. Confused *me.*

It made me question what I knew about love and how people understood one another. It made me believe that celestials—and mortals—were confounding. They did things that contradicted their words. I always assumed that confusion to be a moral failing of mine. It's why I approached clients from the outside in. I didn't know the other way.

I see it all captured in paint.

The look of hope on Lucy's face. The look of longing on Calam's. The look of joy on mine. All of us—celestials, fairies, mortals—carry experiences with us. Those experiences must be uncovered, listened to, regarded with care, for us to connect to each other. I never connected with Virtue, not like I have with Calam or Lucy. Now I can look at this painting and see that this confusion I once felt stemmed from fear.

That fear has been keeping me back too long.

I understand Minerva and her desire to be seen. I understand Lucy and her desire to be cared for. I understand Calam and his desire to be free. I understand myself now too, and my desire to be loved and part of something bigger.

I laugh softly. I also understand now that Calam really does like me. He cares for me. He kissed me not as a friend, but as something more. He never asked for anything more. Yet, I want more. How would that even work, him being a Misfortune and me a fairy? Such different sides of the realms, and philosophies.

I shake my head, staring up at that mural of the bookstore—not as it used to be with her mother, but as it is presently. With a big romance display and a cat in the window—Mrs. Arconia will have opinions about this. Twinkling lights and inside a circle of chairs with villagers holding books. The book club. There's a tray of cookies on the counter.

It's stunning. Arresting. It incorporates the village. It makes the store a part of its community.

A tear slips down my cheek. "Lucy."

Calam's hand squeezes mine and I realize then that I never did let him go. It just felt so natural that I didn't notice. "She's truly talented."

People heap praise upon her, telling her how proud her mother would be. How much they love her work. She beams at the recognition.

Some part of me wants to part that crowd and pull her into a hug, only I know it's not the time. She needs this. She needs all of this to make memories that'll help her get through the years to come, whatever path she goes down. This is her moment.

"What are we going to do?" I ask Calam, sliding him a glance.

"We let her choose," he says quietly near my ear. "Tomorrow, we'll tell her the full truth. Then she can decide."

"Tomorrow's our last midnight," I murmur. "Everything's going to end."

Calam lifts my hand to his lips and kisses it. "Then let's enjoy what time we have left."

∾ ♥ ∾

After everyone has gone, Lucy has retired to her bed, and we've cleaned up the store, Calam suggests we look at the stars.

"It's cloudy outside," I remark, pushing the last bookcase back into place.

"We can change that." He snaps his fingers and the ceiling transforms from wood beams and white paint to a tapestry of a brilliant night sky. Of the realms and their stories. The night sky expands beyond us.

"You use your magic so little, I sometimes wonder if you even like it." I throw him a look, somewhat awestruck how precise he can be with his snaps when he wants to.

"I have limited resources, unlike you." He snaps his fingers again, spreading out a blanket beneath us.

He offers my hand and I take it, lying down beside him in the small space. My side rests against his. My heart gallops with the contact. The nearness. Him. The mural. The way he looked at me. The way he held me outside. The way he looks at me now.

"If you ask celestials where they came from, they'll say some divine force of science and magic. That we were created to serve mortals in each new realm." He grows quiet, gazing up at one realm in particular. Malespero, I think.

"If you ask fairies," I interject, "they'll say constellations depict stories of bravery and compassion, the realms created from daring defeats and stunning sacrifices. We love our tall tales."

He chuckles and I wonder what's going on in his head right now. He can't read my thoughts like he can with mortals when they touch, but can he feel something else? Can he hear my heart? It's currently trying to drown out my words. I take a shaky breath.

"You think an awful lot." Calam's eyes tear away from the stars and land on mine.

"We have a big day tomorrow." My voice sounds high to my own ears. I swallow down the creeping nervousness.

"I'm aware," he says with a small wink. "I wouldn't want to be anywhere else than right here with you, right now."

"Oh." My fingers twitch by my sides. "You don't . . . we aren't . . . we aren't friends, are we?"

"We are, and . . . perhaps we're something else too. Friends don't desire each other the way we do, they don't . . . picture each other . . ." His unsteady tone trails off and there's not a smirk to be found. Something warm flitters through my senses when he reaches over to take one of my curls in his fingers. He unwraps the coil in awe as if he doesn't have similar hair hanging by his ears. "Hmm, I've never seen you with your hair down." It's more an observation to himself than me. "You know, I'm a very good Misfortune. Best in my class. It's been said I might just be the most talented of my generation."

I try not to roll my eyes. "What does that have to do with anything?"

"It's always been easy for me, until this." He meets my gaze and the breath freezes in my lungs.

"Until this?" Though his touch makes me nervous, I can't help leaning into it either. It feels too good.

"Before this situation with Lucy and you," he answers, his fingers still playing with my hair, "I thought I was doing the right thing."

"You are, in your way." Much as it pains me to admit it, there's a reason Misfortunes exist. There's a reason mortals need them. Life could be terrible without a Misfortune stepping in and helping them live a better fate than their choices could create for them. "I just think all of us need new assignments. How the Mortal Outcome Council chooses who gets to be saved needs to change. There's no room for nuance. There's no room for gray."

"Hmm." He seems to be considering my words. "That's why you want to win."

I nod. "We can't make one person's life better without making their realm better. You see that now, right? We have to give them an even playing field for all of this to work. What they choose beyond that is not our decision. We're serving them by letting them make their own fate."

"And what if they choose Unhappily Ever After?" His brow furrows. "What if they choose to be doomed?"

"We help them not drag anyone else into that doom. We give them the tools to make better decisions, we give them options. We let them learn. We listen. We care." That's the truth of it, I realize. I want mortals to have choices.

"Do you really think that'd work?" He studies me closely. I love the way he looks at me. The way he listens.

"I think it's worth trying." I let out a long breath. "It may be naïve to think, but I really believe that if we all cared about each other more, there would be less Unhappily Ever Afters. There'd be more stability. It won't be easy and it'll take time, energy, and work. It would require cooperation among all of us. The Guardians, the Misfortunes, and the fairies—who have been shut out too long. We have much to offer the realms, too, only we've never been welcomed to try. Not all of us can send in an application every week and hound the Mortal Outcome Council for a chance. Some fairies will never want this. Some of us though . . . we'd love for our magic to make an impact."

Calam regards me slowly. "You are . . ."

"An irresponsible, meddling, mischievous, candy-coated, magic-misusing disaster of a . . ."

The words die on my lips as he places a hand on my hip and rolls me closer. "I like you."

"I know." I'm surprised I can say as much since I feel like my spirit is floating out of my body. "I like you too."

"I must admit, I despise the word *like* in this instance. It's juvenile and doesn't really match the emotion I feel for you. Wait—" His eyes widen. "You *like* me?"

"Well, not now that you told me how you despise the word." I laugh, his lips pulling into a frown. "I'm fond of you."

Then he smiles. A real, genuine smile that stretches his

cheeks and lights up his face. He really is quite beautiful, especially when he smiles. "You hold me in the highest of regard?"

I do something between a snort and a giggle. "I . . . admire you."

"You esteem me." His smile turns into his signature smirk.

I cock an eyebrow. "Less and less when you fish for compliments."

His arm wraps around my waist as his nose bumps mine. "I esteem you too."

"You can't use the same word." My body's on fire.

"I see." He grazes his lips against my cheek. "I cherish you."

"Oh, good one."

"Thank you." His lips flatten against my cheek again. Warmth spreads through every limb and I shut my eyes, settling into his embrace. I breathe in his scent of old books and pine, which is a weird combination that oddly befits him. When he moves a little, breaking the kiss, I almost beg him for another. More. Please. I want it all. "I think if we had more time together, I could very well adore you, Darling."

All the air whooshes out of my lungs. My mouth gapes for a small moment. "I—I think that—" I take a deep breath. "Maybe it's good we don't, then."

"Hmm," is all he says as the night floats away and we keep looking up at those stars.

CHAPTER TWENTY-TWO

Dawn arrives far too soon. I've been lying in bed, my arm wrapped around Darling's waist, as the sun rises. She faces me, her lavender wings tucked around her shoulders, her lips slightly parted, her breathing soft and steady. She's wearing her frilly white nightgown, which makes her medium brown skin even more brilliant.

There's no part of her that isn't lovely.

I'm tempted to kiss her again. Share True Love's Kiss. I almost laugh at how fairy-esque that sounds. But I'd do it for her. And maybe eventually, when we're both comfortable being vulnerable with each other and we feel safe, we could try "the lovemaking."

Now I do have to stifle a laugh.

That never interested me until her. Neither did kissing. Holding hands. Being close. Letting myself be touched and willingly wanting to touch someone else. My reality has tilted off its axis and I'm both terrified and excited.

I want. I want. I want. Everything.

My mother's last words to my father circle in my mind. *Don't we as eternals deserve happiness ourselves? Can't we be happy?*

The concept of deserving is entitlement. No one is entitled

to anything—or at least they shouldn't be. Yet if happiness is a choice, why can't we choose it? Following that line of thought, why do celestials believe that mortals can't choose it either?

Darling's right. The fate of a mortal should be in their own hands. We can present the paths, but only they can choose which to walk.

I wonder then if Lucy will take Happily over Ordinary. If she'd rather choose uncertainty over a solidly okay life.

"You think an awful lot," Darling says groggily without opening her eyes.

Her lips look especially pleasing with a beam of sunlight glancing off them. Everything in me wants to lean close and kiss them.

"Big day today." I echo her words of last night because I don't have my own. My mind is in a jumble. I don't want today to end. I don't want midnight to come.

She sighs. "I know."

"Want me to pause time again?" I offer, though we both know I'm not strong enough to do that too long. Nor would it change anything.

She winks one eye open. "You're so fond of me."

"I hold you in the highest of all regards," I murmur.

Now both eyes are open, mischief circling their brown depths. "Calam—"

"Don't forget, I cherish you," I answer, touching my nose to hers.

Her breath whispers against my cheeks. "Calamity, I cherish you too."

"Do you?" My lips hover close to hers. This is it. "*Oh, Darling*, my little love muff—"

Mrs. Arconia hops onto the bed, her meow a cross between a purr and a growl. Darling huffs. "How he and I sleep is none of your business, nor do we care about impropriety. Now, how about this—I'll turn you back tonight, just before the ball?"

Mrs. Arconia grimaces, a wholly strange thing for a cat to do. She meows again, less growly. I could touch her, read her thoughts, yet something in me knows this is going to be a magic-heavy day. I'd better use it wisely.

"Only if you've learned your lesson," Darling says, sitting up. "Or else I'll never turn you back." She cocks an eyebrow at the ginger creature. "I should tell you, Dorette, that if we hadn't intervened, you'd be miserable. Do you understand? You're being given a choice now. Learn from this experience and be better, or have a Miserably Ever After. That means that you'll never be happy, you'll make everyone else around you unhappy, and you'll have ruined everything for everyone." Darling turns to me. "Calam, when you touch people, you can read their thoughts, right? But can you reveal yours to them or your emotions? Project?"

I'm about to shake my head when I really sit with the question. Honestly, I don't know. It's not like I could project the future since I can't see it, but I could try. So much for using less magic.

My hand eases into her fur. I shut my eyes, take a deep breath. At first, I can feel Mrs. Arconia. She's annoyed. Grumpy. Surprisingly, she's not angry. Anger might've left her a day or two ago. She's thinking of her son, and the ball tonight. How she wants Dynnis to make an impression on the Princess. She's thinking of how she misses her husband. How she likes the way people treat her as a cat—they seem less intimidated by her. They include her. They show her affection. As a mortal, she's abhorred. She doesn't mean to be so strict and imposing, she just doesn't know another way.

I came from nothing. I worked hard and spent too much time alone. I forgot how to enjoy my life. I ruined it all. I ruined all my relationships. My own father and siblings won't speak to me. I'm afraid. Terrified. I push everyone away.

Good, that's meaningful.

"I'm going to show you how you make other people feel," I say to the cat, and it's truly bizarre, truly, yet on this assignment, we've embraced bizarre. Today is no different. I push what I know forward. That she's on the path to Miserably Ever After. I make sure she's aware that I've never heard of a Miserably Ever After changing their course. They pull down everyone and anything in their way until it's coated in that same misery. Until there's no joy left.

The memory of how people looked at her when she intruded on the book club flits across my thoughts. The way she made Lucy feel. Her husband too. The fear she holds close inspires that same fear in others about her.

Once I pull my hand away, she whimpers.

"Do you see now?" Darling stares down at the cat. Mrs. Arconia sniffs. "Do you think you can change it? I haven't seen your future—only I know that if you don't mend your ways, you will destroy everyone else's. That's not what you want, is it?"

The cat sinks into the blanket. She meows once more and Darling nods.

"It's our last day," I say with only a hint of woe. "Go get ready. I'll meet you downstairs—but could you give me a few moments with Lucy to explain?" Darling dips her head in understanding as I snap my fingers, changing out of my pajamas into more princely attire.

I go without saying another word. If I stay any longer, I won't leave the bed and her. Plus, the whole talking cat thing is a lot to digest this early in the morning.

Once I'm down the stairs, I take a moment to breathe. Let myself forget the disappointment of finally sharing an actual kiss with Darling. So far, we've kept it chaste. Even I know it's time for more—well, I know our time for more is slipping by fast and I have to make my move.

"Ugh!" I let out in frustration. Why am I here again? An assignment. Not kisses and cuddles. Shit. *Get it together, Calamity.*

Stay on task.

The kitchen is warm when I enter. Not nearly as warm as lying next to Darling, but nonetheless welcoming. I rummage through the cabinets, determined to keep my hands busy to distract my mind. Six midnights ago, the other version of me would have been disgusted by the idea of feelings and emotions, especially toward a fairy. The other version operated on a "needs only" basis.

This version is different.

It's delirious.

Delusional, really.

Delighted too.

I'm doomed.

I grab two cups of rice, rinse it a few times, and then set it boiling on the stove. Then I pull eggs from a basket, a large pat of cool butter, and heat a skillet. Cooking isn't a skill most celestials use. We magick our own basic, boring food when necessary. In this realm though I find myself hungrier for flavor. Perhaps because of my exposure to mortals and mortality. Or worse. It could be that I've begun operating on a "needs and wants" basis.

Now I've given into desire, and my life will never be the same.

The butter sizzles on the hot pan and I crack three eggs onto it. The whites begin to bubble while I slice some magicked mushrooms, ginger, and scallions. Back home, I would sear fresh fish from Avalonia, but fish doesn't seem to be popular here.

The movements shift my thoughts usefully. Hands busy. Mind blank. That's the goal here for now. I add the sliced ingredients to the eggs, snap my fingers to finish cooking the rice to make it perfectly cohesive and somewhat sticky, and take out three bowls.

This was the breakfast my mother made me every morning. My father never cooked. I can't even remember if he ever felt inclined to eat, but she loved it. Even the smell of it—gingery with the sharpness of the scallions and the slightly sweet, rich scent of buttery eggs—causes an ease within me. I sprinkle peppercorn powder on top, wishing for a bit of sour wine, or . . .

One more snap of my fingers, and a cup of fermented wheat sauce appears beside me. I add a dash of it on top of the bowls, salty and briny. I'm doing really well at conserving magic.

I set the table and take a seat, letting my head fall back. It's all going to be over soon, isn't it? Will I be stuck with Blight years and years from now because of my failure here?

Will I see Darling after tonight?

Lucy joins me first, rings around her eyes, her hair disheveled. It would appear she got as little sleep as I did. "Smells delicious."

"Thank you," I say with a tight smile. Just seeing her reminds me that so much has been undecided. Her future can go any way. *This is it: Time to be honest.* "Do you know what you want to do today?"

"Can we not talk about that?" Lucy lifts a spoon. "We have time to figure things out."

"We don't," I say, startling us both. "You have until midnight, Lucy. After that, Darling and I will be gone."

"What?" Lucy's eyes widen. "Aren't you going to stay? I mean, she's a fairy but you're like me, aren't you?"

I take a deep breath and snap my fingers. My true form washes over me. The black smudged around my eyes, the vibrancy in my hair, my skin, the otherworldliness of me. Lucy gasps and scrambles from her seat.

"What are you?" Her voice sounds shrill, scared. "I thought only Darling—"

"I'm a Misfortune from the realm of Malespero. I exist to help mortals avoid an Unhappily Ever After. I exist to make sure you don't inadvertently wreck your own life." I say it as calmly as I can, as gently as someone like me can. In truth, I've never been seen by a mortal. How I'm perceived now makes me uncomfortable. My skin feels itchy, my face hot. I want to disappear behind the mask of a mortal, sallow and perpetually tired. "Darling is here to give you a Happily Ever After as a fairy, and I'm here as a Misfortune to help you choose stability." I gesture to her food. "Please eat, it tastes better hot."

Lucy stands there a few long moments, digesting all that information so that she can make space for actual food. "You look different."

"I know the black streaks beneath my eyes may seem menacing, but it's only the concept that dark equates to evil that is truly menacing. The darkness comes from our magic tied to my home, the night. It's black for all Misfortunes. It's neither good nor bad—it's neutral." I snap my fingers and two wooden sticks land in my bowl. I arrange them in my hands and pluck my food with the grace my mother taught me. Lucy watches me eat, her brows furrowed in confusion. How I eat shouldn't matter, so I don't explain. "You have a choice—"

"Oh!" Darling exclaims quietly from the bottom of the stairs. Her face lights up. "You're very pretty in your mortal form, Calamity, but this"—she gestures to all of me—"this form of you, your true form, it's . . . you're very . . . beautiful. Handsome."

Now I can't fight a genuine smile. "Do you want to show her?"

Darling winks before swishing her wand. She transforms

from her mortal costume into the fairy that makes my heart beat faster. Her skin shimmers, her ears point at the edges, her cheeks turn a shade rosier, primroses weave through her hair, her lavender wings flutter out behind her and, like when I first met her, she has bright rainbow tights on under a mini yellow ball gown of tulle and pastel lace.

For the second time, Lucy gasps, her spoon falling back on the table. "You really do have wings." Darling flaps them, sending a breeze toward us. She giggles, the sound as brilliant as she is. "Can you actually fly?"

"Of course." Darling chuckles. "What else would they do?" Then she turns to me, eyes sparkling. "You made breakfast!" She slides into the seat beside mine and looks at my utensils. "Can you show me how to use those?"

I magick her a pair and show her with my hands. She mimics me, and all the while Lucy stares.

"You lied before." She blows out a stream of air, though I can't tell if she's upset. "You said you aren't in love or betrothed."

"What?" I ask, a bite hovering by my lips.

At the same moment, food drops between Darling's sticks onto the table. "What do you mean?"

Lucy frowns, rubbing the back of her neck. "You're in love."

"What have I told you about reading too many romances?" I cock a brow before continuing to stuff my face.

"If you had, you'd see what I do." She gives us an impatient huff. "Maybe you didn't know."

Darling waves a hand dismissively. "We met nearly the same time as we met you. We're just—"

"We . . . esteem each other," I say with a slight roll of the eyes. "We've grown close."

"Whatever." Lucy stands again, running her hands through her braids. "You both came here to help me. That's what you said. You're going to help me be happy or be . . . stable? You're both here to make sure I don't have an Unhappily Ever After?"

"Precisely," Darling answers, clumsily trying to pick up food.

"Normally, I would've made the choice for you." I thrum my fingers against the table. "But we've decided that it should be your choice. What do you want, Lucy? What would you have us do with the time we have left here in this realm?"

Lucy rocks on her feet, biting her lip. "I thought when she said fairy, it was like a metaphor, you know? Like she's magical in the way of stories. I'm not saying I didn't believe you—you've done magic. I just . . . I didn't think you really had wings. I didn't know you'd both leave me here. Or you"—she points at me with a shaky hand—"that you were magic too."

A sob climbs up her throat and try as she might to contain it, the sound rattles through me.

"You have to understand, normally you'd never see us. You'd never hear our voices or see our magic." I glance at Darling. "Well, not with my kind. You're not supposed to know where we come from or why we're really here. Believe me, I never meant to hurt you. Or overwhelm you."

Lucy's back falls against the wall and she tilts her head up to stare at the ceiling. "I have to choose between happiness or . . . survival, I guess?"

"You do." Darling's tone sobers. "Until the clock strikes midnight. That's how long you'll have us. That's how long you can take to choose your own fate."

"Why would anyone ever choose survival over love?" Lucy's words are soft, more like she's asking herself than us. Then she tips her chin down. "Because love doesn't always mean happiness, does it? Because love isn't predictable. It can grow and crumble, live and die. Like my mom. Love doesn't mean survival. It can be the best thing or the worst. No one knows. Do you know?" Her gaze meets ours.

Darling and I shake our heads. That's exactly it. Love, like happiness, like anger, like a million emotions, is unpredictable. In a perfect realm, it would be a straight line. But this realm isn't perfect and neither are mortals, celestials, or fairies. We are, all of us, a little chaotic.

That's the truth I never saw before this assignment. We can't control the way we or anyone else feels. There are too many complexities, variables, moving pieces. Experiences. Sorrows. Joys. Successes. Defeats. Losses. Gains.

"Do you know what you'll choose, Lucy?" I ask one more time, hoping there's an answer. Hoping that I can prepare for whatever comes at midnight.

Lucy takes a deep breath before sitting back down at the table. She lifts her spoon and takes a bite of the now lukewarm food. I snap my fingers to heat it up a little. She smiles. "I'm never going to get used to you being magic."

"You accepted Darling's magic easily," I remark with a smirk.

She scoops another bite into her mouth. "That's because Darling has always seemed magical."

Darling perks up, her sticks now perfectly situated in her grasp. "Is that a good thing?"

"Yes," Lucy and I answer at the same time.

∾ ⌁ ∾

When the baker arrives to—I assume—deliver his daily platter of cookies, he's in a fresh white coat, his hair slicked back. Sweat beads his brow. And instead of a platter, he's holding a small wooden box. "Ms. Darling, I have cookies for you."

Darling bumbles out of the closet, where she's been sorting Lucy's paintings, and beams at him. "Oh, what do we have today?"

"Well . . ." The baker clears his throat. "I thought I'd try something new. I remember you saying you loved honey, so I . . . well, I decided to make streusel honey cookies." He holds the open box out to her. "Never did so much sweet baking in my life. Never thought I'd like it so much either."

"I knew you would!" Darling's mouth forms a perfect *O*. "Honey is my favorite. Thank you, Baxter!" She picks one from the tray carefully as if she's afraid of breaking them. I stand there transfixed, wondering how I never realized how she lights up a room—how she lights me up too. And when did she take the time to find out the baker's name?

"I, uh . . . I applied to bake the cake for tonight's ball. I hope you'll come and see it. It's only because of you that I knew I could bake it. I'm nervous; it might change my business." Baxter rocks on his feet, his cheeks red. For a man in his fifties, he sure is bashful. "Thank you, Ms. Darling."

"We aren't sure if we'll be there yet. But I'm so glad you're sharing your talents with the world, Baxter." She nibbles her cookie, eyes round. "These"—she raises a cookie—"may be my most favorite ever."

Lucy watches the whole thing with interest, and though I could go over and read her thoughts, I don't. She still hasn't decided. Baxter has. The village has.

One peek outside and you'd see the florist filling a wagon with their brightest blooms, the villagers milling about frantically to get the final touches for their outfits—which could be anything from a fancy hat to a golden broach—Minerva and Ms. Chambers fixing hems, the hairdresser hastily checking the line to make sure she'll get to them all in time.

But the three of us, we're in an undecided limbo.

The ball could be Happily Ever After. Staying could be Ordinary Ever After.

And still, Lucy hasn't chosen which she'd rather do: gamble with her future or take the easier, safer road.

The worst thing is, I don't know which I'd take either, if I were in her shoes. Not if Happily Ever After led to Darling and Ordinary led to the mentorship.

Well . . . actually I do.

CHAPTER TWENTY-THREE

Darling

Horse-drawn carriages rattle past the shop on the way to the palace. Excitement pops and crackles in the air like electricity that could power the entire realm. Hopes and dreams carry on the cool wind. The light blue sky is speckled with pink and orange from the soon-to-descend sun.

And none of us are ready for midnight to come in only a few hours.

Calam walks beside me, his fingers threaded though mine. Lucy wanted to be left alone. So I decided to bring Mrs. Arconia back to her son and family.

"Do you know what you'll do, Mrs. Arconia?" Despite me asking a cat a question, no one bats an eye in my direction. Since it's a costume ball tonight, no one seems to mind my wings either. It's as if Fulhorn has finally given me the freedom to be my authentic self on the last day. It also helps that night has fallen around us and they're all too busy to care.

She meows in my arms. *Change. I didn't know how I was affecting them. My husband . . . he doesn't deserve to be miserable. Neither does Dynnis, or Lucy.*

"And neither do you," I interject. "If you fall back on old

habits, I'll have you know that I can and *will* visit you anytime." I lift my chin. "Take that as a promise and a threat."

Mrs. Arconia stiffens in my grasp but doesn't reply.

At the edge of her estate, I set her down. The lanterns outside the doors are brighter than in the courtyard. Probably because the Arconias can afford more gas than everyone else.

"When you're better, your realm is too." I swish my wand, and she transforms back into a mortal. Though she's a little messier than normal. Her hair's disheveled, and her dress is torn in places. Still, she smiles at me, running her hands over the fabric while marveling at herself.

"You know, I could very well have you killed for this." Mrs. Arconia's smile fades. "Peeing in a box and hurling hairballs, and people touching me all the time—"

"You loved that. I heard you purring." I shake my head. "You should be thanking me."

She glowers. "I will not thank you."

"Fine. But it would behoove you to heed my words." I give her one last threatening glance. I'm about to turn around when I feel her hand on my shoulder.

"I cannot thank you on principle," she says, her voice soft and unlike her. "I can . . . appreciate you trying to save me from myself. I meant what I said. I will change. My family deserves better. And so do I."

I dip my head. "I'm glad."

"And a word of advice." She steps back, her posture straightening. "I understand now that it was you who changed our village, brought our fields back to life, and gave us hope. That . . . determination, it reminds me of myself when I was younger. It reminds me of Lucy too. That perseverance. The only way you'll get her to that ball is by showing her that she doesn't need to be strong all the time. She doesn't need to have it all figured out. If she doesn't take chances because she's scared, she'll become miserable." Mrs. Arconia sniffs. "It's a lesson I wish I would've learned many years ago. Now, if you'll excuse me, I smell horrid, and I'll need at least three baths to wash away the feeling of fur before the ball."

With that, she stalks off toward her home. I do hope she'll change.

Calam squeezes my hand. "She's no longer a Miserably Ever After." He rubs his chin. "I didn't know that was possible. I didn't—we weren't taught that it was possible. If I knew—if any of us knew . . ."

"Fairies believe that anything can be possible." I wink in his direction. "To be fair, we also believe in chaos as a rule."

In a split second, Calam stands directly in front of me, his mouth parted as his eyes search mine. "Darling." One word. My name on his lips. "I would like to kiss you now."

"I would like that too." I lean toward him, the sunshine dwindling above, the air smelling like roses and tulips, my heart hammering. There's a bubble around us and I feel like—

"The two of you are *honestly* together? You really want to be with *him*?" Dynnis slides off his horse in an emerald suit that looks both dashing and bold. Not costume-y at all. "Don't you see how we could be great together? You're beautiful. I feel a kinship toward you. I could make you happy."

I smile kindly, knowing that for the first time in my life, I have to let someone down. It's not natural for me. And I never expected Dynnis to be quite so interested. It's never happened before. Not in the celestial or fairy world. In fact, before Calam, only Virtue seemed to want me in a romantic sense. And that didn't turn out well at all.

Coming here, it was nice to be admired. It felt good to be seen as desirable. Only, my heart doesn't belong in Lumina or Fulhorn. And not to Dynnis.

"Your attention has made me feel seen and appreciated, Dynnis, but I'm already happy. Calam is—" I break off, the words still uncertain. My lips pinch as I try to find the right thing to say. "He's . . ."

Important to me. He makes me happy. He gives me something to look forward to—a future. He cares about me and I care about him. And if I'm honest, there's something else I don't quite know how to describe . . . Something that's warm and flutters around the pit of my stomach, dancing at the idea of Calam and me.

None of which I say aloud.

"You're the sun and he's a dark cloud. You don't match. You can't be with someone who constantly tries to steal your shine." He steps closer to me. "You deserve someone better."

"The sun can't always shine," I respond. "Nothing would grow if it did. You need the shade and the rain. And sometimes I'm the dark cloud too—you just haven't seen it."

Dynnis considers me for a long moment. He opens his mouth, then shuts it.

"I . . . I'll respect that." He backs away. "If you change your mind." Dynnis bows with a good-natured smile. A breeze tussles his red locks, making him look even more attractive. He's not my type, never has been. I seem to prefer curly hair, brown skin, beauty beyond reason, with a mischievous smirk and a penchant for philosophical debate. "Perhaps I'll find my own of what you have with him."

"You will." I mean it. He's on the path to Happily Ever After. Nothing's locked yet, but I have a good feeling he'll make better use of his future. Especially with a less miserable mother.

Once he retreats into the stables, I take another deep breath. "We should go. We'll find another time to kiss and savor it. Right now, we need to find a way to make Lucy know we care about her, whatever choice she makes. That she's not alone."

"Are you ready, then?" Calam asks. When he looks at me, there's a sparkle in his eyes.

"Not at all," I reply. I lean over and press my lips to the velvety skin of his cheek. My eyes close, his scent washing over me. His signature combination of the forest and old books. His fingers smooth over my fabric and his breath hitches. Tentative. Nervous, if the twitch in his nose is any indication. My own body nearly bursts into flames. The breath lingers in my throat and I swallow sharply.

This is *everything*.

My forehead rests against his when it's done, and it's done too soon. His arms clasp around my back, his warmth seeping through my dress. I should move. Tell him there's no more time to waste. But I'm stuck there.

When I finally pull back, his gaze stays on mine. "The last time I kissed someone, they told me it wasn't very good. I was afraid of ever trying again."

"They were mistaken," he whispers headily.

"They wanted me to be less than too much," I admit. "I'm not capable of that, you understand. I'm loud, and big, and sometimes I panic, and I just can't snap out of it until I feel close to destroying everything. I'm brash and hasty. Sometimes I eat an exorbitant amount of sweets—even for a fairy. And I always want to be the best version of myself. Always want to do the best for everyone else. I've never not cared, to my own detriment. I will take on every problem in every realm with a mug of hot chocolate in my hand and my wand in the other. My brain will whisper self-hatred at my weakest moments and I'll try to shut it up. And . . . I will forever be too much."

"Only someone lacking good taste and an interesting personality would want you to be less." Then he gifts me that stunning smile that makes my knees wobbly. "Darling, you're perfect the way you are."

I chuckle with disbelief. "Are you sure?"

"Obviously." He pecks my cheek once more. "Now's the time to do your magic. If Lucy wants to go to that ball, she's going to need the fairy treatment. She'll have a princess to win over."

"She may not want that," I murmur. "She may want ordinary, and who could blame her?"

Why would she choose risk when all she has known is disappointment, loss, and grief? There're only a few hours till midnight and we're finally about to find out what Lucy Addlesberg truly wants.

❦ ♥ ❦

When we arrive at the store, Lucy's sitting amid a pile of books. Her head's down, shoulders shaking.

For a moment, I'm not sure what I should do.

Old Darling would've pulled her off the floor and said, "Cheer up, we can make everything better with a bit of magic!"

New Darling realizes that magic won't solve life's problems. There are skills we need to employ, tools we need to use, and we can't always fix the world, no matter how much we want to. Sometimes all we can do is sit with our big emotions, even when it's uncomfortable.

"Can we . . . can we join you?" I ask carefully. I don't want to crowd her again. I don't want to push again and make it worse somehow. Desperately, I want her to think of me as a friend. A *good* friend. I already know I'll be popping into the realm to check on her from time to time. She's my first client. The one that made me remember why I ever wanted to do this.

The Guardians need me more than I need them. Lucy taught me that. Favie reminded me of that. Calam shows me that. I make the impossible possible. Mrs. Arconia is proof. If I took that approach across the realms, I could change everything.

But then, what does that mean? Would the mentorship help

me achieve that? Would I be out in the field like this or at a desk, making decisions? Is that what I want?

Lucy nods. Calam and I rearrange ourselves on the floor around her. I pluck *The Prince and the Woodsman* from the pile. "How does this end? I never got a chance to read it . . ."

She sucks in a long breath. "They end up together."

"The prince, Louis, marries the woodsman, Paul," Calam adds. "They make room for each other's dreams, finding a way to live the best of both worlds. Louis becomes a writer like he always wanted, and Paul becomes advisor to the King. Together they improve the kingdom and live Happily Ever After."

When I stare at him, brows raised, he only shrugs. "Of course I read it."

Lucy's sudden laughter surprises us both. "Calam *did* read a romance book after all."

"You kept saying I should." He smirks. "Rumor is that the author is making it a series."

"Oh, now I feel like I have to read it too. I love a series." I turn the book over in my hands. "I can say I've never read romances before. I didn't have access to them. And fairy tales . . . well, let's say they're not too romantic what with all the death, mayhem, and terrible parents."

"That makes a lot of sense." Lucy laughs again, and I'm not sure I understand why. How does that make sense? Thankfully, I'm saved from asking. "You're . . . you don't see the way love looks at you."

I tilt my head, still not understanding. She doesn't elaborate either. Perhaps this is just something lost in translation. "Lucy, do you want to live *The Prince and the Woodsman*, or do you want an ordinary, solid, stable life? On the surface one may seem better than the other, but below it . . . one is risky. No one knows what'll happen."

"I understand that." Her hands fidget in her lap as if she's unsure what to do with them. "Do you think it's possible? To make room for each other's dreams? To have it all?"

I hold up the book. "I think you should consider what would happen if you don't. What happens if you try, and you fail. What do you think failure would be?"

Silence fills the space among the three of us.

If I fail, I'd still be a Guardian. Doing what I do now. I could still go home too. That doesn't seem so bad. If Calam fails, he would have to go back to his unloving, cold father. He wouldn't get the mentorship that'd save him the agony.

And Calam would fail if Lucy chooses Happily Ever After.

Yet he's letting her choose anyway.

I know what I need to do.

"If it doesn't work, maybe I'll lose this store. Maybe it'll give me a chance to belong somewhere new too." Lucy's lips twist as if she's resolved. "I want to go to the ball. I want to dance with Andi and try to make her forgive me. I want to make space for her dreams and my own."

I glance at Calam, knowing what this means for him.

Despite it, he smiles. "Well, we're already extremely behind schedule, then." He leans over and pats my knee. "This is where Darling gets to shine."

CHAPTER TWENTY-FOUR

Calam

Darling has Lucy twirl around a few times. She makes little tutting sounds and taps her bottom lip in concentration.

"I've spent a lot of time considering this, Lucy, and now it's here." Darling sniffs. "In Whimsia, there are festivals and lights and music. And the air smells like apples and honey." She closes her eyes as if she's remembering. "There's a costume ball at the beginning of autumn that brings fairies and fae from all around our realm. It's one of our biggest celebrations. My mother, she was the belle of the ball every year. Once, she wore a silver dress with her curls falling loosely around her shoulders, each strand coated in glitter. Her costume was of our most celebrated fairy, Merryweather. A powerful fairy who was known to help mortals achieve their Happily Ever Afters, usually with a song-and-dance number. When the light hit my mother, she sparkled. Her skin glowed and no one could take their eyes off her. That's what I want for you. I want to capture your beauty and let others appreciate you."

Darling has her wand out, gold dust spiraling in the air.

Lucy's dress grows in volume, going from mint to a dark purple that cinches at the waist. Darling's signature glitter sticks to the surface and dots Lucy's skin. Her braids de-frizz and twist into one bigger braid that wraps around her head prettily. Gauzy chiffon in hues of purples, pinks, and blues spread out in both directions from the center like petals, creating a stunning collar that reaches her neck.

Darling has made her into a blooming flower. Into walking art.

After a few beats, Lucy's eyes brim with tears. "I look . . ." Her voice cracks. "Darling, I—"

Darling giggles. "You look just like you. Beautiful. Smart. Talented. I only put a prettier dress on you and gave you petals." She winks.

"Darling," Lucy coughs, glancing down at Darling's perfectly fine but not-quite-right-enough dress. "Do you want to change too?"

"Oh," Darling mutters. "Right." She closes her eyes and lifts her wand. Darling's dress transforms into a pastel rainbow. It falls around her in layers of tulle, and dots with flowers in teal, pink, and lilac. Her curls release from her bun to fall around her shoulders. Flowers bloom from a vine headpiece that makes her skin shimmer.

I'm aware that I should be *ooh*ing and *aww*ing over Lucy—and probably breaking into song about how beauty isn't defined by the clothes we wear but the character of our hearts or some nonsense—I just can't stop looking at Darling. Lucy looks exactly as she should, the girl who will step into the ball and leave with the princess on her arm.

But Darling is a masterpiece.

She looks at me mischievously. "Well, it's your turn too."

"Wait!" I have no time to prepare for what she's about to do. She swishes her wand in my direction. Soon, that same pastel rainbow creeps up my sleeves, along with her flowers. A gold primrose crown suddenly sits upon my head too.

I touch it with the tips of my fingers. "What are we meant to be?"

"We're a bouquet," she answers, like it's common sense. "We go together."

I try not to let my emotions respond to that. *We go together.* No, don't do or say anything cheesy. I clear my throat. "Why primrose?"

Even Lucy stops admiring herself to look up. "You do seem to love it."

"Wherever primrose grows, a fairy goes," Darling says. "If there's a patch of primrose in a mortal realm, it opens a pathway to Whimsia. It tells us we're welcome, and it gives us power."

"Oh." Lucy's eyes widen. "So if I carry one in my pocket?"

"She'll never leave you." I smile over at Darling. "I suppose I'll have to carry one too."

Her cheeks turn a rosy shade on her warm brown skin. She lowers her head shyly, and I must admit, I've never seen Darling shy before. If it's possible, it makes her more adorable.

"Yes, well, keep growing them so I can always pop round to see you." Then she claps her hands, changing the subject. "Now, it's time for us to get to that palace on the hill. Are we ready?"

"Not quite," I answer through apprehension. We have less than two hours and we still have no way to get there.

The three of us go into the dark courtyard, the cool breeze tugging at our fancy costumes. Most of the villagers have cleared out, either on their way or already at the ball. Only we're left behind, trying to make the impossible possible. It'll be no easy feat.

And I know that success tonight means my loss tomorrow.

But I can't stop now. This is what Lucy wants. Who am I to deny her that?

I snap my fingers in quick succession, creating a craggy metal carriage from dirt and rocks. It's not pretty; I'm not good with pretty. Thankfully, Darling is. She tugs her ear, turning the carriage a pearly white, and the tarnished silver twists into gold.

"Do you see a mouse or perhaps a fox to turn into a horse?" Darling peers around at nothing to be found. It's dead quiet.

"Too bad you can't turn Mrs. Arconia into a horse too," I mutter.

"What?" Lucy looks between us, her face pinched in concern.

"Nothing!" Darling smiles. "Don't worry about anyone being transformed into a creature to teach them the meaning of life and happiness."

"Well, I am now!" Lucy looks even more disturbed.

Darling ignores that. "Hmm, if only there were some . . ."

"I'll do it." I'm the only one who can. Darling is capable of many feats of magic, but creating from nothing is too difficult. So it'll have to be me. I clear my mind, take a deep breath. This kind of magic is too much for me and my kind; I'll still try.

I snap. A fragment of a shadow wisps in the air only to dissipate. *Shit.* Another deep breath. I snap both fingers. More shadows form into something, a glimmer of a tall, horselike creature. And then it dissipates again.

Darling reaches out and clutches my hand. "Let's try together."

I snap, she tugs her ear, and . . .

Time stands still. We disappear in a *poof.* Into the Liminal . . . together. I didn't know that was possible. I feel her presence. We aren't forms, we're whatever we're supposed to be in the Liminal. It smells like cookies fresh from the oven and opening an old leather-bound book in a candlelit library. It's different than its normal scent of rot, welcoming. Warm. Home.

My magic—black like plumes of smoke—and Darling's—ribbons of glittery gold—keep clashing together. We are oil and water. Never mixing until . . .

Swirls of shadowy black break through gold. No, not breaking, mingling. They combine, growing thicker and stronger. Black and gold glitter. It's beautiful. More beautiful together than apart. Something prickles in the back of my mind that this is important.

Before I can understand how to get us back to Lumina, we're thrown through space and time to where Lucy's still frozen in place, though I sense she'll reanimate soon in a moment. The sky's still dark. The carriage still awaits.

Yet time has passed and continues, nonetheless. I slide a pocket watch from my pocket. Only ninety minutes till midnight.

Darling stares at me, slow-blinking. "Did we—?"

I shake my head, no words coming to my lips. I don't really know what we just did. We don't have time to wonder about it either.

"Try it." She nods in my direction.

I snap my fingers one more time and the shadows become solid, wrapping around each other until there's a horse . . . Well, a horse-and-wolf mixture. A creature made from magic. His black fur shimmers with fairy luster. His eyes are a vibrant gold, his legs as strong as a bull's. He almost reaches up to my chest.

He opens his mouth, revealing sharp teeth and a lolling tongue, which flops out, his bushy black tail wagging. He butts his head into my arm in an attempt—I think—to get me to pet him. Gingerly, I give in, running my hand over his thick fur. He closes his eyes appreciatively.

"What is it?" Lucy asks, stepping back toward her store. "Is it dangerous?"

"No," I say quietly. "He's a good boy. Shadowboxer."

"Did we—" She barely has time to ask before Shadowboxer bounds over to her. He bends down slightly and nudges her hand with his big, shadow-fur-covered head. She squeaks. "We made him, didn't we?" She pets him carefully. He wags his tail.

"We did." Pride spreads through my gut. The way she loses her apprehension with him. I don't know why this means so much to me, but it does. Her approval matters.

Shadowboxer drops down and rolls onto his back, presenting his fluffy tummy. Darling lets out a laugh, leaning over slightly to appease him. "He's perfect, Calam. I can't believe our magic could make him. Are we—is our power connected?"

"I don't know." And that's the honest truth. I don't know how any of this works. It'll be something to ask the Mortal Outcome Council tonight.

Lucy, seeing Shadowboxer on his back, stalks closer. She lays a hand against her chest in awe. As much as I enjoy this moment—and I do, I've never used this much magic and never created a living, breathing creature, nor have I experienced sharing power with a fairy—we are running out of time.

"We have to go."

Darling stands up, giving Shadowboxer one last pet. "We do. Come on, Lucy."

She gently steers Lucy around Shadowboxer and helps her into the carriage. She glances my way and climbs in after her. I snap my fingers again, feeling surprisingly energetic. Gold spirals around, hitching Shadowboxer to the carriage and landing reins in my hands. I plop onto the coachman's seat.

The cool night air washes over me. Something in me is different. Something's lighter and stronger. Better. Happier. Because of her. My mind is a muddle. And I'm terrified too. Confused. Content?

"You think an awful lot," Darling suddenly says beside me. Her eyes sparkle and the corners of her mouth lift. "Is there anything I can do?"

My hand reaches out to grab hers and threads our fingers together. "You already have."

"I'm not just for kisses on the cheek. I'm a good listener too." Her tone is quiet, pensive. As if she knows I'm processing something huge and she doesn't want to intrude. Or upset me.

It's a ridiculous thought. Me, being upset with Darling. We've done that already and we will again in the future. The future. What a strange thought. Will I have a future with her?

Don't we as eternals deserve happiness ourselves? Can't we be happy?

Can a Misfortune like me have a Happily Ever After?

"You're right that we all carry grief and loss." I bring her hand up to my mouth and kiss the soft skin. "When I am ready to share my sad stories, you'll be the first person I burden."

"It won't be a burden." She scoots closer to me.

"I could very well adore you, Darling." The words leave my lips in a flurry of nerves; I feel warmth despite the cold air.

Darling squeezes my hand. "I could very well adore you too, Calamity."

Every inch of me wants to drop the reins and forget about the assignment, forget about the mentorship, forget everything, and live in this moment with her. She's bright and brilliant. Incredibly smart and disastrously kind.

She's my complement. I can't imagine how my life was before her . . . I can't. No. Shut that down right now.

There's no time for falling head over heels.

This could be the end. And like the mortals I'd scoffed at, it's the fact that I, Calamity the Misfortune, am hopelessly, ridiculously in love with someone I only met six days ago. Whether or not it was fate or science or a call from my magic to hers doesn't matter.

I'm doomed. And the last thing I want is to doom Lucy to a life without this feeling I have.

CHAPTER TWENTY-FIVE

The road to the palace feels long, if only because our time is running out.

I pop back into the carriage, soothing a fidgeting Lucy, who is currently fisting a handful of her dress while her gaze roams out the window at the passing trees. Carriages light the path before us and I know we're getting closer to the final showdown and the culmination of every decision we made over the last six midnights.

In that time, I've grown as a person; I've understood more about myself than I ever did; I've had and given in to bad intentions. My anger got the better of me and I turned a woman into a housecat. My desire got the better of me and I kissed a Misfortune. Mortals, from Minerva to Mrs. Arconia, have changed how I view the realms. It made me realize that deciding someone's fate without considering their history is senseless; it lacks context. Some mortals get an Unhappily or Miserably Ever After simply because they grieve, they suffer, or they forget how to connect to the world. There's something wrong with this judgment.

This experience has also taught me how my own illness interacts with new stresses and pressures. How I can better prepare myself in the future.

"What's the plan?" Lucy turns to me, her expression tense as we rattle over a bridge. "Once we get there, how can I get Andi to forgive me? I was so mean to her. I dismissed her. I dismissed her feelings. She cared about me. She wanted more with me, and I was . . ."

"All we can do is try." I reach out to squeeze her hands. "That's all anyone can do."

To be honest though, I have no idea how to woo a princess. Does she just say sorry and then they dance? Then they'll share True Love's Kiss, and Lucy will have her Happily Ever After? All my magic will lock into place and no one ever need worry again once the clock strikes midnight? Does anything ever truly work that way when real emotions are involved and risks must be taken for success?

No clue.

Almost an hour later—which is surprising since Andi must've made this trip every day just to see Lucy—we're in the palace's massive courtyard. Footmen help us down from the carriage carefully, maneuvering around Shadowboxer as if their lives are flashing before their eyes, but they have a job to do. My feet land on rocky gravel that sticks to the bottom of my fanciful purple flats. I inhale deeply.

The palace stands before us grandly; a massive white-bricked structure with gray turrets, towers, and blue flags waving in the wind. There are torches everywhere, and the ornamentation etched into the stone is gorgeous. Expensive, and painstaking for whoever made them.

Calam loops my arm through his as he leads us through

the crowd of coaches. The chilly night air brushes my cheeks, raising goose bumps along my bare arms. Lucy titters behind us.

Nerves. Same for me.

Calam leans over. "Bit ostentatious, isn't it?"

I giggle under my breath. "Mortals love opulence and displays of wealth. It's how they broadcast that they are 'comfortable.'"

"Do you know it's usually the rich who have the most potential for Unhappily Ever Afters?" Calam winks and my cheeks heat.

"Are they your favorite type of client?" I wonder aloud.

He scrubs his chin. "The wealthy, the corrupt, the needlessly cruel. Those who hold themselves superior to others . . . I fix their paths. There's no joy derived from seeing someone on the brink of ruining their life—yet helping them avoid it does make me feel purposeful. Impactful. Necessary." He pats my arm. "I'm not forcing them to do something they don't want to. I'm giving them permission to act on their terrible desires. For some mortals, they must fall before they can find solid ground again."

I nod, pursing my lips for a moment before answering. "I understand that now. I never thought I would but after a week here . . . Not all people can have a Happily Ever After. They need your help before they're well and truly doomed. The realms need Misfortunes. *As much as* they need Guardians and fairies. We . . ."

"We complete each other," he answers. "They need all of us."

Lucy nudges me from behind. I glance forward to realize we've reached the end of the path and I was too engrossed by

Calam to notice. We're already late and I'm making it worse. Selfish.

"My apologies." I curtsy to an older Black doorman in a powdery white wig and a tan suit with long coattails—judging by his resigned face, he has clearly been waiting for our attention. His stomach rumbles. "It must have been an exceedingly long evening for you greeting every guest by the door and then waiting for the stragglers like us."

He bows his head. "It has been, Madam . . . ?"

"Darling," I offer with a big smile. "This is Calam, and Lady Lucy Addlesberg of Fulhorn."

"Very well," he replies in his deep voice. "I shall have all three of you announced at the staircase. Please follow the blue carpet to—"

"I have snacks if you're interested." I reach into my bag and pull out the small wooden box filled with the honey cookies from Baxter. "Since we're the last arrivals, I'm sure no one will notice."

Now his eyes meet mine, and he swallows. "That would be kind, my lady."

"Darling. Just Darling." I hand him the box and then tug Calam with me. Lucy follows, her head down.

"You're good with them." Calam leans close. "Always kind."

Now I wink his way.

"You are very swoony for two who've said they're not in love." Lucy's smile causes those pixies to flutter back to life in the pit of my stomach.

I bat a shaky hand, trying to stay cool. "We've only been around each other for a week."

She raises a brow. "I've read enough romances to know that sometimes a week is long enough."

"Save all your romantic speculation for Andi," Calam says with a smirk. "With this many suitors who've had a head start and a decision made in only a couple of hours, we'll need it."

Lucy swallows. "You're right."

We tread over a polished patchwork marble floor and see walls filled with pictures of nobility and royals of yore. Music drifts down the hallway, woodwinds and strings. It has a calming effect on my galloping heart. I reach out to touch Lucy, but she moves beyond me to the landing with two more footmen. Her eyes widen on the scene below.

At the foot of the stairs, there's a crowd of gowns and dashing suits and chittering gossips and tiny cups filled by ladle-holding servants and mothers pushing forward their progeny in hopes of securing a beneficial match. It's loud. The music that lured me forward is lost among it all. My feet stay transfixed at the top of the staircase.

"Mistress Darling and Sir Calam," the servant says. People glance up at us, their faces twisted in expressions ranging from puzzlement to outright disdain—as if we, as late arrivals, are interrupting their perfectly planned evening. Anger, whether real or imagined, hangs in the air. Suddenly, I feel like I'm underdressed. I don't fit in. No one wants me here.

My brain takes this as an opportunity to panic.

Calam urges me onward, yet I tug my ear before I begin hyperventilating. Time stands still. Only me and him. Safety. Quiet, save for my hammering heart.

"I can't. There are so many of them. They're all looking at me. They're judging me. I'm silly. I'm . . ." I ramble, my emotions wild. The spiral is spiraling. A trigger I knew I had but thought I would push through until this moment. None of these people truly matter. There's a goal here, and it's selfish of me to feel anything. This isn't about me. *This isn't about me.*

Worthless. Ugly. Talentless. Egocentric.

You are no one. Nothing.

You shouldn't be here.

"They hate me. Everyone hates me. They're laughing. I'm a joke. Calam. Why did I do this?" My hands fist and my thoughts grow as loud as the ballroom. "I want to run away. I don't want to be here."

Calam unravels our arms and puts his hands on either side of my face. "No, Darling. You aren't a joke. They're not watching you. They're all thinking about themselves. Their hopes and dreams. Of being admired and seen. They aren't thinking of you. Well, some do . . . they're thinking about how beautiful you are. How the light dances upon your skin and in every coil of your hair."

I sniff. "They weren't thinking that."

"I was," he admits coyly. "No one can hurt you. No one is worthy of your time but Lucy."

"And you," I say quietly.

"And me." He swallows, hope swimming in his eyes. His

thumbs tickle the edges of my cheeks and time begins again. Though I hardly notice. Now people do look at us. Standing there at the top of the staircase. Touching. Gazes locked. "I can't protect you from having your thoughts, but I can protect you from them. I'll do anything you ask."

I inhale. "*You* are kind, Calam."

Briefly, he's silent while his cheeks turn a shade of rose. Then his lips hitch.

"Kind? Me? Never. Practical. Efficient, even." Calam chuckles, and the room eases back into view. The bubble bursts and now I have to pretend that I don't want to stay in it longer.

He carefully leads me down the stairs as Lucy prepares to be announced. He holds me close, applying pressure to give me a sense of security. It helps.

We turn to look up at Lucy. I tug my ear again and he snaps his fingers, our magic working in sync—a question I'll need to answer later. All the lights lower until Lucy stands out brightly. Her dress looks like a cascade of petals and she like a blooming tulip. Her beautifully arranged hair brings out the roundness of her eyes, the fullness of her lips, and the blush on her dark brown cheeks. She is magnificent. A far cry from the girl we found face down on her bookstore floor in tattered clothes and emotionally closed off.

Everyone watches her, hushed in awe.

"Lady Lucy Addlesberg of Fulhorn," the man announces.

Trumpets sound. There's a gasp somewhere behind us. The air shifts. Andi stands in the center of the ballroom, her mouth a perfect *O*. She's dressed as a bowl of fruit; fabric strawberries, apples, cherries, grapes, a gown painted like a wicker basket . . . it's gorgeous. The crowd parts for her, most bowing in her presence. Whispers echo off the glossy floors and spacious hall.

"You came?" Andi meets Lucy at the foot of the stairs. Though she seems surprised to see her, maybe even happy, there's still a hint of apprehension. "Why?"

Lucy coughs. "Because I—"

"Princess." An attendant in red bows before her. "You are expected to meet with the Arconias first, the Milvers after, and so forth. We don't have this"—he regards Lucy with disinterest—"girl on your list."

"You're right, Bramsley. This girl isn't for me. She has made that abundantly clear." Andi spins around. "I'd rather spend my time with a person who believes we could be something."

Andi leaves us standing there, disappearing back into the sea of suitors and parents and noise. Lucy stalks off in the other direction, citing the need for a bathroom. I offer to go with her, only she wants to be alone. Again.

"We don't have time for this," Calam intones solemnly. "We have to do something."

I sigh into Calam's ear. "Well, we only have a quarter hour till midnight." Not the most helpful of statements.

After a while, Lucy returns. Sniffling, eyes a bit red. "This was a mistake." She shakes her head in resignation. "We should go. I don't see how—"

"No." I stand taller as dancers fill the ballroom and I need to do something. Something to bring them back together.

Here goes nothing, I say to myself, as if I didn't almost have a meltdown on the stairs and I'm totally fine. *Everything's fine.* One might almost believe that I keep throwing myself to the wolves, real or imaginary, for fun. That I enjoy it and my illness is a small, ignorable piece of me. It isn't. It never will be. And I don't think I'd want it to be either. My illness can be a burden but it can also be a bright light. It's neither bad nor good, it just is. In time, I'll learn to live in harmony with it.

Deep breaths.

I yank Calam along with me, nudging through the crowd until I'm dipping into a curtsy for Andi. Her would-be dance partner, Dynnis, gets bumped by other dancers and reluctantly backs off. He's red-faced when he steps closer to his mother as Lucy scuttles behind us.

"Good evening, Princess Marguerite. So nice to see you again." I put on my most vibrant smile and flutter my wings, drawing attention. "This is my good friend, Lucy." I gesture to our client, who's currently staring at me with her jaw dropped. I pull her toward us. "Lucy, this is Princess Marguerite. I believe you two haven't met formally?"

Andi flushes, not in embarrassment, but in nervous energy. Her fingers trace the thread of a fabric strawberry. There's puzzlement in the crowd around us. Inhaled mutterings of speculation. Then her face hardens.

"We have, and that was the end of it." Andi cocks a brow my way, defying me to contradict her. Little does she know I'm great at not only defiance but contradiction.

"I really do think you two ought to dance." My voice grows loud. I can't tell if it's because I'm trying to will this into reality or if I'm beyond anxious. "I've always heard that dancing is the best way to get to know a person. It establishes a rhythm, and . . . and . . . it sets a scene." *Not the rambling! Please don't let me ramble again!* "Sometimes people even fall in love while dancing, especially in this realm. I mean, the realm of possibility."

Calam squeezes my arm. "My betrothed and I are most grateful for your invitation, Your Highness, and, well, we were hoping you'd help us settle a debate?"

My head swivels in his direction. What debate?

Bramsley, the old white man with a monocle—a monocle!—tuts. "How dare you bother our Princess with impertinence. If you do not step back, you will be removed from this ball."

"No." Andi puts up a hand. "I'm very fascinated by this debate." If she remembers Calam as the instigator of her argument with Lucy, her manners don't show it. If anything, her head tilts to the side in curiosity. "What debate?"

"You see, Darling, my soon-to-be partner, believes that wanting something is just as important as needing something." He smiles at me. "She thinks that love is a gamble—a risk worth taking. That sometimes what you need is the opportunity to want. It's what makes life fun and lived. Does that make sense?"

"Hmm . . ." Andi's quiet a few moments. "I think I understand that."

"And my soon-to-be partner, Calam," I cut in, "believes that need is more important than want. Stability, predictability, ordinary is better than risk of the unknown. Love is a risk. Love is unknown."

"So, is need more important than want, or is want as important as need?" Calam finishes.

People around us mumble. Lucy shifts on her feet.

Andi glances in her direction before opening her mouth to speak.

CHAPTER TWENTY-SIX

Calam

"This is a foolish question," Dynnis announces for all to hear. "A princess doesn't need to entertain such philosophical thoughts." He stands tall, his form imposing. He glares at me for several reasons—all of them bad. "The Princess has thrown this ball to select a partner, and as you and Darling are already betrothed, you have no business here."

"The Princess does not need you speaking for her, nor does she need for you to decide what or who she wishes to entertain," Lucy says, her eyes wide when she realizes that she replied aloud. "I apologize for speaking out of turn." She bows in Andi's direction.

Mrs. Arconia clears her throat and already I'm regretting that she's no longer a cat. This is her moment to do the right thing; she knows that Lucy and Andi have a connection. She knows why we're here. And yet, she'll try to skew this evening for her son's benefit, and ultimately hers.

"Excuse me, Your Highness, but I do think the debate has merit." Mrs. Arconia's cheeks turn a shade nearly the same color of her hair. "You see, I've always labored under the impression that need is more important than want, and lately

I've realized"—she nods at Darling—"that when you only approach life based on need and not desire, you end up losing a piece of yourself. You forget how to relate to others. Your focus becomes too narrow." She clears her throat again. "I suppose I just wanted to . . . offer my experience with it, then. Your Highness."

My brows nearly reach my scalp as I stare at Mrs. Arconia. Darling really did it, didn't she? She actually appealed to this mortal's better nature. She gave her a reason to change, and Dorette took it. I didn't expect her to. Some part of me never believed it possible.

Darling did. She sees opportunity where I see impossibility. I almost laugh. That's why we match. We complement each other. I don't just want her in my life, I need her in my life too.

"I appreciate that, Mrs. Arconia." Andi's hard countenance softens while Dorette and her husband rub shoulders. Then she speaks to me. "I suppose I agree with your betrothed in most things. Especially when she said that love can be the purpose of life. Yes, it's a risk and yes, there's always a chance of things unraveling, which is why you must build a solid foundation, like you said, Calam."

"A foundation built on honesty," Lucy says breathlessly. "For instance, I could say: Hello, my name is Lucy Addlesberg, and I own An Enchanted Story. It was my mother's dream and I suppose partly mine too. But I also have always loved painting and I've always wanted to see the world, and I've always wanted to tell the pretty girl who bought my favorite books and smiled at me even when I looked and felt my worst that I like her."

Andi sniffs, stepping closer. "I could also say: Hello, my name is Marguerite Lara Olivia Nyissa Andrea Maxima Peggy—"

"Peggy?" someone asks in the back.

"*Peggy*," Andi confirms, "of House Whitney. My closest friends call me Andi—I don't have many of those—but there's this one girl who I've always hoped would be my friend. Well, perhaps not only a friend."

There's a collective sigh that sounds around the entirety of the ballroom. Dreams are a little dashed. Hopes a little crushed. And yet, two girls stand there looking at each other with all their hopes and dreams bursting to life between them.

"Ask her to dance," Darling whispers into Lucy's ear.

"Dancing won't solve everything." I grimace, leaning near the other ear. I may have taken the loss here and pushed Lucy toward a Happily Ever After, yet I can't completely overlook the impracticality of dancing through one's feelings and everything somehow turning out alright. "Tell her you want to try. Tell her you're right for each other."

Lucy, instead, offers her hand out to Andi.

Andi takes it.

They gaze longingly at each other.

There's no dancing.

No declarations of anything.

Lucy doesn't take our advice.

They clasp each other's hands and walk off through the ballroom, never looking back.

"Well," Darling utters. "That was anticlimactic—"

"Not all stories need a big climax," I say. "The heart doesn't care what's expected." I've spent too much time in a bookstore and it has finally addled *my* mind. "Do you think we did it?" I wonder aloud as I watch the rest of the ball continuing around us. They may not have a chance with the Princess, but they'd never lose the chance at partying in the palace with free food. Besides, they all paid fortunes for their clothes and dragged their poor horses out of the stalls to bring them here.

Mortals really do make the most of every situation.

Mrs. Arconia pats us both on the back. "You know, if you two end up staying, I would expect more decorum going forward. No more sharing a bed until you're married. I don't care what species you are, you should be proper."

Darling rolls her eyes. "We aren't staying."

"Our decorum was perfectly fine." I shrug.

"And proper," Darling agrees. "Besides, we didn't even do the lovemaking."

Mrs. Arconia pales as if she's going to faint. Quickly, I grab a drink from a tray and thrust it into her hand. She totters off, sloshing droplets onto the floor.

Darling doesn't seem to care. "How come nothing has changed?" She glances at me. "Shouldn't we know?"

"I don't . . . I'm not sure." I glance up at the grand clock ticking within a bed of stained glass. "We've still three minutes till midnight."

"Do we just wait?" Darling smushes her lips together for a moment. "Calam, I don't want midnight to come at all."

I let out a long exhale as the dancers dance and the music plays and reality catches up to us. "Neither do I."

"Lumina and Fulhorn are special." She gives me a crooked grin. "I think I'll always carry this realm with me. I've learned more here in these last few days than I have in years of training."

"Me too." My gaze roves over her, from the way she wrinkles her nose to the way the ring of gold in her eyes lights up. My feet step closer on their own. "And you're right, it is special. You helped make it shine. It's because of you that this realm is a little brighter."

"Lucy opened up to you, you made her feel safe and comforted. You showed her the good, the bad, and I'm almost certain—as much as it pains me to admit—that if you hadn't caused that argument between her and Andi, they wouldn't have been able to build a relationship on solid ground." Her voice is soft and she shakes a little. "You should win."

"*You* should win." I cross the last few inches of distance so that we're impossibly close. "You did far more than me."

"That's not true, you—"

I raise my hand to lift her chin. "Darling, we have until the clock strikes midnight. One minute—"

"Do you think you can give me another kiss?" She taps her lips. "Just here?"

"I thought you'd never ask." My hands flit to her face. My thumbs skim the edges of her jaw softly. Carefully. She's not fragile, I know this, but the moment is. We only have seconds.

And yet . . . I can't stop thinking.

That feeling I had when we first met warms every part of me. That feeling that's been there since she appeared in the bookstore more colorful than a rainbow. As if she's the piece that makes the puzzle of me whole. Like our magic that's now in sync and I feel her like she feels me.

Finally, I stop thinking. Finally.

My lips find hers. Pillowy soft. They are exactly as I imagined. My heart races as if it's been asleep its entire life. My skin heats up and catches on delicious fire wherever we touch. Her hand caresses my neck, while my hand drops to clutch her waist. All that matters is this kiss. This one moment.

I breathe her in. Chocolate and clementines. Lemon with a scoop of honey. And on a metaphorical level, all my dreams coming true.

I nudge her nose with mine as I pull back to gaze at her. "Why was that the best thing that's ever happened?"

She lets out a giggle. "You cherish me."

"There's no regard higher than the one I hold you in." I snicker, not wanting to let go of her.

"I think I might even adore you," she whispers, beaming up at me.

I laugh, the sound not enough to be drowned out by my galloping heart. "I adored you first."

"You always have to win, don't you?" Her head falls back as she chuckles.

"I think we've both won." I pull her close and kiss her until the clock strikes midnight.

Everything changes.

And everything ends.

CHAPTER TWENTY-SEVEN

Darling

The Mortal Outcome Council entryway is foreboding and unwelcoming. The black floor is shiny like onyx, the coppery wall sconces cast a small circular beam of light that does nothing to brighten the room. There are small portraits in copper frames covering the walls all the way down the hall. Serious pictures of celestials, none smiling. All of them gray or graying. That's the one decoration to be found. Otherwise, there are no chairs or seating. Nothing that draws the eye. Not even a secretary to offer us tea. Perhaps it's that way to keep anyone from getting comfortable. The only thing rooting me in place is Calam's hand locked in mine.

We were plucked from Lumina and brought here by the coins burning in our pockets.

I don't know if Lucy secured her Happily Ever After. I don't know if the town will survive another drought. If the magic I created stuck or if it disappeared with me. I know nothing but Calam beside me.

I'm about to ask him something, anything, to help me slay my frenzied nerves when a door opens.

Honour, wearing her white robes, shiny halo upon her perfect blond head, and signature scowl, slides a glance my way as she stalks through that door like she belongs. Her signature scent of righteousness with a dash of petty spite clouds the air.

"The council will see you both now." She sneers, one brow cocked. "Suppose you'll go back to Curious Canal soon." She pretends to pout. *Sprinkles*, I loathe that she's still so pretty.

"It's Paradise Pines, and so what if I do go back?" I jut out my chest and inhale deeply, my nostrils flaring. "It's a great place, with great people, and great food. We live life there better than any celestial ever could."

Honour's face slackens. For once, I think I've rendered her speechless. This pleases me.

Calam titters. "Guardian."

"Misfortune." Her lip curls before she struts off.

"She hates me," I say under my breath.

"Guardians are pretentious know-it-alls who don't actually know anything at all," he says drolly. "Don't take her slights personally—unlike you, she wasn't born with a personality." We hear a huff down the hall and I cringe. Calam smiles wickedly.

It's a lovely reprieve when a voice calls out from the other room. "Do come in, the two of you."

Fingers still laced together, Calam and I step through the black door into the Mortal Outcome Council's chamber. It's the opposite of the entryway: It's circular with built-in brown bookcases reaching high, high, high up to the ceiling with ladders that seem to never end. There's a taupe carpet beneath our feet, sparkling orbs of light hovering in the air, and the smell of a newspaper press swirls around us. Inky with an element of surprise.

In the very center and down a few steps there's a long,

massive wooden desk. There are four people seated, one chair empty. On the very end of the table, *The Book of Compassion and Care* sits face out. It's not as magnificent as I thought. The leather looks worn, torn in places, the embossing lackluster. In fact, it says *The Book of Compa sion and Ca.* That's . . . disappointing.

"Darling Sparkleton and Calamity, son of Blight." A full-figured Black Guardian with close-cropped hair and big blue eyes says our names flatly as she reads from a document on the desk in front of her. A dull placard before her reads LARKEN, SHE. "Guardian and Misfortune trainees, respectively."

"I'm not a Guardian," I blurt. I shouldn't talk, not really, but I'm not a Guardian. I never was one. I'll never be one either. I know who I am and what I am now. Favie, Lumina, Lucy, even Calam taught me that.

Larken looks up, scanning me and my wings. "Ah yes, you're the fairy from Paradise Pines, Whimsia—which reminds me, there are several packages stocked in the mailroom in your name. Our mailroom's been understaffed as late. Anyway, you are . . ." She sniffs, eyeing the page closer. "Yes, you are 6,209 midnights old. Academy score of .0001. Near perfect." Calam squeezes my hand at that. "It says here you were on the path to gaining the mentorship for our council, yet you . . ." She grimaces down at the paper again before taking a pair of glasses from her pocket. Once they're firmly on her face, she continues. ". . . were deemed to have differing values. Your assignment of Lucy Addlesberg was created to test your ability of subordination."

"And did she succeed?" An older Misfortune with pale white skin, fluffy white hair, a very full white beard, and beady gray eyes leans forward. His placard says GONSE, HE. At any moment, I feel like he may combust into a cloud of dust.

Larken tuts. "No, she failed within thirty-seven minutes in the realm of Lumina when she performed a spell to expose a Misfortune—ah, his name is—"

"You just read my name—Calamity, son of Blight," Calam says beside me. There's a hint of impatience in his tone.

"If I failed, why was I allowed to continue?" I raise my voice a little—I'm not entirely sure any of them can hear me. And if I'm honest, at least two of them appear to be asleep. Possibly dead.

"Paperwork," Larken says matter-of-factly. "Now, Calamity, son of Blight, The Dark Mile, Malespero, 6,212 midnights old. Academy score of .00012. Was also sent on assignment with mortal Lucy Addlesberg, also to test his subordination. It says in his file that he has been known to be truant from school during official functions, travels through the realms on illegally obtained coins, and doesn't tend to follow rules—instead adapts to individuals with his own judgments."

"And did *he* succeed?" Gonse asks.

"No, he also failed after thirty-seven minutes in the Lumina realm." Larken sighs.

"Odd that they both failed after only thirty-seven minutes," Gonse concludes.

Okay, now I'm impatient. For several years I imagined the Mortal Outcome Council contained the absolute best celestials in all of history and the realms. These four—two at best, really—don't seem to have any real idea what is going on beyond this room. "He should win. Calamity, I mean. You should give the mentorship to him. He's incredible and he'll change the realms for the better."

"No, she should win," Calam says, looking at me. "She'll do more with it than I could ever imagine." He turns back to the council. "You can't fail both of us. Pick one. Pick her. She's the future."

Larken holds up two bright blue folders. "According to these records, we can and have failed both of you."

I groan, hope withering within me. "So then what happens now?"

One of the councilors—another Misfortune—I thought was sleeping sits forward. There's a placard in front of her that says JANNA, SHE. Her inky eyes match her long black hair, she has tan skin, and light pink lips. She's also got to be at least a few thousand years old. Her cheeks sag in places and the flower pinned to her orange blazer died a long time ago.

"That's a good question," she comments in a rickety tone. "As you've noticed we're a bit . . . past our prime."

"We've noticed," Calam mutters quietly.

"What's that?" Janna asks.

Calam and I shake our heads. "Nothing," we say in unison.

"Right, as I was saying," Janna continues. "We're past our prime. To help us coordinate, we have that young go-getter out there, Honey—"

"Honour," Larken interjects, still looking down at her paper.

Janna nods. "That Honour girl's in charge of assignments. I think she might've sent you both to sabotage each other."

"That was cunning of her," Gonse says. "Very unhelpful though."

"We'll have to do even more paperwork," Larken agrees.

"Hmm . . ." Janna thrums her fingers on the table. "Larken, did the assignment work? Was the client saved from an Unhappily Ever After?"

Larken consults her beloved files. "Yes, Lucy Addlesberg is now solidly on the path to a Happily Ever After."

Gonse claps though no one can hear it because his hands are paper-thin. "Despite them failing, they actually succeeded?"

"There is proof suggesting as such, Gonse," Larken concludes. "It would also appear that True Love's Kiss was employed just before the fifth midnight."

"Was it really?" Gonse leans back in his chair. "I haven't heard of one of those happening in three or five hundred years!"

Janna nods, her tone more alive than a second ago. "Was it the mortal?"

"No, let me see . . ." Larken hums as she sorts through her papers. "No, it was the fairy, Darling Sparkling, and the Misfortune—what was his name, Clam?"

"Calamity, son of Blight." Calam closes his eyes in exasperation, but then they snap open again as he gasps. "Wait. True Love's Kiss is *real*?"

Then it sinks in for me too. "We had a True Love's Kiss?" My insides are on fire as I point between us. "Him and me?"

His tone goes impossibly high. "*We* shared True Love's Kiss?"

None of the council looks as surprised as we are. They're useless.

"You love me?" I can barely keep the air in my lungs.

Calam stares off somewhere in the distance before answering. ". . . No?"

"There was a question mark there."

"A hesitancy at best," he counters. "We said we adored each other."

I bite my lip for a moment. "I said I adored you."

"And I said I adored you first."

"And then I said——"

"Yes, yes, true love does occur, often moments after the first meeting." Gonse waves a hand dismissively, and briefly I wonder if it's going to detach from his arm. "It's only a possibility until True Love's Kiss binds it. And a True Love's Kiss doesn't always mean a kiss or romance, it could be a hug or even a new friendship. A deep bond between beings. At any rate, now you're both free to use your power however you like. Such good fortune, and so rare. Usually takes millennia to unlock. Didn't you notice the way your auras and magic have combined? We can see it from here."

"Auras?" Calamity rubs his temple. "That's why our magic combined?"

"Binds?!" I squeak. "Does that mean we're together forever? I—I—I do adore him. That's true. But love and magic?

People don't fall in love within a week. If I learned anything from romantic stories recently, it's that people falling in love within a week is clumsy writing. I believe it's called instant-love."

There's a beat of silence. What does any of that mean? What does it mean that we're free to use our magic however we like? What does . . . Do we? Are we?

Suddenly, Calamity throws his head back and lets out a roar of laughter. The sound washes over me until I end up joining in. Gonse does too, though I don't think he knows why. Janna, I'm worried, might've fallen back asleep. Larken seems to be writing everything down.

And then the laughter turns into something else, something huge and I don't know what to make of it until I wipe the tears from my eyes. "Do we love each other?"

"I—I do feel like we . . . there's a bond between us. Not just romantic, something else. You make me feel whole. And . . . as you said, love *is* always the objective." He tugs me into his arms. He leans down, his lips just inches from mine and—

"It would seem that although both candidates failed individually, they succeeded in collaboration." Larken sure knows how to ruin a moment. "Which means, if we are to follow protocol, both are entitled to mentorships on the council. One esteemed colleague will be asked to step down—"

No sooner does she say it than Gonse and the other councilor—a Guardian with a dull halo whom I assumed was dead—snap their fingers and disappear.

Larken holds up a finger. "Excuse me for a moment as I

record their resignations. We'll need another mentor soon." She shakes her head.

"It's going to be good having young faces on the council." Janna smiles in our direction, but I'm not sure she can see us since one eye is already closed. "I'll teach you everything I know." Her voice grows a bit soft and then she slumps over again, snoring softly.

Asleep.

Unbelievable.

"We fought over *this*?" I cackle. "Does anyone even realize this is a mess? Who let it get this bad? Where do we even start?"

Calam runs a hand through his curls, his fingers almost getting caught. "Wherever we want."

I smile at him. *Want* is such an unusual word coming from his lips.

"Ah, there we are." Larken tuts, looking back at us. "Resignations are accepted. Now you two, stand still. I'll just need to equip you with a new set of skills and sight—"

She snaps her fingers.

Epilogue

After a nice lunch in the forest between the village of Fulhorn and the palace on the hill, we try to say our goodbyes. The mossy magical table's laden with picked-over platters of food, several empty bottles of berry wine, and flower petals. The sun flickers through the trees, the thicket soft beneath our feet and the vine-made chairs. It's like Whimsia has come to Lumina.

And looking around the table, I suppose it has.

My mom, Favie, Aelvar, Minerva, Hannah, and Their (soon-to-be) Royal Highnesses Lucy and Andi, can't stop smiling our way with knowing looks. Which is precisely why we need to leave. There are only so many hugs or questions about the future between me and Calam that I can take.

"You look peckish." My mom holds out two tiny porcelain figurines that turn into mugs when needed—a magical experiment she did just for me. "Remember, if there's a problem you can't yet solve, the first solution is hot chocolate. And make sure you snack a few times a day. My baby can't be out there changing the realms *and* be hungry."

"I'm a Mortal Outcome Council Mentor. I'm not a baby," I murmur quietly. At her frown, I switch gears. "Thank you, Mama." I shove them into my overflowing pocket.

"I know that's right." My mother's brows furrow. No matter what I say, she'll always treat me like her baby. She turns to Calam. "And for you, I made some rice crackers with a few dashes of that stuff you like. Here." She holds them out to Calam, who gets ensnared in another of her hugs. That's his own fault. You can't get too close without getting trapped.

Part of me thinks he enjoys it though. After all we'd been through, Blight still hasn't taken an interest in him. Proud as he was when Calam got the mentorship, it wasn't enough. With freedom from Malespero, Calam no longer wants to try anymore either. All I can do is be there for him as he decides if he wants to track down his mother, or if he'll leave that past behind while making a future with me, with us. I don't know. Whatever he chooses, I'll support him.

"We'd love to host you in our realm for your honeymoon," Favie says to Andi. "Aelvar has been reading all about mortals."

Aelvar saunters closer to Andi and Lucy. His pale white skin shimmers in the sunlight like a million twinkling stars. His attire is dark blue, almost black, his hair the same shade. He's tall and reserved. His tone is always a mixture of calculating, droll and somewhat sinister. "Yes, we're dying to host you."

"Don't say it like that, you sound creepy." Favie smacks Aelvar's arm. "Don't mind him, he's Fae. They can't help it," he states as if everyone understands that. Weirdly, Andi seems to.

Lucy watches it all with a big grin, nudging her shoulder against mine. Shadowboxer brays on the edge of the clearing. "I didn't know—in all my years reading about Happily Ever Afters, I never thought I'd have one. I never thought it would be like this."

"I did." I nudge her shoulder back with my own. "See you for the wedding?"

"Of course, you're making the dress." Lucy wraps her arm around my shoulders. "Go enjoy your next adventure."

"We will." I extract Calam from the fray.

Calam and I gaze at each other for a moment, clutching our coins. And the realm of Lumina falls away. So do we . . . until . . .

We land in the middle of . . . I don't know what. Tall structures of metal reach up to the clear, dark blue sky. I can't see the stars even though it's midnight. There's noise everywhere, emerging from metal carriages without horses. I want to throw my hands over my ears but I'm too distracted (too overwhelmed) to not catalog everything going on. Mortals walk quickly in all directions in packs, holding weird glowing rectangles and speaking into them.

There aren't any trees anywhere. Just broken stone beneath our feet and walls that display images and colors and sound.

"I don't like this," I murmur. I doubt Calam can hear me over all this sound. That's when I'm hit with smells. Like burning meat. And sweat. Rot. I gag. "We should go."

But when I glance at Calam, he's smiling. He leans close. "This place needs a Misfortune guiding it. It's so unlucky, unhappy . . ." He inhales deeply, his eyes flashing in delight. "Oh, I'm going to like it here. Think of all that we can do. I can't wait to fix it."

I shake my head, trying not to roll my eyes. "You *would* like it."

A mortal walks by, screaming into their flashing rectangle. "I can't believe you won't forgive me! I made a mistake. Everyone makes mistakes!"

Calam's voice breaks through the noise like a balm to a wound. "You should tell them that you don't deserve forgiveness right now. Be honest. You don't need to hurt their feelings worse, promising that which you can't deliver. You need to work on yourself. Better yourself."

The mortal does just that and then a second later, follows it up with, "I'm sorry."

"Wow." Calam laughs. "Already their aura is changing. In a few years, they'll be ready for a Misfortune agent."

"Or a fairy," I offer.

That's basically all we received from the Mortal Outcome Council—the ability to read auras. That's how we know who will be getting a Happy, Unhappy, Ordinary, and Miserably Ever After in the future, when to expect the pivotal moments and precipices. It's our job to send the right Guardian or Misfortune *or* fairy to help the right people change their paths in time.

Calam and I have been at this a month, and we're already shaking everything up. We ditched the desks and decided the best way to do our jobs is among the mortals. Together.

"This realm is going to kill me." I take out my wand and swish it around, making this place somewhat quieter. Vines break through the stones and by morning, they'll be trees. Flowers too. I'll make this place pretty somehow. I start calculating everything I'll alter—understand and adapt to their technology, help their climate through good ol' fairy dust, and level the playing field through equality and inclusion. That's just a start.

Calam twirls me around to face him. In the center of this strange world with these strange mortals. We've never been farther away from home. And yet with him, I feel like I carry home in my heart.

"My little love muffin." He kisses me, dipping me as he holds me in his arms. "I really do adore you." We're not ready for the L-word yet, but we've got a few hundred centuries. There's no rush. Besides, once you share True Love's Kiss, saying it feels like a foregone conclusion anyway. I do love him. He's the other end of the string that's pulled taut between us.

"I know you do, I'm very adorable." My life is a fairy tale—one I've written myself, thank goodness—and I giggle, feeling treasured. The hem of my gold dress skims the grime of the realm, but I don't care. "It looks like we've got our work cut out for us."

"It's not work when we're together." His nose crinkles. He really means that. "Let's go make this realm ordinary, Darling."

I elbow him, knowing he's trying to trick and tease me like he always does. "We're here to make it happy, Calam."

"Hmm, we'll see."

"You're a menace." I laugh again, looking up at him and forgetting about this terrible realm around us.

He winks. "And you adore me anyway."

"I do." I peck his lips and reach for my wand one more time. "First things first." I pull the tiny mugs from my pocket; Mom was right, it's a necessary part of my process. I hand one to Calam before tapping them both, watching as they grow into the perfect size and fill with delightfully strong hot chocolate. We sip at the same time. "Now, what's our objective? How should we begin?"

"With a bit of misfortune, and—" His gaze flits around at the chaos, fingers about to snap.

My wand sparkles. "A bit more fairy magic."

ACKNOWLEDGMENTS

Every story I've written has a tiny piece of my heart in its pages. This one might've taken a bit more. I saw who I am in Darling and who I try to be in Calamity. This constant back and forth between chaos and sensibility, the sorrow and the joy, being too loud and too quiet, the big ideas that don't quite work out and the little dreams that come true even when you never knew you wished for them. Whitney Houston's Fairy Godmother inspired Darling, but over the course of revising and twisting these words, I realized that she inspired *me*. If I had magic, I'd be swishing it around to make the world a better place. Big curls, big body, glitter, sparkles, rainbow leggings, maybe a few musical numbers, and loud laughs the entire time. Just like Darling.

While I don't have magic, I wrote magic instead—with a lot more than just a little faith, trust, and *fairy* dust. With that, many thanks to:

First and foremost, Emily Settle. You are an incredible editor: kind, and thoughtful. You saw the potential, you challenged me, and you gave me an opportunity I thought I'd never get in my life. Twice. Thank you, Emily. It is always a pleasure working with you and seeing your reactions to food descriptions!

Katelyn Detweiler, the kindest and most caring agent I could ever ask for. Thank you for not only believing in this story, but holding my hand along the way as it went from this wild fairy tale to cozy confection. Thank you for helping me get my stories into the world!

The team at Feiwel & Friends, including Lelia Mander,

Bonnie Cutler, and Jacob Sammon, for helping me make this book shiny and bright, you all are the best! And thank you to Meg Sayre and Nia Peach.

Tracy Badua, my friend, writing partner, coauthor of our mysterious middle grades, and the person who reads every book from the first draft to the last. I'm a better writer because of you.

Jenny L. Howe. It's not just your friendship that means the world to me, but your unwavering support, and your perfectly big laugh that blends with mine.

Rocky Callen. You kept me going; the sprints, the laughs, the chats when I was particularly glum and you were in your blue era. I'm beyond grateful for you and our friendship. ♥

Mara Rutherford, Rae Castor, Rosiee Thor, Eric Smith, Andrea Tang, Aidan Thomas, Jessica James, Jason June, Dhonielle Clayton, Janae Marks, Tamara Mataya, Sonora Reyes, Crystal Maldonado, Beth Revis, Page Powars, Dante Medema, Krista Manos, Juliet Peel and her incredible photography skills, Ash at Pages in the Stars! You all are the best!

Milford Town Library, for giving me the loveliest, safest place to grow up. You've made me into the person I am today.

Booksellers and bookstores! So many bookstores! But especially the following that welcomed me inside, let me sign books, hosted my events, and/or inspired An Enchanted Story. An Unlikely Story—and the staff who always made me feel at home: Kym, Alice, Julien, Maddy, Patty—Heartleaf Books, Love's Sweet Arrow, Brookline Booksmith, Books of Wonder, Scrawl Books, Loyalty Bookstores, Books Are Magic, Books on the Square, Beacon Hill Books & Café, Powell's Books, East

City Bookshop, One More Page Books (Hey, Lelia!!), Parnassus Books, and Barnes & Noble Wareham and Dartmouth.

Nicole Redd McIntosh. I'm so lucky to call you my sister and best friend. Over miles and oceans, we've kept up our food-tastic adventures. Your confidence keeps me going.

Christoph and Liv. Every day I'm excited that I share my life with you—okay, maybe not excited, but appreciative, I know Americans can be a bit over-the-top with our "excitement." And Liv, I'm endlessly proud of you and your ability to never complain about how many stress-cakes I baked. You only ever picked up a fork. I love you both.

Librarians, teachers, book bloggers, BookTokers, bookstagrammers, reviewers, the entire book community: You've boosted my work, you've shouted from the rooftops, you left reviews and sent me messages. Your enthusiasm, support, and dedication to getting stories into the hands of readers is what keeps this business running. I hope you know how much I—and we—cherish you. If you're ever in my vicinity, I promise to make you cookies.

And most importantly to the readers, thank you for reading. Always. I hope it makes you believe in magic, gives you hope, and lets you see yourself.

ABOUT THE AUTHOR

Juliet Peel

Alechia Dow is a former pastry chef and librarian. She is the author of the young adult novels *The Sound of Stars*, *The Kindred*, *A Song of Salvation*, and *Until the Clock Strikes Midnight*, and a middle grade novel, *Just a Pinch of Magic*. When not writing, she can be found having epic dance parties with her daughter, baking, reading, or taking teeny adventures.

alechiadow.com

Thank you for reading this Feiwel & Friends book.
The friends who made

Until the Clock Strikes Midnight

possible are:

JEAN FEIWEL, PUBLISHER
LIZ SZABLA, VP, ASSOCIATE PUBLISHER
RICH DEAS, SENIOR CREATIVE DIRECTOR
ANNA ROBERTO, EXECUTIVE EDITOR
HOLLY WEST, EXECUTIVE EDITOR
KAT BRZOZOWSKI, SENIOR EDITOR
EMILY SETTLE, SENIOR EDITOR
DAWN RYAN, EXECUTIVE MANAGING EDITOR
ALLENE CASSAGNOL, ASSOCIATE DIRECTOR OF PRODUCTION
RACHEL DIEBEL, EDITOR
FOYINSI ADEGBONMIRE, EDITOR
BRITTANY GROVES, ASSISTANT EDITOR
MEG SAYRE, JUNIOR DESIGNER
AURORA PARLAGRECO, ART DIRECTOR
LELIA MANDER, PRODUCTION EDITOR
CARLEE MAURIER, ASSOCIATE MARKETING MANAGER
SARA ELROUBI, PUBLICITY ASSISTANT

Follow us on Facebook or visit us online at mackids.com.
Our books are friends for life.